D0504280

DANCE ON MY DREAMS

Vere Carrington, the eminent surgeon, had unwittingly stolen his efficient staff-nurse's heart. Jill went to another hospital, to try and forget him—only to be told that he was sending a very important patient there whom Matron was appointing her to nurse.

By the same author

MOON OVER MOROCCO
THE HOUSE IN HARLEY STREET
EAST OF THE SUN
STRANGE ENCHANTMENT
LET LOVE GO BY
STRANGERS CAN LOVE
THE NURSE ON THE CASE
BITTER HONEY
THE LONELY HEART

DANCE ON MY DREAMS

by

Hermina Black

THE ROMANCE BOOK CLUB
121 CHARING CROSS ROAD
LONDON W.C.2

The characters in this book are entirely imaginary and bear no relation to any living person

This edition by arrangement with Hodder & Stoughton Limited

Printed in Great Britain by Northumberland Press Ltd., Gateshead

Chapter I

CROSSING the broad quadrangle from the nurses' wing towards the main entrance, Gillian Foster paused to take in the picture which she had grown to love.

The mellowed red brick of the old house with its gabled roofs and mullioned windows, glittering in the sunlight of the June day; the turf, green as an emerald and smoothed to the texture of velvet by centuries of rolling; the herbaceous borders, rioting with summer flowers; the heavenly blues of tall delphiniums, the pink, mauve, and white of phlox; and roses everywhere.

From the near distance came the rhythmic click of croquet balls, and the subdued sound of voices and laughter from the big lawn behind the house, where the convalescents were indulging in a leisurely game, while from a blossom-laden syringa tree a thrush trilled out its notes. Through the trees the river glinted, winding its way across the grounds of Broad Meadows towards not very far off Runnymede.

To Jill the peace of it all was sheer heaven, and she drew a deep breath of thanksgiving for the privilege of being allowed to work and find contentment in such surroundings—supremely unaware that her slender figure in a lilac print dress and white apron, a starched cap on her golden brown hair, added considerably to the beauty of her setting.

But as the stableyard clock struck, she was reminded that this was no time for dreaming, and hurried on her way.

Jill had a strong sense of history, and only the fact that this lovely, ancient mansion was being used for such good purpose to-day reconciled her to the sadness of it's having ceased to be one of the Stately Homes of England.

During the war "The Hall", as it was still known in the neighbouring riverside village, had been used as a home for convalescent members of the forces; after that it had been empty for a long time, until finally the owner, who could no longer afford to live there, had been obliged to sell his ancestral home for the usual reasons of taxation and high death duties. It had been bought by a private syndicate of doctors to be used as a hospital and clinic which specialized particularly in treating orthopædic cases.

Jill had come from the big London teaching hospital where she had trained, unwilling to change her environment but desperately determined to escape from the heartache which had begun to make her work unbearable. She had grown to love nursing here as she had loved it at the hospital, for, being the kind of nurse who is born and not made, her work was more than half her life. And so gradually peace of mind had come to her, however hard it had been in the first place.

Thank heaven she had found the courage to turn her back on on it all! she told herself now, as she ran up the steps and passed into the shady coolness of the great hall. Turning to the left, she tapped on a closed door. A woman's pleasant voice called a crisp "Come in", and the next moment Jill found herself in the presence of the beloved, but occasionally formidable head of the nursing staff.

Ann Travers looked up from the report she was checking with a slight frown, her expression at once softening into a smile.

"Ah! Nurse Foster."

"Sister Anderson told me I was to report to you before I went on duty, ma'am," said Jill, a little apprehensive of the reason why she had been suddenly bidden to Matron's room. Her conscience was clear, but—one never knew! Patients, especially rather difficult ones like her present case, had a habit of manufacturing grouches against their nurses; and although one could rely on Matron being fairness itself, complaints had to be investigated.

"Yes. I wanted to see you. Sit down, Nurse." Matron indicated a chair beside her desk.

Jill obeyed, perfectly aware that while a half drawn curtain threw her superior's face into shadow, the light shone remorselessly on her own and the shrewd eyes opposite would miss no shade of expression which passed across it.

Miss Travers was a good-looking woman who, in her forties, had kept her figure trim as a girl's. Her hair, which had been true gold, was already turning silver, and in spite of severe brushing it curled naturally beneath the winged cap tied under her chin, which she wore with a severe Quaker-grey frock with stiff white collar and cuffs. Her brown eyes were naturally kind and smiling, though they could become hard as agates when she was annoyed.

But obviously she was not annoyed now.

"I am going to take you off your present case, Nurse," she said. "Mrs. Chalder is going home next week, so the change will not inconvenience her, and you are wasted on the routine work which is all she needs now. Dr. Skelton would have discharged her long before this, but he was keen for her to remain under Miss Culley-Ord until the last moment, knowing perfectly well that she will not continue with any treatment after she leaves us—until she has to come back for more, and it will all be to do over again." Miss Culley-Ord was the clinic's principal radio-therapist.

It was not for Jill to criticize the patient, however difficult.

"I hope she will continue to be co-operative," she said.

"*Continue* to be?" Matron raised her brows. And then: "I must say I am pleased with the skill and tact with which you have handled that very difficult lady!"

"Thank you, ma'am." Jill coloured with pleasure.

"You will probably need a good deal of tact, and certainly all your skill for your next patient," said Matron calmly. "I don't doubt she is a most temperamental person—as all artists are." And meeting Jill's interested look: "I am speaking of the famous ballerina, Sandra St. Just."

"Sandra St. Just!" Jill could not keep back the exclamation.

"Yes, my child. She is coming in to-morrow. I don't know whether you read that she had met with an accident while she was with the ballet in America six months ago."

Jill shook her head. "I didn't——"

"She was in a motoring smash; her ankle was broken, and there was a fracture of the knee-cap. Apparently, everything possible was tried before the doctors told her that she would never be able to dance again. Yes!" In answer to Jill's exclamation of protest: "It was a shocking thing to happen. And in spite of her fame and success she is so young—not more than twenty-three or four. We can only hope that the story may have a happier ending now that Mr. Vere Carrington, who is easily one of the most brilliant orthopædic surgeons this country has produced, has taken charge of the case. I understand," Matron continued, unaware that if she had dropped a bomb she could hardly have given her hearer a greater shock, "he has told her that if she will put herself unquestioningly in his hands, and obey to the letter of the law everything he tells her, he has every hope of getting her 'on her toes' again. And when Vere Carrington undertakes a thing, he usually succeeds. We should be flattered that he has arranged for her to come here. It will be the first time he has entrusted a case of his to us, and a decided feather in our caps if we please him—as I think we shall." Then, thawing from officialdom: "It will be a long business, though; I need not tell you that Miss St. Just will be dependent on her nurse for a lot—not only good nursing, but the power to persuade her to co-operate cheerfully, and above all, not get depressed. I have chosen you because you are not only efficient, but more likely to understand a girl of your own age. This is a most important case, and I want you to put everything you have into it."

"Yes, Matron. Indeed I will do my best. Thank you." Jill marvelled at the steadiness of her voice. Undoubtedly Matron had paid her a compliment; undoubtedly she ought to be proud. But what would Matron say if she were to follow her almost ungovernable instinct and cry out that she could not do it—that she would rather have been told she was going to nurse a case of plague, than one that came under Vere Carrington?

Realizing the interview was ending, she rose mechanically to her feet, but Miss Travers was not ready to dismiss her yet.

"Of course, I know Mr. Carrington well," she said. "Although he had no idea I was in charge here until he rang up to make arrangements. He is the nephew of a great friend of mine, and he was a student at St. Monica's when I was a Sister there—my first ward! Now he is one of their head surgeons. As a rule he likes to put his private patients in his own hospital——" she broke off, adding: "By the way, you were at St. Monica's, of course. I expect you saw him work, and perhaps learned something about his methods? It will be a help if you did. These great men have their difficult moments." The brown eyes twinkled.

Jill thanked heaven that she could manage to keep that mask on her face which is every nurse's protection when there is something in her own mind she must not betray—that calmness of expression which must remain the same whether life or death confronts her.

"Yes," she said steadily. "I was—acting staff nurse on his ward for a time."

"Excellent." Matron nodded approvingly. "Did you manage to please him?"

Jill hesitated. "It—depended. He can be—quite charming; but he is ruthless when things go wrong, and he thinks anyone is to blame."

"Well, I hope he will not need to be 'ruthless' with you, Nurse. Anyhow, you will take over the case as soon as it arrives."

"Thank you, ma'am." Jill had turned towards the door when Matron's voice recalled her.

"Have you ever seen Sandra St. Just dance?"

"No——"

"She is—or rather, was, poor girl!—absolutely exquisite. Her Gizelle was a poem." Matron was a ballet fan and did not attempt to curb her enthusiasm. "I wish you had seen it. It would make you even more keen to help her dance again."

However that might be, Jill knew that nothing could very well make her *less* keen to nurse this, or any other case of Vere Carrington's.

Walking blindly outside again a few minutes later, her mouth felt dry and her heart was thudding painfully. How ironical that Matron should have chosen her, when any other nurse in the place would probably dance with excitement at the chance of working with the brilliant surgeon, no matter how "difficult" he might be.

She glanced at her watch. Twenty minutes before she need return to her patient; she was not due back on duty until five.

She felt that she must be alone, must try to sort some order out of the turmoil into which her mind had been thrown; and, turning away from the buildings, she passed through a gateway in the rose-festooned wall, taking her favourite path through the parkland surrounding the house and gardens, towards the river. But her wish to be alone was destined to be unfulfilled. She had only gone a little way when a girl's voice hailed her.

"Oi! Jill——"

Jill looked round, and stood still unwillingly, waiting for the person who had accosted her.

The other nurse reached her side, laughing breathlessly. "Where on earth are you off to in such a hurry? Running away?" she asked.

"Not exactly," Jill replied. "I was only trying to get a little exercise while there was still time."

But Judy O'Farrell, who had been Jill's particular friend since they started together on the same day as student nurses at St. Monica's, was not to be so easily taken in.

"What's wrong?" she asked, her usually laughing blue eyes searching her companion's face anxiously. "Not been on the carpet, have you? I saw you going into Matron's room."

"Good gracious, no!" replied Jill, and then, taking refuge in an attempt at flippancy: "I haven't been dismissed for neglecting my patients, or flirting with the staff men!"

"Sure, darling, the hospital would fall down flat if that happened. You're the most reliable and respectable thing in it," said Judy. "Now if it was *me* Matron sent for, you wouldn't need to be told there were fireworks going up!" Red-headed, blue eyed Judy was a born Irish rebel with a fund of high spirits that were always getting her into trouble.

"Well, what did the Great White Chief want with you?" she asked.

Jill could not help smiling, though she shook her head reprovingly as she answered: "I'm being put in charge of a new case. Sandra St. Just, the ballerina, is coming here to be operated on."

Judy opened her eyes wide. "The St. Just! Golly! Who's the surgeon? Or is all Harley Street doing the job?"

Judy said steadily: "No, not all of it. Only Vere Carrington."

"No!" Judy's eyes sparkled. "Tell me more, Jilly. I've a cousin at St. Monica's, who says he's the handsomest thing in medicine—I mean surgery. My little heart is all a-flutter already."

"Rubbish!" retorted Jill in her briskest manner, trying to persuade herself that if she could speak of him like this everything must be all right, and it was only the shock that had upset her. "He has no time for women, and nurses are just so many automata—though heaven help them if their work goes wrong!"

"Don't disillusion a girl," begged Judy. "You know my

capacity for hero-worship. Anyway, Kathleen says he can be quite devastatingly rude, but when he's charming you just forget it and fall flat on your face for him!"

"At which point he walks over you and wonders what made the floor uneven," said Jill drily, wishing her heart would keep to its usual beats.

Judy slipped a coaxing hand through her arm. "Tell me, lovey—*is* he every girl's dream of the hero of a hospital romance?"

"Do be your age!" Jill disengaged herself, an unusually sharp note in her pretty voice. "He's hard as iron and cares only for his work. And it's time you stopped going romantic over the doctors. It's inexcusable. If I didn't know there was no harm in it——"

"Don't be cross—a girl ought to be allowed her dreams. I don't scold *you*, because your idea of fun is a row of medals and a hospital to lord it over!" But it wasn't in Judy to be sulky more than a minute, and the next instant she was coaxing again. "Is he very good-looking?"

Jill could not help laughing. "You're incorrigible," she announced. "And you need slapping. He is—very distinguished looking. Anyway, forget it—you will see enough of him in the next few weeks. And—though I know it will be an interesting one—you're welcome to the case if Matron will give it to you."

"What a hope!" sighed Judy. "But I bet there isn't a nurse in this place who wouldn't give her eye-teeth to be in your shoes. Apart from the surgeon, fancy nursing Sandra St. Just —all sorts of interesting people will be coming to see her."

"Well, you can all queue up for autographs when she's well enough," said Jill. "I must fly now. I've stayed too long gossiping." And she hurried away, thankful to make her escape. She had got over that very well; for in spite of her friend's madcap ways, she knew quite well that Judy often saw very much more than she was wanted to. Thank goodness the other girl had left St. Monica's before Vere Carrington made his first appearance there, and knew nothing of her—Jill's—own reasons for suddenly deciding to leave London.

If only she could have asked Matron to give this "interesting case" to someone else; if only she could think of an excuse to ask her to, even now at the eleventh hour. But she imagined

Matron's voice with a crisp note of annoyance in it, asking coldly:

"But why, Nurse Foster? What reason have you for not wanting to take this case?"

And how could she possibly reply: "I can't face it, because I was wildly, hopelessly in love with Vere Carrington—and I don't know how I am going to stand up to seeing him every day again, though he never even noticed my existence. . . ."

After all, she had given up everything she valued most at St. Monica's, so that she might be cured of that secret love which all against her will had grown and grown, until it threatened to crowd everything else out of her heart; coming between herself and the work she loved, taking the savour out of everything; torturing her pride with the derisive taunt that she had given her heart unasked and unsought and—ten times unwanted, to a man who didn't even recognize her as a human being.

She had never thought or dreamed that love could be such a complete obsession. And so—determined to cure herself—she had left the hospital she adored; turned her back on the ambition which she had worked and slaved to make come true. If it had not been for the weakness which made her despise herself (poor Jill! as if a girl falls in, or out of love because she wants to!), she remembered bitterly that she would by now have obtained her ambition to become a Ward Sister at the big teaching hospital where she had trained, and where Vere Carrington was one of the chief visiting surgeons.

Until to-day she had persuaded herself that her sacrifice had not been in vain. That she was cured of the thing which had torn her apart. And then, at the very mention of his name, she had realized how completely she had deceived herself. Now he would be back in her life, and the whole battle would have to be fought, all over again.

But Jill had gone a long way in the year since she had come to Broad Meadows. She knew now that she would not run away a second time. She told herself that the old rhyme:

> "He who fights and runs away
> Will live to fight another day"

should have been "will *have* to fight another day."

Perhaps, if she had stood firm the first time, she would have won through to peace far more surely than by turning her back on the issue.

As the first panic passed she told herself that it was only panic. A reflection of past pain. Perhaps when she came face to face with him she would realize that it had only been an illusion—that she was cured, after all.

Meanwhile, she could at least do her duty; make herself remember that, whatever her personal feelings, that duty was to her patients. Besides, surely she loved her work, as much as she admired Vere Carrington's?

And so, lying awake far into that night, she tried desperately to persuade herself that it had only been a girl's foolish dream, born, in the first place, of her admiration for a brilliant man's skill in that profession of healing which she had also made her own.

It was only a shadow that had scared her in Matron's room.

She was a whole year older now. And so very much wiser. . . .

Chapter II

I

It was raining the next morning, and taking the covered way leading from the nurses' annexe to the Private Wing, Jill pushed open the swing door, and passing through it almost collided with a tall young man in a white coat who was standing on the landing.

"That's right!" he exclaimed, grinning down at her as he rubbed the elbow which the door had hit smartly. "Compound fracture of the right elbow. Don't mind me! Knock me about——"

"What on earth are you doing here?" she asked crossly, suspecting that she could give a rather too accurate answer to that question herself.

Kenneth Harding, the young resident physician at Broad

Meadows, confessed unashamedly: "Waiting to ask a pretty nurse if she would let me drive her into Windsor for dinner to-morrow evening. You've no idea how delightful the Castle looks by moonlight!"

"Thanks, I've seen it!" replied Jill drily. "But I wouldn't know anything about whether your 'pretty nurse' has—you'll have to ask her when she comes along."

"Not been looking in the mirror lately?" he enquired.

She frowned. "Don't be silly, Ken. And, anyway, if you're blarneying me, I couldn't possibly go. I shall be on duty——"

"But not on Wednesday evening——"

"Every evening until the night nurse takes over. Anyhow, you know perfectly well I couldn't dine with you in Windsor. It's against the rules."

"What are rules for?" he asked, showing two rows of very white teeth in another of those infectious grins.

"To be kept! And I can't stay talking to you now. I've an important case coming in to-day."

Ken Harding's brows went up. "Not Mr. Carrington's?"

"Yes."

"My poor sweet!"

Jill gave him an exasperated look. "If Matron could hear you, Dr. Harding!"

As a figure appeared at the end of the corridor Ken said hurriedly: "Well, I'll be seeing you, Jill. Don't forget that if the worst happens, I'm around to pick up the pieces." Then raising his voice: "Ah! There *is* Sister Anderson. I can ask her myself."

But as Jill hurried away she could almost feel Sister's suspicious look following her, though Dr. Harding had already engaged her in animated conversation.

Not for the first time she decided that Ken Harding could be an impossibly trying young man! Yet it was difficult to help liking or being amused by him. He was such a very nice person; under his high spirits and flirtatious manner, he was kind-hearted and friendly, and—what recommended him most to Jill—a very good doctor who treated his work seriously, even if he could not be persuaded to treat much else in life that way.

Then, inspecting the room which had been allotted to her

expected patient, Jill forgot him with what he would certainly have found unflattering promptitude.

If she had found time to think about it, she would have been grateful that there was such a lot to do that morning. Miss St. Just was not expected until after lunch.

She arrived about three, in a dove-grey saloon car upholstered in wine colour, and carrying a silver statuette of a ballet dancer balanced precariously on her "points" on the bonnet.

Jill heard about the car later from Judy. With the exception of lunch time, she herself had been on her feet ever since she got up, and had gone along to scrounge a hurried cup of tea in the diet kitchen, of which there was one to every floor in the private wing. Anyhow, she could not have been expected to be on the mat when no one had known just what time to expect her patient

Meeting her as she emerged from the kitchen, Sister Anderson—who was a stickler for DUTY (all in capital letters)—frowningly demanded: "Where have you been, Nurse?" And then, without waiting for a reply, informed: "Miss St. Just is here."

In dismay Jill hurried along beside Sister's tall form, and was in time to see her new patient emerging from the lift, leaning on the arm of an elderly chauffeur, one of the maids following with rugs and a dressing case; and though she had seen plenty of photographs of the dancer, Jill realized at once how little justice the camera had done this lovely thing who seemed as frail as a flower, and as elusive as its perfume.

Sandra's startling loveliness owed little to regularity of feature. Yet she was beautiful, with her gold-flecked brown eyes, the milk-white skin which went with the dark honey-gold of her hair.

Jill felt instantly that she should be floating over the ground like a piece of thistledown in the wind, or a butterfly on the wing. It was tragic to see her limping along as she leant heavily, partly on the arm of her chauffeur and partly on the firm gold-headed stick in her free hand. She looked tired and drawn, her mouth drooping at the corners.

Then, as Sister said: "Here is Nurse Foster to help you, Miss St. Just. She will be looking after you while you are here," Sandra stood still abruptly, and for an instant the two girls looked straight at each other. Jill saw the dancer's reddened mouth set—it was a petulant, though by no means bad-tempered mouth—and held the wary, enquiring glance of those golden eyes with her own serenely smiling ones.

"Good afternoon," she said. "You don't know how different you will feel when you leave Broad Meadows."

A sudden smile lit the dancer's face. "Good afternoon, Nurse—I hope you are right," she replied. "I am certainly not feeling at my best to-day."

"I don't suppose you are." Jill was beside her. She nodded to the chauffeur. "I will take Miss St. Just to her room."

Immediately the other girl's hand was transferred to her arm.

"Good-bye for the present, Rivers," said Sandra. "You will hear later when I want you again. Tell Annie to be sure and look after the cats and don't let them be burgled—or there will be the very dickens to pay!"

"She'll look after them. So will I, Miss. Good luck." Rivers saluted and turned back into the waiting lift. Sandra did not glance round, but as the hum of the descending cage sounded, Jill felt the slender hand on her arm tighten convulsively, and her quick intuition told her that this girl, who was so famous and must have so many friends, was feeling suddenly lonely. From that moment she knew unconsciously that, whatever happened, she would never be able to dislike the lovely ballerina; though she also realized how right Matron had been—she certainly had a temperamental, and not by any means easy case on her hands.

II

As Sister flung open the door, preceding them into the big airy, cream-walled room, where flowered cretonne curtains fluttered round the open casement windows which looked out over the flower garden to the rolling acres of parkland beyond, Sandra paused with an exclamation of pleasure.

"This is delightful. It's not a bit like a hospital!" she exclaimed impulsively.

"It isn't meant to be," Sister told her briskly. "Broad Meadows is just somewhere to be very comfortably ill in, and soon forget you have ever been ill at all. Matron will come and see you later, and I understand that Mr. Carrington will be looking in."

"Yes; he promised to assist at the ordeal of my arrival." Sandra gave a little laugh. "But his secretary telephoned that he had got caught up with something else. He's dreadfully elusive—I never know whether he's coming or going," she added, shrugging her shoulders. "His secretary said she could only promise he would be here as soon as possible."

"Well, Nurse will get you nicely settled, and you will be able to rest after your journey. Remember that now you have nothing to worry about at all—just relax and let us do all the worrying." Sister disappeared, leaving Jill and her patient alone.

"Excellent bedside manner! Is she as sweet to everyone?" asked Sandra, a mischievous twinkle in her eyes.

"Depends." The little dimple which lent an added charm to Jill's face appeared and disappeared. She could have explained that Sister could be a tartar on occasion, but naturally refrained.

Just at that moment there was a discreet knock at the door announcing the arrival of Miss St. Just's suitcases. She sat in an armchair by the window while Jill unpacked her nightdress and some other necessary things from the smaller case which had come up with her, hardly speaking while she was helped to get ready for bed, and finally tucked into it.

Although she did not show it, by that time Jill was growing a little apprehensive about this suddenly taciturn young woman whom she could not help knowing was obviously summing her up.

Nurse-patient reaction was so important! Jill had only ever had one case who had made up her mind to dislike her, a difficult one of neurosis, and she prayed that Sandra St. Just was not making up *her* mind to be difficult.

Then suddenly breaking the silence Sandra said with devastating frankness: "I'm so thankful they've given me someone young and pretty to nurse me. While I was having some treatment prescribed by the doctor whom I first went to when I came back to England, I had oh! such capable nurses! But the day one had a face like the side of a house, and the night one read good books all the time—which of course was O.K. so long as she didn't read them to me!"

Thanks be she had a sense of humour; that always helped such a lot! thought Jill.

"Oh dear! I promise I won't inflict my reading tastes on you," she said. "And I assure you that Nurse Faversham, who is on night duty on this floor, though she isn't very young, is a dear."

Sandra leant back on her pillows, hands clasped behind her head. In her shell pink silk nightdress and quilted bed-jacket of blue satin embroidered in roses, her lovely shining hair curling about her heart-shaped face, she was startlingly attractive, and Jill, who had not a pang of jealousy or envy in her, admired her whole-heartedly.

Then as the other's eyes met hers she saw a wistful, questioning look in them.

"You're not nervous, are you?" she asked. "I promise you it won't be too bad. Mr. Carrington never lets his patients suffer a lot of pain."

"I don't exactly expect to enjoy myself." Sandra made a little face. "But if Vere Carrington can really cure me——" she broke off, a shadow in her eyes. "I wonder! I wonder if I'm not just mad to consent to suffer more weeks of hell—being pulled, and dragged about, and I suppose strapped up in beastly plaster, all with the risk of another disappointment at the end of it?"

"But why should it be a disappointment?"

"Well, all the others have told me it's hopeless. Nothing will unlock that joint again."

"Mr. Carrington didn't tell you that?" Jill was grateful she could say the name so calmly, and know that her colour remained unchanged.

"No. But——"

"Well—I think you are wise to put yourself in his hands," said Jill briskly. "Now, wouldn't you like to have a little rest before tea?"

"I couldn't even doze. Do unpack my other case like a dear, and talk to me."

"Very well," agreed Jill. "Can I have the key?"

"It's in my bag." Sandra found it. "Tell me," she added with a shade more confidence, "do you really think Mr. Carrington is as wonderful as all that?"

Again Jill noticed with pride how steady her hand was as she unlocked the case. "He is—very clever," she said. "Have you been under him long?"

Without answering, Sandra observed: "There are some photographs and knick-knacks I'd like to see out—makes me feel more at home!" She snuggled down. "It was my godmother who insisted on my going to V. C. My godmother is Lady Amanda Skeyne—she's a bit of a dragon, but a darling. She dragged me down to Brighton to stay with her because, she said, I was moping, and getting morbid! And Mr. Carrington turned up at the hotel where we were staying. I've an idea Lady Mandy engineered his arrival, though she won't admit it. He had dinner in our suite on the second night, and it was all very social, though I did tell him I was sick of doctors and had no faith in them any more. Then, before I knew what was happening my godmother had arranged for him to examine me the next day. I suppose you know him?"

This time Jill was thankful her back was turned while she put a little pile of the patient's dainty night attire into a drawer.

"I have—seen him work," she said.

"Well, no one could accuse *him* of an excess of bedside manner! He told me that if I was determined to accept defeat and waste the rest of my life, and the talent which had been given me, he couldn't prevent me. He also suggested I was a coward. I was furious. I asked him why he should think he could succeed where others had failed. Do you know what he said?"

"No—what?" Jill had turned, and conscious of a slight breathlessness, waited to hear. She knew him so well when he was irritated. He could be horrible!

"That it was probably because he did not believe in accepting defeat, though all he would guarantee to do would be to take a fifty-fifty chance on me—if I had the courage to let him! Well—somehow I found I'd been bludgeoned into it, and here I am. I don't expect, in spite of my godmother's enthusiasm, he's any better than the others."

Jill found herself saying warmly, "But you are wrong. He is—magnificent. I wouldn't let disliking him prejudice you, if——"

"But I don't dislike him!" interrupted Sandra. "I'm ready to own he can be charming when he likes; or rather, when he gets his own way. But with him it's a matter of 'What I say, goes!' And he doesn't always say it politely. I still hate being kicked around, and as he warns there is a risk of failure, I just wonder if it's worth while letting myself be made a guinea-pig of." As Jill passed the bed Sandra reached out, catching her arm with a sudden pleading look. "Nurse, I do so desperately want to dance again. I had made up my mind I never would, but—I can't bear the thought now that there seems to be a gleam of hope. *Can* he bring it off?"

Jill looked at her steadily. "What matters is that he thinks it worth while taking a chance on you," she said. "He is only human, but I've seen him do things that were—almost miraculous. In my experience I have never known him do more than promise to 'take a chance' but never once has he failed to turn that chance into certainty. I grant that Mr. Carrington may be a very difficult man to get along with——"

"May be!" repeated Sandra. "I'm certain he can be a fiend."

Jill smiled. "Well, let's grant he is a very difficult man; but remember he is also a very brilliant one——" she broke off, turning swiftly towards the door, which had opened silently, to find herself staring in dismay into the cool grey eyes of the man on the threshold—finding herself for the first time in ten months face to face with Vere Carrington, and knowing with terrifying clearness how completely she had been deceiving herself—how crazy it had been ever to have believed she had regained control of her heart. . . .

Chapter III

I

"I KNOCKED twice, but you were too interested in your conversation to hear me."

Jill felt that if there was any sarcasm in those cool clipped tones it was for her; the smile he gave his patient was warm and friendly.

How well Jill remembered that rare smile, and the way it transformed the gravity of his dark, clear cut face! "Good afternoon, Nurse." He passed her with a brief nod.

Sandra did not seem at all embarrassed. "Hello!" she greeted. "So you got here. I rather gathered that you might be a lot later."

"I expected that myself, but my consultation took up less time than I had allowed for it, and by ignoring most of the speed laws I hoped that I might manage to get here before you." He took the slender hand she extended and holding it for an instant released it and sat down in the chair by the bed. "But here you are, happily settled in."

Sandra pulled a little face, shrugging her shoulders. "I wouldn't say 'happily' was quite the operative word," she said, a touch of what-have-you in her manner. She was plainly not at all in awe of her handsome surgeon, and Jill was human enough to decide that it would do Mr. Carrington good not to be kow-towed to. How like him to arrive at an awkward moment! She remembered the time when Sister on Oxford Ward at St. Monica's had cursed the man for walking in at unexpected moments when he could reasonably be expected not to be in the hospital at all.

Well, here he was dealing with someone as famous in her way as he was in his. And yet—however spoiled the lovely ballerina might be, if she expected to get her own way from Vere Carrington she would soon find out her mistake, thought Jill a little bitterly. As Sandra herself had indicated, it was what Mr. Carrington said that mattered. Mr. Carrington saw to that!

He was saying now: "If not happily, at any rate comfortably settled. And once we get the worst of this business over you will be happy enough."

Sandra said quickly: "But you are not going to rush the—operation, are you? You will give me time to get used to being here."

"The sooner it is over the better," he replied. "I am arranging to operate to-morrow."

"Oh no!" she frowned at him. "I'd rather wait."

"No good. You would only get fidgety, and be wanting to run away," he said calmly.

"I shouldn't be able to run very far, should I? And if I could I suppose you would be after me in seven-leagued boots—with a big stick." In spite of the touch of sulkiness in her voice Sandra laughed.

"I most certainly should." He softened the threat with another smile. "Believe me, the sooner it is over the better pleased you will be. This is a delightful room." Glancing round he reached out casually, taking one of Sandra's wrists between thumb and forefinger and holding it while he watched the minute hand on his wrist watch.

Waiting while he counted the pulse beats, Jill, standing at the foot of the bed, was aware of her own heart throbs, and of that dull pain which, however hard she tried to deny it, mingled with them. How stupid to feel so—churned up! she thought, resentment welling up in her against the bondage in which she was held against her will. Until she had turned and seen him standing in the doorway she had been almost sure that she was cured. She wondered if there were some things which were beyond cure, and dismissed the idea sharply.

But in spite of the chaos at work inside her she looked cool and calm and very efficient standing there in her mauve frock and stiffly starched apron and cap; and though she did not guess it, the doctor was fully aware of her presence as he put the wrist he held gently back on the blue linen bedspread.

"She stood up to the drive down from London fairly well, Nurse?" he asked.

"Very well, sir. I checked her pulse and temperature. Both were normal." She unhooked the chart which she had already hung above the bed and handed it to him.

Vere Carrington glanced at it briefly.

"Thank you."

Jill went back to the suitcase she had been unpacking and shutting it said quietly:

"It is time for your tea now, Miss St. Just. May I bring a cup for you, sir?"

"Yes, of course," said Sandra. "You're not going yet, doctor?"

He looked at his watch. "I must be away from here by five, and I have to see other people and make my arrangements for you before I go. But yes—perhaps there is time for a cup of tea."

II

Going to collect the tea-tray two or three minutes later, Jill wondered again if Vere could have heard what she and Sandra were saying before he arrived. How awful if he had! Worse if he had recognized her! And it was impossible to tell whether he remembered her or not, in spite of the hard look he had given her. Probably not! All nurses looked alike to the top-of-the-tree man. That was what made her own folly so much worse!

Perhaps that was why he was being so—specially nice to Sandra, because he was interested enough to want to make her change her opinion of him. She felt that sharp, cruel little pain go through her. It was followed by a feeling of panic as she asked herself if, on top of all that she had suffered, she was to know the degrading passion of jealousy.

She had arranged the tray and just filled the teapot when to her secret dismay Judy came into the kitchen.

"Hello! Going to have tea with Sandra St. Just?" she asked, indicating the second cup.

"Not me, my dear." Jill hoped her laugh sounded natural. "Second cup is for the surgeon."

Judy gave a low whistle. "Heavens! The great man is condescending. I say, Jill," she added, reaching for another tray and beginning to prepare it, "wouldn't it be too funny if he fell for the ballerina? She's certainly got what it takes. But I bet she's got a will of her own. She'd larn his nibs!"

"Rubbish!" exclaimed Jill sharply. "She's just a 'case' like any other. Your trouble is an over-developed bump of romance—or reading too many novels."

"Not a bit of it," retorted Judy. "You wait and see. He may be all strong and silent and wedded to his work (*doesn't* he look like every girl's dream come true, though? I saw him arrive, and Kathleen's description is stark understatement!) but I've known that type before; when they fall they fall *hard*—believe you me, ducky."

"Judy, dear, I love you fondly," Jill told her, "But you do talk the most arrant nonsense. I've seen Mr. Carrington work, and he's as cold as ice."

And yet Judy was only putting into words something that had been at the back of her own mind. Something she wanted to hear so little that she knew she was deliberately building a wall to hide behind.

But Judy refused to be repressed. "Shure, I can't help what you've seen," she said obstinately. "He may think he's immune to all human feeling—but a man with a face like that isn't only a human refrigerator. Mark my words; one day he'll meet his Waterloo. If," she jerked her head towards Sandra's room, "he hasn't already met it."

Judy and her romancing! If only she would pay more attention to her work! thought Jill.

But when she reached her patient's room again, the other girl's words were still echoing in her mind. As she opened the door Vere Carrington was laughing at something Sandra was saying. He rose when Jill entered and took the tray from her, and again she was conscious of the hard direct look he gave her from those grey-blue eyes which appeared so light in contrast to the dark tan into which the summer sun and wind had burned his complexion.

He put the tray on a table in the window recess and went back to his seat. While Jill poured out the tea she was conscious, in every fibre, of the two behind her, who had resumed their conversation.

Sandra had said that she disliked being "kicked around", but in spite of his determination over the operation Jill could not help noticing that Vere's manner towards his patient was one of amused tolerance, and a natural sort of friendliness which she—Jill—had never noticed him use before. But of course, she reminded herself, he was a friend of Lady Amanda Skeyne's, who had first introduced him to her goddaughter; and so, quite apart from her being his patient, they had met socially. For the first time it occurred to her that the man whose brilliant work had attracted her admiration, long before she discovered that the man himself was so important to her, had a life quite apart from the environment in which she had met him.

This time he allowed himself to be waited on, and when she carried the cups of tea across, having first arranged a bed table for Sandra, he took his with a brief "Thank you—no sugar, please."

Sandra said: "Before you arrived, Mr. Carrington, I was telling nurse that I wondered if I were not just asking for more trouble by letting Lady Mandy and you persuade me to come here."

"You will soon know," he replied imperturbably. And then, as Jill moved to the door he rose again: "Are you going off duty, Nurse?"

"Only to tea, sir," she answered.

"I wish to speak to you before I leave. I will see you on the landing in twenty minutes."

"Yes, sir."

Shutting the door she felt a sudden surge of resentment. Not because the request sounded so much more like an order; she was used to taking orders and obeying them; but because—well, somehow she felt he could not have been more impersonal if she had been a bit of the wall. And yet his manners were perfect in many ways.

Don't be so idiotic! she scolded herself impatiently. You might be the wall for all the personal interest he ever has taken, or would be likely to take in you.

And yet that was not entirely true—there had been those few weeks when he had thawed. When there had been a most difficult case in the surgical ward where, more than eighteen months ago now, she had just been promoted to staff nurse. The case had been a challenge to his skill, but he had known that just a little more even than his brilliant doctoring was needed, and he welcomed the perfect and loyal co-operation Jill had given him. For those too-brief weeks she had experienced the thrill and excitement of actually being trusted as a fellow worker of Vere Carrington's, and feeling that he considered the co-operation necessary.

And she had worked so willingly—so desperately hard, blinding herself to the fact that it was the doctor who mattered, that for the first time in a career which had hitherto been so selfless, she had worked for a reward apart from just the knowledge that she was helping a sick person to come back to health.

It was only afterwards that the realization of how much Vere Carrington's approval meant to her had come with the shock of a thunderbolt. And that had been the beginning of it.

After that particular case had been cured and discharged

from the hospital—another monument to Mr. Carrington's great skill—Jill had felt, though he had said no word, that he realized how much she had helped, and that his brief "Good morning, Nurse", his rare smile, were marks of his remembrance.

She had left the hospital while he was away on holiday, but although she was sure that he would very quickly forget she had ever been there, she had sometimes dared to hope that he might have wondered where she had gone before he forgot.

But she was sure now, with angry humiliation at her weakness, that he had not even recognized her. She told herself that this was where she really began to come to her senses—to learn "to be her age", as she had told Judy to be.

She vowed determinedly that she was going to learn to meet Vere Carrington without the quickening of one heartbeat.

She *would* escape escape from her bondage; cure herself of the madness of loving that cold, hard man who would despise her if he guessed her secret.

And yet—was he so cold and hard?

He seemed to have become human enough where Sandra St. Just was concerned.

It was maddening to feel the heart she had been so determined to control contract, and throb like an open wound.

Suddenly she felt that she hated Vere Carrington, and asked herself if that was not the very best way she could feel? Forgetting that love and hate are simply opposite ends of the same pole.

Chapter IV

JILL avoided the big sunny room where she knew as many of the nurses as could get there would gather for tea. So many of the staff were ballet-mad that she knew she could not possibly avoid a shower of questions about her new case, and she did not want to discuss Sandra, if only because Mr. Carrington's name was bound to crop up.

She went along the corridor to the now deserted kitchen and, having made herself a strong cup of tea, stood by the window drinking it, determinedly shutting her mind to all disquieting thoughts.

She reminded herself that she was here to do a job of work—the work which meant more to her than anything else in the world; she ought to be thankful to be able to do it in this lovely, so perfectly run place.

Duty, Jill! she told herself. Duty—duty!

It might be a cold little word—it might suddenly look like a cul-de-sac. But that was what mattered—the whole course of a nurse's life. Not her personal feelings.

Anyhow, she liked Sandra, and felt gratefully that the other girl reciprocated the feeling. That would help.

Exactly twenty minutes after she had left her patient she returned to the broad landing off which Sandra's room led. Mr. Carrington had said that he would see her on the landing, and knowing he was the kind of person who expected people to do exactly what he said, she did not attempt to knock on the door and tell him she was there. When he was ready he would come out to her.

She had not to wait long. She had walked over to the big window which lighted the square space off which the rooms led, when the soft opening and closing of a door made her turn back quickly.

Vere Carrington signed to her to remain where she was, and joined her. Somewhere at the back of Jill's mind was the knowledge that she would be able to pick that light, firm footstep out from a hundred. But she stood, hands behind her back, the picture of outward serenity, waiting for him to speak.

She was not by any means a small girl, but she had a long way to look up to Mr. Carrington's six foot two, and magnificent width of shoulders. Yet he carried his inches easily, and like most really well-proportioned big men, did not strike one as being unduly tall.

In spite of herself Jill could not help thinking with a touch of irritation that Judy's description of his as "every girl's dream of romance" was incorrect. There was nothing of the film star, of the Adonis, about that dark, clear-cut face and rather penthouse brows above the deep-set grey eyes. Attractive—yes; and distinguished looking. A strong nose, and a strength that again also hinted of obstinacy in the square jaw line. A ruthless enough face, but saved from being a hard one by an unexpected cleft in his chin, and a mouth that could soften so remarkably when he smiled.

He was unsmiling now, though, as he said abruptly:

"I had already made by arrangements by telephone before I saw Miss St. Just. I am operating at ten to-morrow morning—I cannot get down here earlier. And I had a word with Matron on my way up. I am going to interview Sister Theatre now, and look round and get the hang of the place. Will Sister be in the Theatre now, do you think?"

"Yes, sir," said Jill. "There have been no operations to-day, but Sister is always there until five-thirty."

"Good. Will you show me the way," and then he added quickly: "Just a minute. You know, of course, that this is not going to be nearly so easy as I have persuaded the patient it is."

"Yes, sir," said Jill. "I—gathered that."

He frowned. "If I had dealt with it first—or even if she had come to me at once on her return to England, she would not be in this state now." With another man the calm taking for granted that he was bound to succeed where others had failed, might have sounded boastful, but there was no trace of conceit in this air of calm self-assurance. He knew his job and he could do his job. How many patients, thought Jill, must have been glad they had trusted themselves to him.

Then in a few brief, clear-cut sentences he was explaining the whole thing to her, and Jill felt her heart beating quickly for other reasons than ones that could hurt and humiliate her. She was a nurse who was going to have the privilege of working with a very great surgeon—for he was great. All her enthusiasm welled up in her while she listened with concentrated interest.

"Afterwards," he told her, as Matron had done earlier, "a great deal will depend on the nursing, and on seeing that the patient obeys orders. I need not tell you that this particular patient is extremely highly strung. But you are—or were—good on this kind of case."

For that once, all Jill's training and self-control could not stop the quick, startled look she gave him, or her sudden change of colour.

Meeting her eyes, he smiled slightly. "You were the staff

nurse for a time on Oxford Ward at St. Monica's—were you not?"

"Yes——"

"Why did you leave?" Then to her relief, in his characteristic way not waiting for a reply, he continued abruptly: "No matter. You are here now," and continued to give her some instructions about to-morrow's arrangements in his cool, level voice. Then: "As you know, I expect both you and the patient to carry out my orders to the letter," he said. "And as long as you do that you will not find the surgeon an unduly 'difficult man'."

Jill felt herself go scarlet again. So he had heard! This was awful!

But he was saying calmly: "And now for Sister Theatre—take me as quickly as possible. I am in a hurry."

"Yes—s-sir."

Walking swiftly ahead of him Jill pushed open the door leading to the newly-built surgical wing. She held it open for him, but he did not look at her as he passed through, or perhaps she might have seen that although his mouth was set and grave there was a little twinkle in his eyes. . . .

But he remained quite silent while they traversed the white-tiled corridors, passing the Radio Therapy and X-ray departments, and the two children's wards, where bad, and getting better, cases were treated.

Glancing in at one of them Jill's companion broke the silence. "I did not know they had wards here," he said.

"Only for children," she told him. "We do give completely private treatment if parents insist. But we have found that the kiddies are better when they are together. There is a special staff for those wards."

He nodded. "Good idea. Children are gregarious creatures."

Then they reached the Theatre where, after she had announced him to Sister, he dismissed her with a nod.

As Jill retraced her steps, life seemed to have fallen more into perspective again. Broad Meadows and its claims closed round her. She was once again Nurse Gillian Foster with an interesting case ahead which—she hoped—would take up most of her time and her thoughts for the next few weeks.

Chapter V

I

It was of Nurse Foster that Vere Carrington was thinking when a quarter of an hour later he turned his car Londonwards.

The moment he had seen her in Sandra's room, he had remembered the young Staff Nurse who had never got flurried and never failed to carry out his orders to—as he had told her he expected to just now—"the letter". He had indeed intended to draw the Matron of St. Monica's attention to the girl with a suggestion that in these days when extreme competence so often seemed to be at a premium (Mr. Carrington was an impatient man and did not make, or accept, excuses if things went wrong) the Staff Nurse on Oxford Ward should be given the speediest possible promotion.

Naturally he knew enough of hospital etiquette not to have contemplated more than a casual remark, though he knew the St. Monica's Matron almost as well as he knew Miss Travers.

Then the girl had disappeared abruptly.

He had never troubled to ask why, and he probably only recollected her because her successor had been far too eager to please him, and failed to do so, or come anywhere near his difficult standards; and even now he was annoyed and irritated with Jill for leaving.

However, the Foster girl evidently had not got married as so many of them did—after wasting the hospital's time training them.

Mr. Carrington had a fixed idea that marriage and medicine ought not to meet.

It was a small world, he mused. Sometimes too small—sometimes conveniently so. Anyhow it was a good thing that particular nurse was on this case; she knew his methods and—she was an excellent nurse. He was staking a lot on the success of to-morrow's operation. It was a wicked waste for Sandra St. Just to have had to interrupt her career in this way, and if he made the success he expected to it would be the triumph of *his* career.

To bring it off! That was all that interested him.

As usual, he ignored the possibility of any element creeping in to complicate—not the surgical, but the personal side of the case.

II

Running quickly up the broad staircase which led from the entrance hall Jill almost collided with Kenneth Harding, who was just about to descend by the way she had come up.

"Sorry, Nurse," Dr. Harding apologized. And then: "Jill! I didn't recognize you with the sun in my eyes."

"Must you rush about nearly knocking inoffensive members of the nursing staff downstairs?" she asked.

"Did I hurt you?" he enquired anxiously.

She laughed. "No, you didn't. What a clumsy person you are!"

"Well, stop and talk to a fellow for two minutes," he coaxed. "It's ages since I've even caught a glimpse of you. How is 'operation dancer' going?"

"As well as can be expected. She isn't out of plaster yet."

"So no one knows whether the great man has performed a miracle or made a flop."

"Don't be flippant about your betters," said Jill.

He grinned. "Professional jealousy, sweetie. You couldn't help a fellow to use a couple of tickets for Drury Lane next Thursday night? I'm sure Sister would arrange for you to get off early, if you asked her very nicely, and told her you were invited out by the most attractive man of your acquaintance."

"I couldn't tell a lie as big as that," Jill told him. "Not even for the chance of going to Drury Lane——"

"Seriously, Jill—couldn't you?" he coaxed.

She shook her head. "It can't be done, honestly. Patient gets fretful if she is left." She paused. "Ask Judy O'Farrell if you haven't anyone else in mind. She has Wednesday and Thursday leave next week, but though she's going up to London to stay with an aunt, she's looking forward to a dull time, and Thursday happens to be her birthday. It would be nice of you,

Ken, and as she is on leave it wouldn't matter about her going out with you, even if anyone saw you."

"O.K. I'll ask Judy," he agreed cheerfully. "She's a nice kid. But I still don't see why, just because you are nursing Sandra St. Just, you should become her Siamese twin. I suppose you are not doing night duty as well?"

"Of course not," she answered. "But just at present I don't want to leave her more than is necessary. She gets fretful and worries about what will happen when she comes out of plaster—though I tell her it is practically certain it's a success." She did not add that it was between the hours of five and seven that Mr. Carrington usually visited his patient, and naturally she was expected to be in attendance.

"I must go," she said. "She'll be awake and wanting her tea."

But as she would have passed him he caught her hand, holding it determinedly. "Listen, Jill——"

He broke off and, annoyed, Jill pulled herself free hurriedly as a door opened and someone came out. It was only when she turned her head that she saw who the someone was, and her heart missed a beat in dismay when she met the level stare of Vere's grey eyes.

On the heels of her dismay, her first thought was: What on earth is he doing here at this hour? Never since the first two days following Sandra's operation had the surgeon arrived before the late afternoon, or early evening; but here he was now, coldly correct, returning Ken's good afternoon.

Murmuring sumething rather vague Dr. Harding ran downstairs. At any other time it might have amused Jill to see the gaily philandering young physician so evidently deflated, but she could feel disapproval oozing from Mr. Carrington, and told herself it was too bad. She could have slain Ken. If the older man had seen him tolding her hand, he would think she had been taking advantage of this quiet time to indulge in a spot of flirtation. Bother the man! What on earth *was* he doing here at this time?

"Good afternoon, Nurse," said Vere curtly. He was hardly going to explain that he had had a consultation in the neighbourhood and decided to look in on his way back to town.

"Yes, sir? Patrick should have let me know you were here." Jill's voice was steadier than her heartbeats.

"The porter was not on duty when I arrived," he replied. "I came straight up. If Miss St. Just had been asleep I should have left a message and gone away again."

"She always sleeps in the afternoon," said Jill. "I leave her for an hour—as you suggested."

He frowned. "It is not much use a patient being left to sleep if telephone calls are put through to them."

"But no calls are put through to any of the patients between three o'clock and four-thirty," said Jill.

"It would be as well if they were also prevented from making them," he told her impatiently. "I found Miss St. Just on the telephone. She finished her call as I arrived, but she seemed excited and upset."

"I will enquire about it," said Jill. "If a call was put through——"

He made an impatient movement. "I evidently did not make myself clear. The call was not put through. Miss St. Just could not sleep, and decided to ring up a friend. I told her that at this stage I preferred her to rest at the time when she is supposed to."

So both nurse *and* patient were in trouble! thought Jill with a wry touch of humour. But it was rather hard that the nurse who had not been on the spot should be blamed because the patient had decided to disobey orders.

Dismissing the subject Vere continued:

"That plaster must come off to-morrow. I trust it will be possible to keep it off. I shall be here at ten-thirty."

"Yes, sir," said Jill serenely.

He gave no sign of the question in his mind in the cold, keen glance he bent on her. There was a brief silence while Jill waited for further orders; then, he continued frowningly: "It is not the limb I am concerned about, so much as the patient's nervous state. It strikes me she is fretting about something. Find out what it is, if possible, and set her mind at rest. Good afternoon."

Hardly giving her time to reply, and without making any attempt to ring for the lift, he ran quickly downstairs.

For a brief space Jill remained where he had left her, her underlip caught hard between her even white teeth.

"You will not find the surgeon unduly 'difficult'!" Had he really made that half-promise at the beginning of all this?

Well perhaps he had kept it up to a point—as long as everything went exactly as he thought it ought to. But really he could be—quite the most unreasonable and difficult man in the world! Though, this afternoon was the first time she had felt that he was really displeased with her. She wondered if it was because he thought she had been philandering with Ken—or just because he had found it necessary to scold Sandra? Undoubtedly he was extremely interested in his lovely and famous patient, and, try as hard as she would not to, Jill could not help asking herself if the interest was limited to purely medical grounds.

Turning towards Miss St. Just's door she was miserably conscious of the sudden painful lurch of her heart. Now! she told herself sharply, Stop that! It doesn't matter to you any more who he is interested in—you've finished with that folly.

How easy to say! How difficult to believe! But she had to build a barrier against her weakness, and hope it would in time grow high and secure enough to protect her.

Meanwhile the "difficult" man was striding out to his car in one of his most difficult moods.

Really, these young women! One never knew where one was with them. He would have thought that Nurse Foster had more sense of the dignity of her uniform, than to stand about having her hand held at odd moments—and by a staff man (who also ought to know better).

Of course, what she did when she was off duty was none of his business! Vere's frown deepened. This afternoon she had not been off duty. And—oh! confound it! if a girl was conducting a love affair how could she possibly give her whole mind to her work? Yet that particular girl always appeared so calm and serene; the last person he would have expected to find holding hands! He decided that if he saw anything like that again he would have to report it.

All of which, considering the real facts, was decidedly unfair to Jill.

Chapter VI

As her day nurse came into the room Sandra closed the magazine she had been absent-mindedly looking through—her mind very far from the shiny pages with their pictures of the doings of the worlds of society, stage and film folk.

"Oh, Nurse," she greeted. "Mr. Carrington has been in——"

"I know," Jill told her. "I met him on the landing."

"Was he still bad-tempered? I did wish you were here to protect me." Sandra smiled—though it was only the ghost of one of those flashing mischievous smiles Jill had got used to. "Was he very fierce?" she asked.

"He was cross. He snapped my head off."

There were times when Sandra was like a naughty, but still attractive child, and Jill could not help smiling, in spite of her annoyance. "You shouldn't go making telephone calls when you ought to be resting," she said.

"He's been telling tales."

"Naturally."

Sandra made an impatient movement of the pretty shoulders under her silk nightdress.

"I couldn't sleep, and I was bored. It suddenly occurred to me there was someone I wanted to speak to in London. What harm was there in that?"

"Couldn't you have chosen some other time to make the call?" asked Jill.

"I wanted to make it then."

"And Mr. Carrington turned up to find that his orders were being disobeyed. You can't grumble if he was annoyed. During these first days you know it is very necessary for you to keep quiet."

"Quiet! I feel I would like to break the furniture—I *hate* keeping quiet——"

"Now, now!" Jill smiled down into the stormy eyes.

"Well!" Sandra's tone was exasperated. "I hate being expected to obey anyone. And anyway, that man's got a power complex. He must have his own way. I like my own way, too."

"The difference is," said Jill, laughing, "that *he* wants his own way for your good."

"Oh! You are always on his side," exclaimed Sandra impatiently.

"I would get fired if I was not," said Jill, adding firmly: "I am going to fetch your tea now."

She had her hand on the door knob again when a coaxing voice from the bed pleaded: "Have yours in here with me—please, Nursie! I've got the blue devilkins this afternoon, but I will be good."

"O.K." Jill's smile turned to a sigh as she got outside the door again. It had been impossible not to get fond of her patient, however trying she might be at times—in fact she could not understand anyone not being attracted by the lovely tempestuous creature. And any man who failed to succumb to her charm must be a block of stone—she switched the thought off abruptly.

If her nurse had become fond of Sandra she seemed to be returning the compliment; there were times when her complete dependence on Jill could be a little trying. Unfortunately she had not taken so completely to her night nurse who, though she was briskly kind and efficient, had not much imagination.

When Jill brought the tea tray in Sandra, with one of her lightning changes of mood, was all laughter and gaiety. Watching the other girl set the tray down on the table by the window, she asked: "Do you remember the first day you poured out tea for me—and Mr. Carrington stopped and had it with me?"

It was something Jill would rather have forgotten, remembering her own feelings that day. "Yes," she said briefly. Then proceeding to move the litter of magazines and books from the bed rest in front of her patient: "What an untidy girl you are!"

"I've never been anything else," Sandra assured her. "And I like other people to do my tidying. At home I have all the morning papers brought up to me, and the two cats come and make nests for themselves in them—usually the ones I haven't read." She looked wistfully at the big, framed picture of two large and very beautiful pussies—one black, the other with an expanse of white shirt front—which stood on the bedside table. "Aren't they pets— I do wish I could have them here."

"I'd like to see Matron's face if she paid you one of her visits and found a couple of cats on the bed," laughed Jill.

"I'm sure she would let me have them, if it wouldn't create some shocking precedent and every other patient didn't demand domestic pets," laughed Sandra. "And wouldn't it be lovely to see Vere Carrington's reaction! Matron's a darling, though. She spoils me."

"In fact we all oblige by spoiling you—with the possible exception of Mr. Carrington," said Jill, bringing her tea.

"Oh, he is not so bad. He soon got over his snappiness," Sandra admitted, dimpling.

Transferred it to me! thought Jill. But I suppose I ought to be used to that! Bedside manner for the patient, bad temper for the nurse. It was not strictly accurate or fair, but suddenly she did not feel inclined to be fair. Men were just the limit! And when she saw Ken again there was going to be trouble for one of the trying sex!

Sandra said: "The—friend I was talking to this afternoon is coming down to see me on Tuesday. I wonder what you will think of him?"

Jill's heart missed a beat as she asked: "Anything very special about him?"

"Only that he is probably the most selfish man in existence," said Sandra, and though her tone was cool, her hand, resting on the tray before her, clenched tightly. "I expect you have heard of Glyn Errol?"

"Lord Glyn Errol," repeated Jill, her interest quickening. I've seen pictures of him—there was one in the *Tatler* the week you arrived. He is terribly interested in ballet and opera, isn't he? Isn't he the chief owner, or something like it, of The Sonnet Theatre?"

"He is the head of the syndicate that owns it now," replied Sandra. "His father built it—with his mother's money, or rather some of it. She was the daughter of an American multi-millionaire, and incidentally a very great friend of my god-mother's. Errol is crazy on ballet. It was he who financed my American tour."

"You know," Jill said frankly, "since you came here I have rather lost sight of the fact that you are a famous person, who must know all sorts of other famous persons."

"If you include Glyn among the 'persons' I hardly think he deserves to be described as 'famous'," said Sandra.

"Well, he's very well known—both in Society and because of his connection with the theatre," Jill told her. "Is he a great friend of yours?"

"I should never describe him as a *friend*," said Sandra with her favourite little shrug.

Conscious of slight disappointment, Jill said:

"Anyway, he is coming to see you."

"And hating it," Sandra told her. "He loathes illness of any sort—takes it as a personal insult if any of his acquaintances dare to be ill. It might have been my fault that I was spilled out of a car; you've no idea how he will hate coming to see me."

"He sounds utterly unnatural!" exclaimed Jill indignantly. "Why do you let him come?"

"Sheer cussedness!" But though Sandra laughed, her eyes were shadowed as she added: "Mr. Carrington said to-day that I could have a few visitors to see me now, if I wanted them. I didn't tell him I had already arranged to have Glyn. I just said 'thank you' very prettily and meekly."

Jill shook her head reproachfully; the first startled half-hope that Sandra's visitor might be of some real importance to her had died down, but this incursion from the outside world reminded her that—as she had told Sandra just now—the other girl had a background and an important life of her own.

All Jill's patients became her children while they remained in those strong capable hands of hers, and she had thought of Sandra, after her operation, far more as a sick girl who had to be coaxed and mended back to health, than as the famous ballerina she actually was. But suddenly it seemed strange and rather short-sighted to have so completely lost sight of the fact that there must be plenty of other men in the dancer's life, as well as her handsome surgeon. She realized that she had unknowingly narrowed the circle down to Sandra's sick room and the interests it must contain.

After all, it was not absolutely necessary for Vere's evident interest in his patient to be returned, any more than it was necessary that the interest was—well, anyway not much more than professional.

"What are you looking so serious about?" asked Sandra,

and Jill was jolted quickly away from the speculation which in another moment would have begun to torture her.

"Was I looking serious?" she asked. "If you have finished, I had better take this tray back. You don't seem to have eaten anything," she added severely, looking at the untouched slice of thin bread and butter, and the crumbled piece of cake on Sandra's plate.

"Please, Nursie, I'm not hungry," pleaded Sandra, putting her hands together.

"Don't 'nursie' me, you spoilt child," Jill told her. "If you don't eat what is given to you I shall have to report you to Mr. Carrington. Then there'll be fireworks."

"Two can let those off," replied Miss St. Just rebelliously. Then with a half mischievous look: "Wouldn't that one and I fight, if we got up against each other! But if you told tales I expect he would blame you for not *making* me behave."

Perhaps she was right, Jill thought with rather bitter amusement, as, having gathered the tea things together, she carried the tray back to the kitchen.

Judy was just arranging another tray when her friend entered.

"Hello, stranger," she greeted. "The only glimpses I seem to have caught of you these last two days were at mealtimes. And I've been too sleepy to come in for a girlish gossip when I'm through with the chores."

Jill raised her brows. "Who's working you to death?"

Judy shrugged her shoulders. "Ask Matron, ducky. You knew they'd put me in the infants because Sister Garret had three of her staff away——"

"Why on earth!" exclaimed Jill.

"Comyns has 'flu, Madison's sprained her ankle, and one of the pros has gone home on 'compassionate leave' because her mother's seriously ill."

"Lawks!" exclaimed Jill, "what a chapter of accidents!" She sighed. "I don't seem to hear anything that's happening any more—my life's confined to my present case."

"Is it hateful?" asked Judy.

Jill shook her head. "No! I like her. She can be tempestuous, but she's lovable."

Judy looked mischievous. "Does the Great Man agree on that point?"

"I haven't asked him." Jill's voice was more even than the quickened painful beating of her heart. She had made up her mind so firmly that it did not matter to her what Vere Carrington was likely to feel about his patient, but she wished Judy would hold her tongue. Anyway, he had shown his disapproval of the nurse clearly enough! she decided, retracing her steps a few moments later.

The lift was just coming up as she passed the gates. She continued on her way without glancing towards it, and had her hand on the knob of Sandra's door when a woman's incisive but cultured and not unpleasant voice spoke behind her.

"Excuse me, Nurse, is this the right floor for number 25?"

Jill turned quickly, and to her surprise, for the voice had sounded young, found herself confronting a tall old lady whose white hair shone like silver under the tilted forward brim of an exceedingly becoming grey straw hat from which two ostrich plumes swept back across the crown. From under the brim a pair of intensely blue eyes looked out from a handsome face as clear skinned as a girl's, though Jill guessed instinctively their possessor must be all of seventy. For the rest, her spare, upright figure was attired in a grey linen tailored suit which, with its rather long jacket and full skirt, bore a distinctly Edwardian touch.

A formidable old lady who must once have been very beautiful, and would have made full use of the power that beauty gave her.

Jill told her: "This is number twenty-five. Are you wanting Miss St. Just?"

"Yes. My goddaughter. I am Lady Amanda Skeyne," was the brisk reply.

Jill had already guessed who the visitor was. "Good afternoon, Lady Amanda," she said. "She will be glad to see you. She was not expecting you, was she?"

"No. Don't open that door for a moment, please," Lady Amanda requested. "I want to talk to you first. You are her usual nurse?"

"Yes. I am Nurse Foster," Jill admitted.

"Good. Come over here." The old lady moved across to the window recess, and Jill, thinking with a touch of amusement that here was someone else who obviously liked their own way and was used to getting it, followed her.

"Now!" Lady Amanda turned again to face her. "How is she getting on? Behaving herself—eh?"

"She is getting on very well," said Jill. "Mr. Carrington is removing the plaster to-morrow, and then we can get on with the treatment."

"Um! Going to be a long business?"

"Several weeks, I am afraid."

"Well, I don't envy you that part of it. For a girl who has—more or less patiently—endured the years of drudgery that go to make a ballet dancer, Sandra is the most impatient and difficult invalid imaginable. If she can't be mended all in one go, she is in despair that she never will be! But of course you have found that out." Lady Amanda's sudden smile was warm and humorous. "She writes that you are 'a poppet', whatever that may be."

Jill laughed. "Better than being a tyrant—which is how she would describe me if I——"

"Didn't know how to manage her," the old lady chuckled. "But what does Vere Carrington really feel about the result of his operation? I only came back from France yesterday and I have not been able to contact him—as easy to get hold of an eel as that man; he is always somewhere else."

"I think Mr. Carrington is quite happy about the result," said Jill.

Lady Amanda gave her a quick look. "Oh! he is sure enough of his own skill," she said drily. "But I suppose he makes mistakes sometimes. Let's go in." She marched back to the door, tapped on it briskly and had opened it before Jill could even catch up on her.

Sandra was lying staring out of the window and did not look round until her godmother said:

"Well—child—how are you?"

She turned her head quickly, then with an exclamation of pleasure, "Lady Mandy! Darling! How wonderful!"

"What a lot of exclamation marks!" The old lady bent to kiss her cheek. "You are looking a bit pale. But that is only to be expected. I hear you will be running round in no time now."

"Sez you," retorted Sandra. "I believe the torture only really starts after to-morrow."

"No worse than limbering up, or whatever you call it."

Sandra made a little face. "You're an unsympathetic woman. But I'll forgive you anything for coming. I thought you were not returning till next week."

"Paris was full of tourists, and I got bored," said Lady Amanda. "Tell me your news, Sandra—if you have any."

Sandra shrugged her shoulders. "Precious little, darling. Visitors have not been encouraged, and," she flashed a smile at Jill, "Nurse treats me rough."

"If you have been indulging in tantrums I wonder she has not beaten you," said Lady Mandy coolly, but her eyes were tender, and it was plain that she was very fond of this famous and lovely young goddaughter.

"I hope we have not treated her too badly," said Jill serenely, tidying the bed which, in some unguessable way, because she could not move easily by herself, Sandra had again littered with magazines. When she had finished she left the other girl to talk to her visitor.

"I cannot stay more than half an hour," Lady Mandy observed as Jill prepared to go out of the room. "I must get back to town. How long do you think this child will be kept here, Nurse?"

"I couldn't tell you, I'm afraid," Jill replied.

"Then perhaps you will ask Mr. Carrington to telephone me after he has seen her to-morrow."

"Yes, Lady Amanda." Jill went out. As she closed the door Lady Amanda's clear voice followed her, though her Ladyship was now addressing Sandra. "Tell your surgeon that I have already wasted three telephone calls upon him, and I expect him to ring me."

Jill suddenly found herself wishing that was the part of the message which had been entrusted to her, and thinking that she would have liked to deliver it in exactly those words.

Lady Amanda might be an admirer of his, but it was certain she, at any rate, was not in awe of him.

Good for him, thought Jill, with a flash of resentment, to find somebody as arrogant as he was. . . .

Chapter VII

VERE arrived the next morning, punctual to the very moment of his appointment. He was at his briefest and most reserved; intent on the business in hand and obviously not inclined to spare time in any kind of social chit-chat. He looked grave and, unless she had been certain that his mind never deviated an inch from the smallest detail of what he happened to be on, Jill would have thought he was almost a little distrait.

Sandra was very quiet. Jill knew that she was nervous and was sorry for her; she could not help thinking that it would have made her feel better if Mr. Carrington had not been quite so impersonal.

Perhaps the fact that he was accompanied this morning by the Resident Surgeon at Broad Meadows, Dr. Falconby, and Dr. Pearson, the radiologist, accounted for the stiffness of his manner; it never entered Jill's head that he, too, might be a little nervous—both clearly on tiptoes to know how things were going to turn out.

As for Mr. Carrington's manner towards the nurse in charge, it was icily correct; but she could not help feeling that he had not forgotten yesterday's episode on the landing, and was still disapproving.

Oh, well! let him disapprove! Jill was not inclined to worry about that; she felt that the only really important person this morning was Sandra—Vere Carrington might at least have showed her some of the friendliness which by now she had surely grown to expect from him. Couldn't he see that in spite of the gay greeting she had given him, the poor girl was sick with anxiety?

Sandra had been moved from the bed to a high examination couch which had been brought in and placed near the windows. She was wrapped in a soft padded dressing-gown of orchid mauve satin, and her wonderful hair shone like liquid honey in the sunlight.

Once again the knowledge of the other girl's breath-taking

loveliness was thrust home to Jill. The other doctors were obviously not as immune to that vivid young beauty as Mr. Carrington appeared to be—a fact her nurse would have noted with considerable amusement at any other time.

Vere proceeded to remove the plaster cast in which Sandra's left leg was encased from the knee downwards, himself. Somehow, his silence during the operation affected the others, and the room was curiously quiet, so that every sound seemed to be exaggerated.

It was not the first time Jill had found it oddly comforting to be able to whip up resentment against Mr. Carrington to the point when it was almost easy to believe that she really disliked him. And yet, while she stood there, professionally ready to anticipate his smallest need of help, she was still intensely conscious of that tall, well-proportioned figure bending over the couch; of the dark, lean, handsome face, and the rather grimly set mouth, which she remembered against her will was capable of softening so amazingly that it seemed almost it could not belong to the same man.

It was not until Sandra's limb was entirely freed from the plaster that the surgeon's set face relaxed a little.

"Good!" he exclaimed, and glancing at the other men: "Now, once we get this debris out of the way we shall know more."

Jill was already removing the last of the "debris", and as she carried the basket, into which she had gathered it, away, Vere smiled at his patient for the first time.

"That feels a little lighter, does it not?" he asked.

"At the moment it feels rather as if I had lost my leg altogether," said Sandra a little ruefully.

"By Jove, Carrington, you didn't cut it off by mistake, did you?" asked Dr. Falconby, a good-looking grey-haired man with a pleasant though sometimes slightly over-hearty manner, and a habit of making facetious little jokes. He was much older than Vere, and his years, added to the fact that they had known each other at the big teaching hospital to which Vere was now attached, made it permissible for him to wisecrack at the younger man's expense.

Vere said: "Miss St. Just will find out very shortly." Already those expert hands were at work. "Try to bend, please—it is bound to be a little stiff."

"But—I don't think I can—oh!" It was a cry of pain, but Mr. Carrington's second smile that morning was a satisfied one.

"Sorry," he said. "It won't be easy at first, but you must learn to do that quite a lot. Come now, please." And in reply to the patient's protest that he was hurting her: "I am sorry, but I must find out your reactions. It is no use having that plaster off if you behave as if it was still there." In spite of the seeming harshness of the words his firm hands were really very gentle as they probed and moved the once useless limb. Then: "I think just a final X-ray to make sure there is nothing wrong," he glanced at the radiologist. "Can you do that now, Pearson?"

A portable apparatus was already in the room, and it was only a matter of minutes before the photograph was taken.

"It is not really necessary, but you will probably feel more satisfied afterwards," Vere told the patient. "You are tired now, and the best thing we can do is to put you back to bed. To-morrow you can begin to learn to walk again."

Sandra's eyes widened as she looked up at him, and for the first time the colour crept back into her cheeks.

"Do you mean," she asked breathlessly, "that—it's successful—that I—I am going to be able to walk—to—to dance again?"

"Of course. There was never the smallest doubt about that," said Mr. Carrington calmly.

How sure he was of himself! And with what reason! Jill felt her heart miss a beat, and forgetting her earlier resentment let the flood of delighted triumph seep through her. In that moment she felt almost as though his success was hers. He *was* wonderful! One again he had taken one of those fifty-fifty chances and brought it off, where another man would have blenched at the risk.

Then Dr. Falconby's voice, a shade drier than usual, asked: "You don't think any further complications can arise, Mr. Carrington?"

"Not unless by laziness on the patient's part—which I am really not afraid of, although she will find things uncomfortable for a time." He gave Sandra another of those fleeting smiles. "Over to you—I've done my job."

She stared up at him for an instant. Then with a sudden impulsive gesture held out both her hands.

"Oh! thank you—thank you! I can't believe it. If it's really true you're a miracle man——"

"No miracle about it." He touched and released the slender hands, but Jill noticed the dark flush beneath his skin. "Back to bed with you." Then, lifting her as easily as if she had been a baby, he carried her back to her own bed.

Even while Jill was settling her comfortably he had turned towards the other doctors who were standing by the window. For a few moments they conversed in low voices, then Mr. Pearson went out of the room, and having paused to murmur his congratulations to Sandra the older doctor prepared to follow him.

At the door he paused, looking back.

"Mr. Carrington may be modest enough for once to deny being a miracle worker, but I will go so far as to say that you are lucky in your surgeon," he told her a little gruffly. "Again I congratulate you—both."

It was, in fact, a very gracious compliment from an older man who had just missed the heights, to the younger who had so brilliantly climbed them. Human nature being what it is, Jill could not help appreciating "Old Falconby's" compliment to his more successful rival—especially as, in the usual channels of gossip, she had gathered that the R.S. had been slightly sceptical about Carrington bringing it off this time.

"Thanks." Vere glanced at his watch, his face inscrutable. "I must hurry," he said. "I should have left ten minutes ago! See that the patient rests to-day, Nurse—I shall not be down again before Thursday. Meanwhile, she is to have massage for that leg twice a day. Don't let it stiffen, but don't attempt to get her on her feet until I give the word."

"Very good, sir." Jill opened the door for him and with a smiling nod for Sandra and an unsmiling one for her nurse, he went quickly out.

Just for a moment Jill stood, the door in her hand, looking after him. Then closing it softly she turned back to the bed and met Sandra's eyes.

Sandra said: "I don't know whether I shall finish up by adoring that man, or, with complete and base ingratitude, hating him. Jill——" there was a sudden catch in her breath. "Is it true? Am I going to be—cured?"

"You are cured," Jill assured her, "to all intents and purposes. You've still a long way to go, but you heard what he said, my dear, it's 'over to you'. We'll all help you—you must know this whole place is behind you. You've no idea how determined we've been from the beginning to get you right—but of course it is Vere Carrington who has done it, as I told you he would."

"I can't believe it!" exclaimed Sandra. "It's—too wonderful," and burst into tears.

Jill sat down on the bed and putting her arms round the weeping girl let her cry for a few minutes. Then:

"That's enough," she said firmly, and putting Sandra back on her pillows poured out a sedative and stood over her while she drank it.

Soon Sandra was telling her, half laughing, "I've read of people crying for happiness—but as a rule it's rage that makes me cry. Goodness! I hope my eyes won't be red when Glyn turns up."

"Glyn——?" Jill gave a puzzled frown.

"Yes—Glyn Errol. Had you forgotten he was coming this afternoon?"

"I honestly don't think you will be inclined to see a visitor——" Jill began.

Sandra interrupted quickly. "Of course I shall. I must, in any case—it's my only chance. He's off to America to-morrow. And—it's very necessary I should see him. Don't be stuffy, Nurse—Mr. Carrington needn't even know if you think he would disapprove."

Jill was sure he would, but there did not seem much sense in upsetting Sandra by arguing, and she agreed reluctantly.

"Very well. But you must keep very quiet until he arrives. And you are not to get excited then—you've had quite an ordeal to-day."

Going out of the room a little later she could not help thinking that Sandra was born to have people give her her own way—born in spite of any set-backs to get what she wanted.

The question was, had she set her heart on the man who was coming to see her to-day, or—was that heart still free to bestow on someone else?

"I shall either end up by adoring that man——"

If that happened she would certainly be asking for trouble; unless, of course, Vere Carrington——

Jill shied away from the thought, but she could not escape from the remembrance of that flush when Sandra had thanked him, or—before that—the softening of his eyes as he looked down at her. He had worked like a black on that case—letting nothing get in the way of his observation of it. Of course, just as a case it meant a whole lot to him; so many people in his own profession were waiting, in many instances, for him to fail. He had, Jill realized, staked his reputation when he had determined that the "incurable" was nothing of the sort.

But—somewhere under his professional pride the man was human, and her professional observation had often shown Jill that doctors, however little they show it, feel a kind of gratitude towards their successes. And Sandra was a success. Surely Vere would be less than human if his interest in her did not take on a more personal slant. Surely he would not be human at all if he did not realize that, besides being a case, she was also a very lovable and desirable young woman. After all, he had not been completely impersonal up to the moment; he had stayed to tea with the patient, put himself out of the way for her——

Oh, hang! she thought impatiently. What business is it of mine——?

But it could still turn a knife in her breast. The folly of it!

Out on the otherwise deserted landing she discovered a slender figure in nurse's uniform doing a mixture between a *pas de seul* and a complicated figure at skating.

"Judy! Have you gone daft?" she demanded crisply.

But quite unabashed Judy caught her arm and squeezed it. "Jill! I hoped you would come out. I saw his nibs and the others depart.

"Well, you weren't cutting capers because of Mr. Carrington's departure, were you?"

"No——"

"Supposing I'd been Sister? She would either have thought you had gone mental or reprimanded you for undignified and unbecoming behaviour—she hasn't much opinion of you as it is!"

"She thinks I would be an excellent nurse—if I would curb my propensity to flightiness." Judy pursed her lips with such a perfect caricature of Sister's disapproving expression that Jill had to laugh.

"Never mind Sister," said Judy. "I've four days' leave next week. And what do you think, Jill?"

"Tell me. I'm not good at guessing."

"Doctor Harding has asked me to go to Drury Lane with him on Thursday."

Jill had no intention of giving away how the invitation had come about. "That's grand," she approved.

"Stalls!" There was awe in Judy's voice. "Think of it; and I'm dying to see the show."

"Oh well, that's fine," Jill told her. "I must run, lovey—I can't leave my patient for long."

"I forgot to ask," said Judy. "Is it O.K.? Has the divine Vere added to his laurels?"

"A whole wreath of them," Jill replied.

"What a man! I bet he's as pleased as a dog with two tails," exclaimed Judy. "But it really is a triumph for him—it isn't like an ordinary patient—he has the right now to feel that he has a stake in the career of a great artist. I bet that on the first night she dances again his nibs is in the audience thinking: 'That's my doing!' And he'll be quite right." In spite of the surface feather-headedness Judy had an unexpected psychological insight.

"Ducky, you ought to write stories," said Jill, forcing a laugh.

"If I did they would always have happy endings," Judy assured. "And don't forget that I've always had a hunch how this one would end——" she broke off to whistle softly a bar of Mendelssohn's wedding march, her eyes mischievous. "Bet you five bob I'm right."

"I only bet once a year—on Derby Day," replied Jill. "Don't be rash—neither of us can afford to lose five shillings in these hard times. I'm glad you are going to have a nice birthday treat—see you later." She was smiling serenely as she walked away, but try as she might to ignore it there was that sharp twisting little pain in her heart. . . .

The senior nurses at Broad Meadows had the privilege of having tea served to them in their own rest room, and later that afternoon, having snatched a quick cup, and glanced through an illustrated paper, Jill was crossing the entrance hall when a streamlined shining black car drove up and stopped at the bottom of the steps.

Visitors, thought Jill, who knew most of the doctors' cars, but there was no time to stop and see what kind of human freight that very expensive automobile was about to deposit. She had left Sandra in the hands of Miss Baerlin, the Swedish masseuse, who had been scheduled to give her the necessary treatments—the first of which must be very nearly over. Jill wanted a word with Freja Baerlin—and if she hurried knew she would just about catch her before she left number twenty-five.

She had just reached the staircase when the voice of the Irish porter, who sat in his box by the big entrance doors, reached her.

"Nurse Foster——"

"Yes, Patrick?" she turned back a little impatiently.

"There's a gentleman here for Miss St. Just—you telephoned down to say no one was to go up to her for half an hour, and the time isn't up yet."

"It very nearly is. If you care to come up you can wait outside her room for a few minutes if necessary." Jill, who had retraced her steps, found herself looking at the man whom she now realized had arrived in that luxurious Alvis.

So this was Glyn Errol! Better looking than the photographs which she had seen reproduced. Not so tall as Vere Carrington, but carrying his inches with a careless assurance; fair-haired—he was hatless—with curiously light eyes which appeared almost jade green in some lights. Cats' eyes! thought Jill, and there was something rather feline about their owner.

His grey summer suit bore the unmistakable stamp of Savile Row, his blue tie, just flicked with yellow, exactly matched the handkerchief which peeped from his breast pocket. Certainly he was good looking, perfectly groomed, the product of the world with which, as yet, Jill had hardly come in contact.

He said in a cultured, rather lazy voice:

"Thanks very much. I don't mind waiting in the least."

"Then come up." She turned and led the way towards the lift. It was only when something very important was afoot, or a patient needed help, that the porter worked the lift. To-day it was Jill who pressed the button beside the numeral III. While the cage ascended, she was conscious of her companion watching her, but not all interested in what he might be thinking; she herself was instinctively comparing him to Vere Carrington. It seemed quite impossible that any girl in her senses would continue to be interested in this man when she had met Vere. But then she—Jill—had never cared for artistic men. It seemed to her quite impossible that now Sandra had met Vere she could any longer feel interest in this other. What she forgot was that while Vere belonged to her—Jill's—world, Glyn Errol belonged to the dancer's, and they were bound to have a great deal in common.

As they shot past the first floor Lord Glyn broke the silence. "How is she?" he asked. "Any luck?"

"Luck?" Jill glanced at him interrogatively, and seeing him smile decided more emphatically than ever that he was not her "cup of tea". There was a decided touch of hardness about that well-cut mouth. He would not be ruthless—as Vere could be, he would be just plain unkind.

"I mean is there any chance of her being cured," he explained. "Or is all this for nothing?"

"Certainly it is not 'for nothing'," said Jill crisply. "In six months—perhaps considerably less, Miss St. Just should be dancing again—provided she does not do too much before she is allowed to."

"She will, will she?" he said coolly. "That's news." But he did not sound in the least enthusiastic, and Jill felt a thrill of indignation. Just then the lift stopped. Lord Errol stood aside for her to precede him, and as she stepped on to the landing she could not help asking:

"Didn't you think the operation would be successful?"

He shrugged his shoulders. "I am afraid I haven't much faith in the medical profession. However, I am ready to admit when I am wrong. But I suppose she has been very well put through it."

"If you mean she has suffered a lot of pain, certainly not," replied Jill. "She has been uncomfortable, and—worried. But now she is very happy."

"Thank heaven for that!" It occurred to Jill that the gratitude was more on his own account than Sandra's, and she remembered again what the other girl had said about him hating sick people, or illness of any kind. Serve that kind of man right if he got really ill himself some time, she decided with unusual viciousness.

Somehow she had not taken to this handsome, inhuman specimen; and having told him to "please wait a moment", she was again comparing him to Vere Carrington. Whatever there was in Vere to—dislike, at least he was not really inhuman in the way that she had immediately sensed this man was.

She had reached Sandra's door when it opened and the masseuse came out. Jill stopped to exchange a few words with her, and then went in.

Sandra was leaning back on her pillows, looking white and rather tired.

"Hello," she greeted. "Is that really going to happen every day? I think I'd rather be in plaster."

"You won't notice it after the first once or twice," said Jill cheerfully. She hesitated; should she tell Sandra that Glyn was there, or just send him away again? Then, remembering that he would not be able to come again, she said reluctantly:

"Your visitor has arrived. But if you are very tired——"

"I'm not. Bring him in at once." Sandra half raised herself.

"Honestly we should have telephoned to put him off," Jill said, really annoyed with herself. "I am certain Mr. Carrington would not want you to have anyone from outside to see you to-day."

"I don't care what Mr. Carrington wants," retorted Sandra. "Give me a mirror. Do I look awful? Lipstick, quick! And do I need some colour? Glyn hates being kept waiting."

There was no doubting this visit meant a lot to her. Jill gave her what she needed, and when she was ready went to the door and called to Lord Errol to come in. But when she looked back before going out and shutting the door behind her, she could detect no sign of anything save the coolest welcome on the invalid's face as Sandra stretched out a hand saying:

"Hello, Glyn—so you got here."

Chapter VIII

I

THE little half-smile remained on Sandra's lips after the door had closed, leaving her alone with her visitor.

He had walked over to the bed, and taking her hand stood looking down at her, a slight frown on his face.

"Well," he said. "You are not running about yet—though I gather you are due to take ten-mile walks very shortly."

"Wait and see what is happening next time we meet," she told him. "So you actually got here? Sit down—if you have done with my hand."

"I should prefer it if I could not nearly see through it." He examined the lovely slender hand critically before he let it go. Then, sitting down in the chair which had been placed ready for him, he glanced round the room and out of the window. "For a hospital this place is not bad. Where do they put the patients?"

"They tidied them all away because they knew you were coming," said Sandra sarcastically. "They didn't want to lacerate your 'sensitive' feelings."

He shrugged his shoulders with no sign of being in the least sensitive. "Anyway, you won't need tidying away."

"Don't say you are on the point of forgiving me for daring to upset your plans," she said.

"I trust that for the future you will be careful who you drive round with, and stick to hired cars after a party." There was not the smallest trace of sympathy in his voice.

"Would you prefer me to shut myself in a glass case between performances?" she asked.

"Rather that than risk ruining your career," he answered coolly. "Anyway this surgeon fellow seems to have mended you. When will you be ready to dance again?"

"I don't know——" She broke off on the edge of adding that she did not even know whether she wanted to dance again. And yet for one kind word from him—some little sign that he had really cared what happened to her, not as a dancer, not even as a great artist, but as a flesh-and-blood girl, she would have danced bare-footed to the end of the world for him.

But he doesn't care! she thought—not about *me*. All the time I was lame and miserable he avoided me. It's the ballet he cares for—always the ballet. He only sees me as part of it—the most important part.

Suddenly she almost hated the work which had been more than half of her life.

The worst of it all was she was certain Glyn Errol knew that she cared for him. What a good thing it would be if he were made to realize that there might be some other man who was capable of becoming more important to her than he was.

She said smilingly: "By-the-way, you must meet my surgeon as soon as you come back from America. He's the most charming person—and of course I owe him a debt it is almost impossible to repay. He hasn't heard of you yet, but you two really must know each other!"

If she had hoped for any reaction she was disappointed. The handsome, rather cynical face beside her did not change.

"I expect he has been extremely well paid already, hasn't he?" Glyn asked. "You're not exactly doing this on the Health Service, are you? And I don't expect the man's a philanthropist—not," he added a shade more quickly than he usually spoke, "that I'm not extremely grateful for what he has done."

But Sandra felt bitterly that his gratitude was only because Vere Carrington had mended the puppet that he—Glyn Errol—had helped to make.

He's hateful! she told herself. I'll teach him not to be so sure of me—and of himself. . . .

II

When Jill went back to her patient she found Sandra alone again.

"Your visitor didn't stay very long," she said.

"No. He had to get back to London." Sandra, looking up from the magazine she was reading, sounded quite cheerful. "What do you think of the noble lord?"

"He's very good looking," said Jill.

"Yes, and not half so conscious of it as you might think. He's so used to having everything ladled out to him with a gold spoon that he takes it all as a matter of course. The only thing he really cares about—thinks really important—is his first, last, and only love—the ballet. I ruined his plans when I had my accident—he had to cancel a season in Paris, and another one in Madrid, because he couldn't find anyone to take my place—or not anyone who satisfied him. But now he's beginning to make plans again."

"Well, he had better not make too many, or make them too

quickly," said Jill. "Mr. Carrington is the person on whose permission all that will depend."

"I told him so," said Sandra. "But Glyn can't easily understand anyone else holding the strings he has always pulled himself."

Was she in love with him? Jill wondered again—or was the tie between them only forged by the part he had played in her career? She could not help feeling, now that she had seen him, how much better it would be if Sandra had not given Glyn Errol her heart. And yet——

During the days that followed his visit Sandra did not refer to Lord Errol again, although on the day before he sailed an enormous box of orchids arrived for her, and Jill saw that the card which accompanied them bore his name.

Never had Jill believed so many orchids could be gathered together, they must have cost a fortune, and they filled two great bowls.

That was on Thursday, and when Mr. Carrington came in he glanced at them with raised brows.

"Very exotic, are we not?" he observed.

"Yes. Won't you put one in your buttonhole?" asked Sandra.

"Good heavens, no! Thanks all the same. Orchids are not in my line," he laughed. "And now what about this knee?"

This time Sandra endured the examination uncomplainingly, and when Jill had carefully covered her up again asked eagerly:

"Can I get out of bed to-morrow?"

"Yes, if you want to," he replied. "There is no reason," he was addressing Jill now, "why—when the masseuse has finished with her—she should not be partly dressed and put into a wheel-chair—one of those worked by hand, please, the time has not yet arrived when she can go peddling all over the place."

"But, Doctor! I thought I had finished with chairs," protested Sandra.

He looked at her quizzically. "Don't you expect ever to sit down again——"

"I want to walk," she said impatiently. "I want to use my feet again."

"All in good time, but certainly not yet," he told her firmly.

"But you said—I was going to be taught to walk."

"So you are being—this is all in the process. But, you must

be very much stronger and those muscles must be in much better trim before you even stand with help," he said firmly. "This is the time when you must be content to do exactly what you are told—and no questions or arguments. I have not time now to explain all the reasons, but I assure you that if you attempt to get on your feet one moment before I give the word you may do irreparable damage. Kindly let other people do your exercising for you, and for heaven's sake don't try to rush things."

"But I have had to be patient for so long." Sandra looked like a disappointed child, the tears very near.

Vere had risen and as he glanced down at her his face softened in a way which Jill could not help feeling seemed to be reserved for this lovely, wilful young woman. "Then you can be patient for a little longer," he told her; then sitting down again: "Come—surely you are not going to weaken now?"

She sighed rebelliously, then smiled at him.

"All right—I will be good. What about some tea, Nurse?"

Jill glanced at her watch. "It's nearly time, I'll fetch it." She noticed that this time Mr. Carrington seemed to take it as much as a matter of course as his patient did, that he should stay and share her tea with her, and was impatient with herself because in spite of all her efforts every little detail concerning him still seemed to register; as she closed the door she was so conscious of him sitting there beside the bed, and the deep musical cadence of his voice went with her though she tried to shut her ears against it.

When she went back into Sandra's room, Sandra broke off a story to which her companion seemed to be listening with interest to say:

"Oh, Nurse, do you remember that book of photographs I lent you to show the others last week?"

"Yes, of course," said Jill. "It's over in my room—do you want it?"

"If you can get it easily," replied Sandra. "There's a picture in it—of me in the Corps de Ballet in 'Swan Lake'. Mr. Carrington"—she gave him a mischievous look—"doesn't believe I was dancing as long ago as that—and I want to prove it."

"It seems ridiculous," said Vere. "I saw that ballet just

after the war, and I should hardly have thought this ballerina would have been old enough to appear on any stage then——"

Sandra laughed delightedly. "This 'ballerina' was a 'rising' thirteen-year-old—a spindly little girl who already saw herself as a prima ballerina and thoroughly resented having to give hours in the week to keeping up the rest of her education."

"I shall certainly be interested to see if I can pick you out in the photograph," Vere told her. "I will see to this, Nurse." He rose and took the tea-pot from her.

Shaking up Sandra's pillows again while he poured out as calmly as though it were an everyday occurrence, Jill thought how at home he looked—so much more part of the environment than anyone else who came into it from outside. He certainly did show himself capable of unbending where Sandra was concerned, when he felt like it. But surely she—Jill—had learned long ago that he could descend from the reserved heights on which he dwelt.

Going across to the nurses' quarters a few minutes later her mind was back at St. Monica's in those days—heaven knew they had been brief enough—when they had worked together to save a life, and she had known that he trusted and depended on her.

She might have been responsible for his cases in the big hospital now; might even have been a Ward Sister, if she had not turned coward and run away from her own weakness.

But at least, she told herself, she had overcome that weakness; her heart no longer turned over every time he spoke to her or came into a room. At least she could see his interest in another girl growing daily without feeling as though she was being cut into little pieces. . . . Or—could she?

She did not take into consideration the fact that only a short while ago she had found how conscious she was of his presence—if she had done she would have reminded herself that it was quite impossible not to be aware of such a strong personality.

And if somewhere deep down in her a small, gibing voice murmured "Oh yeah!" she ignored it.

The book Sandra wanted was one which had been done about a year ago, and purported to tell the story of her career in photographs. Sandra had sent for it among some others to show her fans on the staff at Broad Meadows—those young, and not so young, nurses whose autograph books kept coming backwards and forwards through the carefully guarded door if number 25. Determined that the book should be returned intact whence it came, Jill had collected it and locked it up for safety.

But when she went to look for it she found to her horror that she could not remember where her keys were. Then she remembered that Judy, whose suitcase had the same kind of lock as Jill's, had borrowed then, and since Judy was on duty and it would take too long to find her, Jill went along to her room to search, and there were the keys in the lock of Judy's case!

Really! It was a good thing the maids were honest!

Very annoyed, and feeling rather a fool, Jill hurried back, but as she drew near to Sandra's room again her dismay deepened when she saw Vere standing by the landing window, his fingers drumming impatiently on the glass.

"Mr. Carrington, I'm terribly sorry, but——" she began to apologize a little breathlessly.

He turned quickly, cutting her short with a gesture.

"That is all right! I am in no particular hurry, but as I wanted to speak to you alone I—waited here."

Jill said: "I am awfully sorry to have been so long, but I couldn't find this——"

"Give it to me." He held out his hand. "Miss St. Just says I can take it back to town with me."

She resigned the book to him and tucking it under his arm he moved back into the window recess.

Jill followed and stood beside him, her hands clasped tightly behind her, suddenly aware that she was trembling—it must be because she had hurried.

"It is much too hot to rush about. You had better sit down." Vere indicated the padded window seat, adding, almost as though he expected her to protest. "Sit down—please. I want to talk to you."

She obeyed, forcing herself to look up at him, and discovering when she did so that his own glance was unexpectedly friendly. Then sitting a little way from her he bent towards her.

"Doctor Falconby will be holding a watching brief," he said "—just in case anything goes wrong (which unless somebody plays the unforgiveable fool is practically impossible at this stage!) but this is where I hand over the main responsibility to you, Nurse. I am going up to Edinburgh to-night and shall be gone for a week. When I return the patient should be sufficiently advanced to get on her feet again—as you know, walking will be a more gradual business than she realizes. What I want to impress upon you, and for you to impress upon everyone concerned, is that she must not attempt to stand—even for an instant—until I give permission."

"Yes, sir. I should not dream of allowing her to," said Jill.

"I'm sure I can trust you to see that nothing goes wrong."

"If it is in my power to prevent it." There seemed nothing strange to Jill in the thrill of pleasure his words gave her. Could anything be more satisfying to anyone as keen on her work as she was, than to feel that Vere Carrington relied on her, and had the generosity to let her know it? It must mean, too, that he was ready to forget the Ken Harding episode—there was no longer the smallest trace of disapproval in his manner.

"Of course you can prevent it," he said. "It is just a matter of keeping a strict eye—above all, persuade your patient to remember what I have said to her. If she tries to hurry things now she will regret it later. Let her have as many visitors as she wants—provided they don't stay late; keep her amused, I shall be down again to-day week." He rose, and as Jill followed his example, moved away, paused, and turned back again. This time there was a half amused smile in his eyes as they met hers.

"I need not remind you," he lowered his voice, "that the young lady is obstinate, and very intent on having her own way. Of course Dr. Falconby has my instructions, but in case he should be persuaded to—side-track any of them, be very firm."

Jill looked at him in dismay. "But—Mr. Carrington, he won't, will he? I—it would be difficult for me to interfere if——"

"Look here"—for once Vere was ignoring etiquette—"the fact is—I wouldn't go away for the world at this stage, but I have this conference in Edinburgh, and I cannot possibly not attend it. Unfortunately Falconby will not entirely agree with me over keeping my patient more or less moribund. If it was his case he would let her begin to get on her feet right away."

Jill said impulsively: "He shan't do it—except over my dead body!"

"Excellent. But before you die go to Matron, and she will support you." His eyes twinkled. "I'm not really afraid of what the Doctor will *do*—it is only that he might imply that if it rested with him——! And she might get the idea that no harm would be done if she chose to disobey. I rely on you." He held out his hand. "Good-bye for the present."

A quick firm hand-shake, and then he was running downstairs—it was characteristic of the man never to wait for a lift.

Jill remained where he had left her for a moment, then she turned back towards the window, unconsciously resting her right hand against her heart that was suddenly beating at so much beyond its normal rate.

A strange, unpredictable man! But how easily he could make you feel that there was nothing in the world you wouldn't do to please him; even if it meant cutting your heart in little bits and—feeding them to someone in whom he was far more interested.

Such a little while ago she had been telling herself that she was cured of her folly. And yet the very touch of his hand had power to set her pulses racing, to fill her with unnamable longing.

Staring unseeingly at the branches of a chestnut tree which were level with the window, Jill knew that the time had come when she must stop deceiving herself. Love was not just something like measles or any other curable malady—at least not her kind of love. And so—after all she had better just accept it, and keep it locked in her heart where no one would ever know about it. But somehow she faced what she had hitherto thought of as weakness and folly without any humiliation.

Hadn't Vere just told her that he trusted her?

That was something to be proud of. . . .

Chapter IX

COMING out of the dispensary Jill paused, passing a hand over her forehead, an involuntary sigh escaping her.

The dispensary was in the new wing, where the children's wards and the operating theatre were also housed, and where all suggestion of a private house faded completely into the shining white and chromium of a very modern hospital.

At the end of the long corridor a door opened on to the garden. Jill stood looking towards it, conscious of an unusual tiredness. The five days that had passed since Vere Carrington went away had been hectic ones; not because the nursing of her case was any longer a very onerous one. Contrary to her expectations Sandra was taking this portion of her convalescence with amazing cheerfulness. There was hardly a grumble, she did everything she was told, and seemed ready to go on indefinitely as long as she was sure that at the end of it all she would be able to pick up the dropped threads of her career again. So that the only real problem was to keep her from getting over-excited and expending too much of the energy and strength which it was so necessary to conserve. Gone was the listless, anxious girl of the post-operation period, and coping with the return of that electric, vivid personality who was the real Sandra was just a shade exhausting for her day nurse, who had to strike the happy mean between keeping her contented and stopping her from tiring herself out.

Since the ban on visitors had been completely lifted, friends poured down to see her, and the hospital was aflutter with interest as one well-known personality after another—stars of the theatre and the ballet, and bearers of names well-known in society and the writing world—were deposited from cars, or arrived in taxis from the nearest station.

Sandra was by no means brainless, and since in spite of all the success and adulation which had come her way she had never suffered from swelled head, she was very popular.

Flowers had always come in quantities since her arrival, but now her room was literally a bower in the day-time, to say nothing of all sorts of lovely presents, and pounds of goodies—she sent nearly all the sweets to the nurses, and generously shared her flowers with less lucky patients. There was no doubt that, however spoiled and wayward she might be in some ways, she was really a lovable person; and there was even less doubt that every man who came to see her was ready to grovel at those pretty, once twinkling feet—that she would one day be dancing on all their hearts again. She was lucky enough to be popular with her own sex too—it seemed to Jill that her women friends were equally fond of her, and there seemed oddly little jealousy in it all.

Yes, Sandra was a charming person, and it would be impossible to blame any man for loving her. In fact it seemed quite impossible that a man—unless he were blind, or his heart was very safely tied up somewhere else—should not fall for her.

Undoubtedly Mr. Carrington would be delighted with his important patient's progress when he returned—as he should be doing the day after to-morrow.

In spite of its fullness, this had seemed a curiously long week. Jill sighed again, this time a little impatiently. It was quite crazy that not seeing one person for a brief few minutes during the day should make it seem double its length.

No use pretending she did not miss him. She wondered if he would be pleased with her stewardship; his admonishing had certainly been necessary, for no one had fallen more under the spell of Sandra's charm than Dr. Falconby—and Sandra's only sign of discontent had come yesterday when she had told Jill:

"The doctor admitted to-day that if he had the responsibility he would let me begin to walk—just a few steps."

"Well, you must have put the idea into his head," Jill had said drily. "Don't you go trying to get round G.F.—he's only holding a watching brief, and Mr. Carrington will have the roof off if he thought he was encouraging you to be disobedient."

But Sandra had only pulled one of her mischievous little faces and laughed.

A good thing Vere Carrington was coming back, Jill decided, and wondered for the fiftieth time if that new friendliness towards herself would still be evident, or if he would have relapsed again into the old curt, impersonal manner.

The whole place seemed very deserted this afternoon, and while she stood musing, her eyes on the dappled shadows the sun made as it shone through the foliage of the trees outside, not a soul had come that way. Then as she roused herself and turned away a door farther up the corridor opened and Matron came out.

Jill stood aside for her superior to pass, and, seeing her, Matron stopped.

"Hello, Nurse! What are you doing here?" she asked.

"I have been to the dispensary, ma'am." Jill showed the small bottle she was carrying. "Miss St. Just did not sleep very well last night, and I wanted some more of the prescription Mr. Carrington left."

"You are the very person I wanted to see," Matron told her. "Come to my room."

Jill followed obediently, wondering, as one usually did under such circumstances, what was in Matron's mind.

As she entered the elder woman's bright, comfortable sanctuary Jill was remembering that day, nearly five weeks ago now, when she had come here to be told about the new case which she was to be put in charge of.

Strange how one travelled on, gaining strength by the way. How thankful she was for the way she had been able to adjust herself since that day.

Matron nodded to the chair on the other side of the desk where already her tea-tray had been placed.

"Sit down, my child—will you have a cup of tea?"

"No, thank you," said Jill. "I have just had one."

Miss Travers, sitting as usual in shadow with the light from the window full on her visitor's face, appeared to give her whole attention to filling her cup, while in reality those keen eyes were taking in every detail of the girl's face opposite.

"I need not ask how your patient is progressing," she said. "She looks blooming."

"She's going on splendidly, isn't she?" asked Jill eagerly.

"So I gather. But I can't say you are very rosy—I noticed when I saw you in Miss St. Just's room yesterday that you were looking decidedly peaky." Matron had formed a habit of calling in on their lovely celebrity, which had more to do with her enthusiasm for the ballet than the routine of the clinic. "What is this Sister tells me?" she asked. "That you are still taking no proper time off?"

"I get my exercise every day, Matron," said Jill quickly. "And you will remember that you told me when I was put on the case——"

"Never mind what I told you then," Matron interrupted. "She is out of the wood now, we are not so busy, and have several more staff. It is quite easy to spare someone to deputize for you, and I insist that you take your day off again in the usual way."

Arguing with Matron was something which was definitely not done. "Yes, ma'am," said Jill meekly.

Matron shook her head disapprovingly. "Really, Jill," she protested. "I did not intend you to make a slave of yourself. You are beginning to be worn out."

"I am not really," Jill assured her. "And please, I do want to see this through. Mr. Carrington——"

"Oh, I know Mr. Carrington regards you as the only really capable nurse in the place," said Matron with a half laugh. "I assure him there are others, but he hardly listens. He was in here before he went away demanding to know whether you were due for leave, and that if you were it should be postponed—one does not expect him to believe any of you are not made of iron. I told him that you missed your leave last month and must certainly have it at the end of this one. He merely said the end of the month was three weeks off and we could argue about that later. That you were entirely necessary to his patient's well-being, etcetera."

"I don't want to leave her," said Jill. "I—understand her. Besides," she looked at the elder woman pleadingly. "It's my very special case."

"I know how you feel," agreed Matron, dropping the last of the red tape for the time being. "You've done a wonderful job of work between you."

"Mr. Carrington——"

"Is very pleased anyway with the nurse I chose for him."

Wonderful thought! Jill felt that her heart, which was often so heavy, had suddenly grown wings. Perhaps in the future she would be able to work with him again. If only he was pleased she knew that the work she loved was doubly worth while.

Matron talked on for a few minutes before she dismissed her; but when Jill was on the point of going she was told firmly:

"You are to take to-morrow afternoon off. Go somewhere away from this place. I insist. You must have a break, if it is only for a few hours."

Again it was no use arguing.

And so at noon the next day Jill left her patient. Sandra agreed that it was time she had an afternoon to herself and promised gaily to be good.

"Mind you are," said Jill. "I've told Nurse Williams that

she is to be sure and get Patrick to lift you back to bed."

"How absurd it is! I believe I could walk those few yards easily with help," said Sandra. "It is so idiotic to feel so strong and have to sit here, or just lie in bed like a stuffed dummy. Miss Travers says I am in wonderful condition—so does the doctor. I bet that if Mr. Carrington had only let me—or Dr. Falconby had had the courage of his convictions, I should have been walking by the time he got back."

"Mr. Carrington will be here to-morrow," Jill said. "You must wait to hear what he says. And you will promise not to get up to any tricks while I am out."

Sandra laughed. "I'll promise not to run up the curtains or anything like that."

But Jill could not help feeling uncomfortable about leaving her. Surely Matron could have let her miss one more afternoon off, and she was determined to be back before Sandra's bedtime—which was officially at six, at which hour whatever visitors there were were sent off.

On her way out she encountered Sister Anderson.

"Going out?" Sister asked. "Quite a red letter day, isn't it?"

Jill laughed. "I would really be quite happy not to go," she confessed.

"Rubbish! By the way," Sister turned back. "I was in with Matron just now and Mr. Carrington telephoned. He is back in London."

Jill's heart was thudding as she went on her way. To-morrow she would see him again! And however moody he might be in the future, she would always remember what Matron had told her, and try desperately to live up to his good opinion of her.

Chapter X

SHE had decided to go into Windsor to do some shopping, and after she had had some tea catch the early bus back again. It would not mean that she had had as much time as she was expected to, but she would feel more satisfied if she saw Sandra again this evening—especially now she was quite certain nothing would stop Vere from coming down to-morrow.

It was a beautiful day, and by now the flowers of high summer were making a blaze of colour in the gardens.

Jill felt a thrill of pleasure at being once again in the old town that was dominated by its lovely castle, and saturated with memories that were the very warp and woof of England.

And after all, it was rather nice to be completely free again for a few hours. She realized now that except for the one occasion when she had been lent out from St. Monica's on an arduous private case, she had never before been tied in quite the same way in which she had been these last weks.

The town was crowded with visitors—too crowded! And, deciding to leave her shopping until later, Jill went for a walk in the park, where there was more room for what still seemed to her too many people.

When she returned some of the chara-à-banc parties had gone on. Jill did her shopping, managing to get most of the small things she needed, and was leaving the draper's longing for a cup of tea when a man crossing the pavement almost cannoned into her.

"I beg your pardon!" He put a quick hand to his bare head, and then: "Hello, *Jill*! What luck!"

Jill had hardly seen Kenneth Harding since the day last week when Vere had found him clutching her hand on the landing; she had in fact avoided him. But this was not the sort of day on which one could remember a grievance, and she smiled back at him.

"Hello! What are you doing here, Doctor Harding?"

"The gipsy told me that if I came to Windsor to-day I should meet a tall and beautiful girl with grey eyes and—that she would probably 'accept of' a cup of tea from my fair hands," he told her.

"Idiot!"

"Who are you with?" he asked.

"No one. I was pushed out against my will, and I am catching the five o'clock bus back," said Jill.

"Plenty of time for a cuppa," he glanced at his watch. "Come along."

Jill hesitated. The rule that the nurses were not allowed to go about with the staff men was a fairly elastic one—Matron would not be likely to make a fuss about a chance encounter. Meeting her eyes Ken grinned.

"If you want a water-tight alibi you can always go in first. After all, if I sit down at your table you can't have me thrown out."

"Doctor Harding, your lack of integrity is distressing!" She shook her head at him; and then with a shrug of her shoulders turned to walk beside him.

The teashop they chose was very full, but they managed to find a table. Ken ordered tea and lit a cigarette while they waited for it.

"Now tell me all the latest news," he demanded. "Has the Great Man been beating you up lately—metaphorically of course?"

"The Great Man," said Jill, "is—or has been—in Scotland."

"Of course. I'd forgotten. Fancy leaving Old Falconby in charge of his case."

"You are very disrespectful to our senior R.S.," said Jill.

"Nice bedside manner—our senior R.S.," he grinned again. "But he thinks anyone with sense and a little skill could have done as well as Carrington. Calls it more luck than anything."

"He doesn't!" Jill flushed indignantly. "Of course, I knew at the beginning that he told someone it was 'a criminal risk', and he wouldn't have taken it for the world. But I thought he at least appreciated what Mr. Carrington has done."

"I think he does, really. He likes Carrington, but he's just a bit of an old woman," said Ken disrespectfully.

Jill changed the subject. "Did you enjoy Drury Lane?" she asked. "Judy says she had a wonderful time—it was good of you to cheer her up."

"It was no end of an evening," he said enthusiastically. "She is a poppet. I hadn't noticed her much before."

Though she could not very well say so Jill hoped he would take Judy out again.

"She hasn't had much of a time," she said. "And she's really a darling. She said she had had the nicest birthday she could remember."

"And when can I take you out?" he asked.

"I wouldn't know—anyway, you're taking me out now," she told him.

He looked at her reproachfully. "Are all really good nurses

hard-hearted? I've been trying to make an impression on you for months, and all you do is to fob me off on the girl friend."

Jill said frankly: "I'm too busy to philander."

"Well, I like that!" he exclaimed. "Won't anyone ever take me seriously?"

"Some day somebody may—and then you will probably wish they had not," said Jill drily.

"You will be sorry when I have gone to the wilds of Africa," he said sadly.

"What do you mean?" she asked. "You are not leaving Broad Meadows?"

"There is a suggestion of a job in Rhodesia," he told her. "Sounds interesting, but it wouldn't be yet. I don't suppose you will need an extra half-dozen handkerchiefs when I go."

"Not all those. But I shall miss you," she admitted, surprised to find how true it was. For however much he annoyed her at times, she still liked young Doctor Harding, and he made her laugh.

He bent quickly across the table. "Come with me, Jill."

She gave him a startled glance and, meeting his eyes, saw that they were serious. "Couldn't you think about it?" he pleaded. "You know I've been crazy about you for ages, and—well, we've got the same interests, haven't we? And I'm not quite such a fool as I appear—sometimes."

Jill was a little stunned. The last thing she had expected to-day was a proposal of marriage.

"Ken, I'm—so sorry, but I couldn't possibly," she said.

"Not even think about it?" he pleaded. "I shouldn't be going for six months. You might change your mind."

She shook her head decisively. "No. Please don't say any more—it's impossible."

"O.K. I didn't think my luck was in," he told her.

"Sorry, Ken. I wish that tea would come," she added. "Whatever happens I don't want to miss that bus. There isn't another until seven."

He consulted his wrist watch. "I can't rely on this darned thing—there's something wrong with it. I went swimming in it the other day. But the clock on the wall there says twenty-five to, and here comes your tea."

While they drank it and ate the toasted scones which accompanied it, Ken talked in quite his usual manner.

The teashop clock said exactly seven minutes to five when they paid the bill and went out.

"Why don't you let me drive you back?" he asked. "I don't really want to linger about here, and you know perfectly well it would be O.K."

She shook her head. "I'd rather get the bus."

Turning a corner they came in sight of the stop. There was no bus there, but very much further down the road one was rapidly vanishing from sight.

"Sorry, Jill, I'm afraid you've had it," her companion told her. "That darned clock must have been slow. Are you really due back? Will there be a shemozzle?"

"No. I'm free until ten o'clock if I want to be," said Jill. "But I wanted particularly to get back——" And suddenly she felt that for some reason which she could not quite define it was more necessary than ever that she should return and find out how Sandra had got on this first time without her. Although she had tried to ignore it, telling herself that she really was being rather silly, as nothing could go very wrong in her absence. Nurse Williams was thoroughly reliable and it was not as though Sandra was any longer really ill; except for the fact that she could not walk probably she was in better health than she had been for years. Yet that feeling of uneasiness persisted and had grown stronger in these last minutes.

"I must get back," she said. "I must."

"But why?" he asked. "Why not stay now, and go to the flicks—there's a rouser at the local—"

She shook her head decisively. "I should hate it." Then after a moment's hesitation she added frankly: "Honestly I don't know why, Ken, but I am worried. I've been jumpy ever since I came out," she laughed uncertainly, "rather like a mother might feel who has left a baby sitter in charge of her infants, and suddenly wonders if she ought to have done it."

"But good gracious—you've left a whole hospital on call if anything went wrong with your particular baby," he protested. "What's come to you? You can't possibly go through all your professional life jittering whenever you leave your cases for a few hours."

"No, but——" she broke off. How could she explain the feeling of responsibility she had about this case—because Vere Carrington had put her in charge in a rather special way; and because she would have cut off her right hand rather than fail him. Kenneth would think she was behaving like a hero worshipping, romantically inclined youngster; and supposing he guessed——

She said: "I just feel I want to go back—I can't explain."

"O.K. I'll take you," he announced promptly. "One does get these phobias—I've had 'em myself when I was young. I was once smitten with the awful feeling that I had given the wrong prescription. I had gone away for the week-end, and I turned up at the hospital in the middle of the night, only to discover that the patient was sleeping peacefully and not dead—as I dreaded he might be. Come on, we'll get the car."

What a nice person he was! And, in spite of that veneer of flippancy, how understanding and kind!

She was sure the girl who got him would be lucky. He was clever too, and even in spite of himself, she was sure he would go a long way in his own time. She bit back a sigh. How much easier life would be if she had been able to give her heart to Ken Harding, or someone like him. But hearts were unmanageable things, only too apt to get lost before you ever dreamt of locking them up. She knew that some people made almost a habit of losing their hearts and getting them back again; she had almost persuaded herself that she had managed to regain hers, until she discovered her mistake.

"What are you thinking about so seriously?" Ken asked, smiling down at her as they hurried towards the place where he had parked his car.

"Was I looking serious?" To her dismay she felt her colour deepen, and hoped he had not noticed.

But Kenneth had noticed, and he was unusually silent when he had helped her into the car and driven off.

Intent on her own thoughts, Jill took no notice of the speed they travelled at. He could not have gone too fast for her this evening; besides, however much he ignored the speed limit she had already learnt that he never took risks.

Then, when they had covered the first quarter of their journey he slowed down abruptly to a pedestrian twenty miles an hour.

Jill looked round quickly. "What's wrong?" she asked. "Are you running out of petrol?"

"Can't be. I filled her up before I came out. I just wanted

to ask you something," he said. "You need not answer if you don't want to, but perhaps it would be fairer if you did."

"What are you talking about?" she demanded.

Without taking his eyes off the road ahead he answered her question with another. "Jill, when you turned me down so flat was it because there is someone else?"

She was glad that he was not looking at her. It took her a few seconds to be quite sure her voice was steady.

"I don't think I am ever likely to marry, Ken. I love—my work."

"What wicked waste!" He thrust his foot down hard and the car shot forward again.

Half an hour later, without having exchanged another sentence, they came in sight of the gates of Broad Meadows, and as Kenneth slowed down again Jill said impulsively:

"It was terribly good of you to bring me back. I do hope I have not messed up your whole evening."

"Not a bit of it." He spoke in his usual cheerful tones. "When I have deposited you safely I shall go back and keep my dinner appointment." And then he confessed that he had promised to dine with some friends who lived between Windsor and Maidenhead. He assured Jill that they were used to him and would not be in the least upset if he was late.

"But you wanted me to stay and go to the pictures," Jill reminded him. "How awful, when you had an appointment! Supposing I had said yes."

His only comment on that one was: "But you didn't say 'yes', Jill—I wish you had."

Before she could remind him to take her to the side entrance he had driven her right up to the main one. He got out quickly, hurrying round to open the door beside her.

She stepped to the ground, smiling gratefully up at him.

"Thank you so much, Ken." And then, struck by the fact that above his cheerful grin the eyes that met hers were hurt and unsmiling, she laid an impulsive hand on his arm. Every instinct, all her own experience of heartache told her that he was unhappier than he meant anyone to know.

"Oh, Ken dear, I am so sorry!" she said. "Honestly—so *sorry*."

For an instant he laid a hand on hers. "That's O.K., Jill, so long as you're happy."

He got into the car again, and starting it up leant out to call: "I'll be seeing you." Then with a last wave he was driving swiftly away again.

Shading her eyes Jill watched him go. It was not until he had reached the drive and disappeared round a bend that she turned back towards the house and in so doing noticed for the first time the car parked just ahead of where Kenneth had stopped a few moments ago.

As her eyes fell on the long shining body of the Rolls her breath caught and the colour drained from her cheeks. There were several thousand Rolls-Royces in England, but if they had all been gathered in one vast car park she was sure she could have picked that one out from among them. Her breath caught and she was conscious once again of that familiar, dreaded quickening of her heart.

And then, with that feeling which tells someone that they are being watched, she swung round and looked up the steps straight into Vere Carrington's eyes.

Chapter XI

I

HER first thought was—how long had he been there?

"Mr. Carrington," she stammered, running up the steps. "I—didn't know—I had—no idea that you were coming down to-day."

"Obviously not." His tone was icy. "Neither had I any intention of coming before to-morrow, until I received a telephone call which I was fortunately there to take."

"A—telephone call," she repeated; then as she met his eyes again she realized that never before had they been quite so hard and hostile.

The first shock of his sudden appearance had passed and all her anxieties abruptly swept back on her in one great wave of fear.

"What has happened?" she asked. "Is anything wrong?"

"Wrong——!"

At that moment the porter appeared at the far end of the hall coming back towards his box.

With an angry gesture Vere turned on his heel. "You had better come in here," he ordered harshly.

Jill followed him into the empty waiting room. Since the first day when she had come to interview Matron, she had always liked that room, with its primrose-coloured walls and the gay flowered cretonne at the window and covering the chairs and the deep settee—there was something about it which was entirely different from the usual run of waiting rooms provided by the medical profession. But now, suddenly the warm friendly atmosphere of it seemed to have dropped to the temperature of a refrigerator, though she realized that it was a coldness which contained sparks.

She was beyond waiting until she was spoken to, and facing the angry, hostile man who had just shut the door, she implored:

"Please tell me what has happened. Miss St. Just——"

"Miss St. Just had a fall—it is impossible to tell yet how serious the consequences are."

"A fall——"

Vere had been dealing with a frightened, hysterical girl, and he was in no mood to make excuses for the nervousness of another.

"Kindly do not stand there like a fool repeating my words," he requested.

Jill drew a deep breath. "I'm—sorry——"

"Sorry! Great Scott! You ought to be sorry," he exploded. "Your neglect of duty—your deliberate ignoring of your trust and responsibility, has resulted in an accident which may have undone all my work and caused heaven only knows what suffering." That self-control which he had felt bound to exercise, and which had clamped down the rage and impatience consuming him, suddenly broke, letting out a flood of fury on the head of the girl who he was convinced was to blame for what had happened, and in a searing spate of words which seemed to flay her like a lash, he accused her—of lacking all sense of responsibility, of neglecting her work, and endangering her patient, while she listened, white to the lips, and sick with the horror of what had happened.

At last: "Please let me explain," she begged. "I did not *want* to go out to-day."

"Then why have gone?"

"Because"—she made a hopeless gesture—"Matron insisted."

"Are you asking me to believe," he demanded, "that Matron of all people *insisted* that you should leave your patient! I don't believe it. You are simply excusing yourself——"

In spite of her misery Jill lifted her chin with a little jerk. "I don't lie, Mr. Carrington——"

He swept on. "Matron probably gave you permission to go out because you asked her to. Surely you could have refrained for a little while longer from going to meet your—friend."

"I did not go to meet anyone." Stung beyond endurance Jill flung etiquette to the winds. "I wanted to get back early—I was worried about being away——"

"Your conscience was rather late in asserting itself! That will do, Nurse." Though his eyes were still shining dangerously his voice was cold and even again—and somehow in that tone his words sounded all the more damning. "I have thought before that you might not be fit for responsibility—that you were not in a state to reserve your whole energies for your work. I am sorry that I forgot that impression and was stupid enough to trust you. I am—unfortunately—not one of the governors of this place, and I have no power to enforce my wishes; but as far as my own case is concerned I insist upon having a nurse whose integrity I can rely on in charge—I shall point that out to Miss Travers to-morrow."

"Do you mean," asked Jill, moistening her dry lips, "that—you do not wish me to nurse Miss St. Just?"

He had turned towards the door, and he looked back coldly. "That is exactly what I mean."

"Oh, but you are unfair!" The protest seemed dragged from her and she was powerless to hold it back. "I have done everything in my power——"

"Except pay the slightest attention to my known wishes, and keep the promises you so glibly made," and without giving her a chance to reply he opened the door and went out.

Jill stook a mechanical step forward and paused, still conscious that she was trembling from head to foot. Putting out a hand she mechanically clutched the back of a chair and stood clinging to it, her eyes shut tight.

She felt as though she had been beaten until she was half stunned and could no longer feel the pain, even while she was still conscious of it.

After a few minutes habit and will power came to her rescue. Then her mind began to work, and she realized that as yet—in spite of the tirade to which Vere had treated her—she did not even know what had happened.

She must find out at once. She walked quickly and steadily out into the hall and was crossing in the direction of Matron's room when it occurred to her that Vere might already be there.

She turned towards the porter: "Is Matron alone, do you know, Patrick?"

"She's out, Miss. Went up to London soon after you went off duty yourself," the man told her. "She's going to the theatre this evening and won't be back until late."

"Do you mean that she had gone before Mr. Carrington arrived?" Jill asked.

"Shure I do," said Patrick.

Matron always went up to London one day a month, and of course it had not been necessary for her to mention that this happened to be the day, she thought vaguely.

"But what time did Mr. Carrington arrive?" she asked. She had moved over to the entrance, and a glance outside told her that the Rolls had gone.

"It would be about four-thirty. The saints know how he got here in the time for they didn't send for him until after two o'clock," said Patrick. "Doctor Falconby couldn't get through to London at first, and he was near throwing fits!" Though the man grinned it occurred to Jill then that he was looking at her sympathetically, and a wave of colour rose in her cheeks. Was it possible he had heard some of the things Vere had said to her? It was too humiliating! With a brief "thank you", she walked quickly towards the lift. The numbness had left her now. There was nothing in the world she hated like injustice—and remembering that she had not even been given the chance to defend herslf, and that he had actually dared to tell her she was lying, anger blazed in her.

No matter what had happened he was inexcusable.

I hate him! she told herself. I really *hate* him. . . .

II

Jill did not sleep that night. In the first place she was worried about Sandra. No one—Sandra included—seemed quite sure what had happened, but when Nurse Williams returned from tea she had found her patient lying on the floor helpless and frightened, with a bump the size of a small egg on her forehead.

She was suffering from shock and slight concussion, but the extent of any damage that might have been done was impossible to discover until she could be X-rayed. She had been put to bed and the surgeon's orders were that she was to be kept very quiet, and remain there until he gave the word.

Jill told herself it was crazy to feel that there was the slightest justification for the way Vere Carrington had turned on her, and yet as she watched the daylight strengthening behind the drawn curtains at her window, in spite of her unhappy resentment she began to make excuses for him. Perhaps he could not be altogether blamed for flying off the handle. But there was no excuse for refusing to accept her explanation—or even believe it. She knew that she was innocent of any real responsibility for what had happened, and yet—she had given him her promise. That was what hurt most—that he should believe she was unreliable. And what seemed to make it so much worse was his belief that she had gone out to meet Ken—which was obviously what he did believe.

Carefully camouflaging the shadows beneath her eyes before she went to breakfast the next morning, Jill thanked whatever powers controlled these things for the fact that, thanks to modern beauty aids, it was not necessary to go round advertising too plainly that you had passed a sleepless night.

If only V.C. had not seen her drive up with Ken. For he of all people to have been just on the spot at that moment! It did seem that the fates had a down on her.

Well, she decided, she would have to see Matron as soon as possible; and then——?

What was the use of asking herself what would happen then? She was already determined that even if he changed his mind about her—which was not at all likely—nothing would induce her to go on working under him.

She told herself fiercely that it was not because she really cared about how hateful the most hateful man in the world had been to her; but the more she thought of it, the more ironical it appeared that she, who had always prided herself on never falling down on a job, had been accused of unreliability and neglecting her duty.

On top of all this she was naturally worried about Sandra—and altogether life seemed to have become quite unbearable.

Neither was it any use going on telling herself she did not care what he thought because, if only for the reason that both her personal and professional integrity were at stake, of course she cared.

However, the first thing to do was to see Matron.

It was very unlike Jill to resort to sedatives, but she knew that she could not go about with a head which felt as though it would burst, and so she took a couple of aspirins and, hoping they would do the trick, went down to breakfast with a deceptively calm exterior.

It did not help to feel that she was under a battery of curious, though mostly sympathetic, eyes. Of course everyone in the hospital knew what had happened to her very special and important case! She was equally certain that they knew Mr. Carrington had had her "on the carpet"—for Janey Fane, a student nurse, had seen them going together into the waiting room and would have realized what was happening.

Jill was equally sure that, this morning, pre-breakfast conversation had been all about yesterday's mishap and its probable consequences to the patient, but to her relief she had only just seated herself and had hardly time to greet her neighbours at the table and those directly opposite, when Matron came in and took her place at the upper table.

Grace, and the freedom to talk—even after her years of training and experience this part of the routine always made Jill feel she was at boarding school, and Miss Travers a severe though benevolent headmistress—resulted in the usual slightly subdued murmur.

To Jill's relief yesterday's debâcle seemed taboo and during breakfast no one mentioned it to her. But the meal, which often seemed so much too short, appeared interminable. It came to an end at last, though, and filing out with the others, Jill found herself next to Judy who happened to be, fond as she was of her, the one person she would have avoided above all others.

Slipping a hand through her friend's arm Judy asked in a stage whisper how Sandra was.

"I don't know," replied Jill hurriedly, and detaching her self, "Sorry, ducky, I must fly."

At Broad Meadows the day staff always had breakfast before going on duty, and there was still ten minutes to spare before the night nurses were due for relief.

Hurrying, Jill reached Matron's door and knocked. While she waited for permission to enter her heart was beating quickly.

"Come in." Matron frowned faintly as she looked up from the opening of her morning mail. This was the time when only a very important emergency made it permissible to disturb her.

"Yes, Nurse? Oh, it is you, Jill—well, what is wrong now? What sort of night has Miss St. Just had?"

"I don't know, ma'am." Jill clenched her hands behind her, fighting down a ridiculous desire to pleat her apron. "I haven't seen her yet. Of course you know what—happened while I was—out?" She had never felt so like a stammering school-girl in her life.

"Naturally I know." Matron answered a little tartly. "It was most unfortunate that I should have been absent. But though I deplore it, and hope the foolish girl's stupidity—there is really no other word for it—will not cause any lasting ill effect, no one is really *responsible*. The patient is well enough to be left for periods, and I suppose you would have left her to go to your lunch? And so"—she gave Jill a rather sharp look —"it is no use being angry with the nurse in charge. It was nobody's fault but the patient's."

"I know." Without realizing what she was doing Jill had moved forward, resting a hand on the broad desk. Leaning slightly towards Matron she said breathlessly: "It *might* have happened if I had been here, ma'am. But that does not alter the fact that—Mr. Carrington blames me entirely, and—if you please, Matron, I would rather not continue on his case. So—will you find someone to take my place—even if—it means that I must resign altogether."

Even while she spoke she felt how right the look of angry

incredulity on Matron's face was, and was sure that she was crazy to have come here, instead of waiting to be sent for.

Miss Travers' words almost echoed Jill's thought, and there was no friendliness in her icy glare.

"Have you taken leave of your senses, Nurse?" she demanded crisply.

Jill shook her head, taking a grip of her courage.

"No, ma'am. I could not possibly go on working with Mr. Carrington under the circumstances."

"Why not? And since when is it for you to say what *you* will or will not do, in this hospital?"

Jill bit her lip. Her eyes, meeting the elder woman's, were pleading. "I know it is—unprecedented, but truly I am only —forestalling Mr. Carrington's request that I should be taken off his case."

Matron looked round her charming room, rather as though she had half expected to find herself somewhere else. Then her eyes went back to Jill and, seeing the signs of distress which the girl could no longer hide, noticed how drawn and miserable the young face was with the bright morning sunlight upon it. All the foundation lotion in the world could not hide the marks of sleeplessness and worry from those shrewd, experienced eyes.

"What is all this?" she asked in a kinder tone. "You must tell me quickly, because I am very busy, and you should be on duty."

So Jill, her nervousness evaporating, told her briefly and clearly exactly what had happened.

Matron listened in silence, her face setting, that bleak look which nurses dreaded in her eyes.

"That will do, Nurse," she said when Jill had finished. "I believe Mr. Carrington is coming down about ten o'clock. I will explain to him myself what happened. Now run along——"

But for once Jill could not bring herself to obey. Since she had spoken of it, however briefly, though she had not been able to bring herself to repeat word for word the tirade Vere had hurled against her, every word of it had come back to her like a series of lashes searing her afresh, until it was almost actual physical pain that she felt. Yet it was still the sheer injustice of it which seemed most unbearable.

"Please, Matron," she pleaded. "Don't you see that—even

if he—if Mr. Carrington was not going to ask you for another nurse, I could not possibly carry on when he so obviously thinks me untrustworthy——"

"Has *everyone* gone mad?" Matron demanded. "You were out on perfectly legitimate leave, which you took on my orders. You have nursed his case with untiring devotion—really this is too childish! Go to your patient at once, and don't let me hear any more nonsense. And remember: it is not for *you* to talk of resigning—or for Mr. Carrington to reprove you. He should have spoken to me, if he had a complaint to make, and however annoyed or upset he was he had no right to forget the rules of etiquette. I will arrange this."

Jill knew that Matron could be formidable, but she had never before seen her so angry. With a hardly audible "Yes, ma'am" she faded quickly out of the room.

But, pausing outside the door to pass her fingers across her forehead, she felt that the problem was very far from being solved. Somehow it had not been possible to explain to Matron about the tentative promise she had made to Vere, that when he came back he should find everything well with his patient—it had not seemed possible to explain that. Though, even if she had done so, she was sure Matron would only have said:

"Stuff and nonsense. The man's common sense should tell him that you could not be there every minute of every day."

Which would have been right; yet all Jill's intuition told her that when Mr. Carrington was angry, or when he had set his mind on something, he was not—exactly reasonable. And she could not help feeling that all she had done was to make Matron think she was a fool—which did not help her already wounded self-esteem, or make her feel any more ready to forgive Vere. Not that she imagined for an instant that he would want forgiving.

Chapter XII

THE person who seemed least perturbed was Sandra herself.

When Jill entered the room where the bright-haired dancer was lying back among her pillows, her patient held out a hand with a half contrite and wholly welcoming smile.

"Oh, Jill, I'm so glad you are back," she greeted.

"Good heavens! I might have been away for weeks," said Jill. But in spite of herself she retained that slim, welcoming hand, finding it impossible to look severe. "You could hardly have got into more mischief if I had been," she added.

"But I'm quite all right—aren't I, Nurse?" Sandra smiled cheerfully at her night nurse. "I only bumped my head."

In answer to Jill's questioning look Nurse Farrow told her: "She slept well, and doesn't *seem* much the worse."

"Um!" Jill took down the chart and studied it. Then, to her colleague: "Sorry I'm late, but I had to see Matron. You go along, Nurse."

The night nurse, thankful for relief—for to tell the truth, in spite of the fact that Sandra was safely tucked up in bed, she had been actually scared to leave such a prone-to-mischief young woman for a second, went away gratefully.

"Well!" Jill regarded her patient from under raised brows.

"I know!" Sandra agreed. "I deserve scolding—and won't I get it when the gentleman in charge arrives! I *think* I was rather fortunate to have knocked myself out, and not be in a fit state for 'blowing up'!"

"Really!" Jill drew a deep breath. "You are—incorrigible. First you try to wreck all the work that has been done on you, and then you just lie there smiling at me. I shouldn't blame Mr. Carrington if he gave you a good spanking." She was genuinely annoyed, for after all it was she who had been made the scapegoat.

"I couldn't agree more," said Sandra, with disarming meekness. "If I were—any of you, I should throw me out! But honestly it wasn't that I was trying to be funny and thought I knew better than my doctor and nurses. It was just one of my idiotic impulses, and I didn't think about what I was doing. I was feeling fine, and it seemed as natural to get up as it did to be breathing. I never thought——"

"That you had not even stood up for weeks, and were going to have to learn—really *learn* to walk all over again." And as Sandra shook her head. "Surely you've seen a baby that is just beginning to walk, and know what happens to it without support?"

Sandra giggled. "Yes, it sits down hard—and howls."

"Or tumbles on its nose—which you apparently did."

"And bumped my head against the table—which must be much more solid than it looks. But even that seems better—anyway it doesn't hurt in spite of the bandeau," said Sandra, touching her bandage. "And I'm sure I haven't done any worse damage. I can move my leg and wiggle my toes all right."

Incorrigible! It was not any use scolding her, and Jill gave in.

"Well, you will have to be X-rayed," she said firmly. "Mr. Carrington has ordered it. So I had better get you ready to go along."

In X-ray Sandra was welcomed like a princess—obviously Mr. Pearson admired her immensely. And even Sister in charge of the department, who was usually slightly sour in the early morning, behaved as if it was a gala night and she was master of the ceremonies.

But Sandra still had to face the battery of her surgeon's wrath and even she seemed a little subdued at the thought of it. Back in bed, she asked Jill: "Do you think he will be *very* unpleasant?"

"I shouldn't worry. You'll probably get away with it," Jill told her rather dryly.

Nevertheless it was an unsmiling Vere who made his entrance three-quarters of an hour later. His mouth was set grimly when, without glancing at Jill, he crossed to the bed. It was impossible to tell from his expression how angry he still felt; he appeared to be his most withdrawn and correct self.

Jill, watching from the usual position which she had taken up at the foot of the bed, felt as though a little cold breeze had blown into the room, and suspected that even Sandra was a trifle nervous—anyhow, for once she limited her greeting to a brief "Good morning, Doctor" and waited to be spoken to.

There was a slight pause while Vere studied the chart which Jill had laid ready for him.

"Um!" He put it down again. "Good morning. How far have you walked to-day?"

The sarcasm behind that simple question would have made most of his feminine patients curl up, but though she went a little pink, Sandra looked back at him calmly. "I am not taking any exercise to-day—that is unless you advise it," she said.

While she waited for the explosion, Jill thought involuntarily: She could be a match for him! It was the first time she had fully realized that under the other girl's flower-like loveliness there was another personality beside the spoilt child which so often appeared—a young woman, in fact, who was entirely capable of defending herself, and who was, of course, in a position to do so.

Lucky Sandra! Important enough to hit back at the great man, if she was hurt or annoyed!

For a moment Doctor and patient regarded each other. Then:

"No. I do not advise it," said Vere. Then, seating himself in the chair beside the bed: "Let me look at that head." In an instant Jill was on the other side, her own quick deft fingers removing the bandage and the dressing under it. She might not have been there for all the notice took of her. Then, holding back the bright hair he made his examination. "Lucky you only grazed yourself. No irreparable damage there."

"And I've been telling Nurse that I can move my knee and I am sure there is—nothing wrong with it," she said.

"I shall look at your X-ray presently. They are making a rush job of it," he informed.

"What a nuisance I am to everybody!" Sandra gave him one of her winning smiles. "I know you want to slay me, and perhaps I deserve it, but truly—as I have already told Nurse, I was not just being difficult. I got up without thinking."

"Well, if I were you I should think next time," he advised. "This time I am inclined to agree that you have escaped more easily than you deserve." Although the words were uncompromising the coldness had gone out of his tone. "I shall keep you in bed for a couple of days, and see you again then. Providing your plates show all clear, we will then proceed to teach you to walk. That is, if you promise faithfully not to try to run before you have taken your first steps."

"I won't—I promise." She held out her hand to him. "Faithfully!"

"Good." He rose, retaining her hand for an instant, smiling for the first time. "I think you have shortened poor Dr. Falconby's life. However, you are my responsibility again now."

"And you take your responsibilities *very* seriously, don't you?" asked Sandra demurely.

"I think," he told her, "that, after all, I had better ask Matron if she has not a good slipper with a sting in it." Then they both laughed suddenly, and Jill in the background knew that Sandra was forgiven, though obviously she was not included in the armistice.

Shutting the door behind him a moment later she wondered if he had already seen Matron—if he was furious at having found her still on the case, and what he was going to do about it. Oh, he could be detestable!

She had walked to the window without knowing what she was doing, and was mechanically arranging the curtains.

"What is the matter, Jill?"

She started round to find Sandra's eyes fixed on her enquiringly.

"Nothing," she said. "What should be?"

"You were looking furious, and as if you wanted to cry. I say"—Sandra's eyes widened—"he hasn't scolded you—but of course not," she added happily, "you were out."

"Yes," said Jill quietly. "I was out." She could almost have laughed at the unconscious irony of Sandra's remark.

The other snuggled her head into the pillows behind her. "He let me off—fairly easily, I suppose. Perhaps he realized I don't take to bullying. Anyway, he couldn't be worse at his worst than Marcelle Vernoist whom I trained under. 'You clumsy!' she used to scream at us when we were learning. 'I want a shower of ze rose petals, and I get lumps of lead. You—Sandra! Never will you dance—go and look after peegs, it is all you are fit for.' So a scolding from a mere medical man really means nothing in my young life."

Absurd, Jill supposed, to feel resentment at Sandra's ingratitude for what the "mere medical man" had done for her—using his time and energy and incomparable skill to make her whole again. And then, hands behind her head, Sandra mused:

"But I shouldn't like him to be really furious with me. Bless the man! he can be sweet when he likes. At those times I wouldn't blame any girl for falling for him, would you?"

"I—don't know," said Jill.

"Oh, you!" Sandra laughed. "I don't suppose you even notice how terribly good-looking he is. But I suppose to a nurse doctors are just machines—in spite of all the romances."

This time Jill made no reply; she could not have told whether the impulse to laugh or cry at such a very naïve remark from such a very sophisticated young woman was stronger. Then with a sudden uprush of irritation she thought: One day I'll go ga-ga! and then, humour seeping through: Maybe I have already!

Chapter XIII

I

In spite of his promise to Sandra, Vere Carrington did not appear at Broadmeadows again that week.

A Very Important Person, on whose panel of doctors he happened to be, was indisposed, and his carefully scheduled programme of work was consequently thrown all out of focus.

He telephoned his instructions. After the shock of her fall Sandra was to lie up for the couple of days he had ordered; she could then be allowed up in the wheelchair again—but for the present was still not to be allowed on her feet.

Sandra grumbled but, knowing that if she was being punished it was partly her own fault, endured with remarkable patience.

Though Dr. Falconby was more sympathetic than Vere, his easy-going tolerance was rather shaken, and as he had no desire to be blamed for any possible catastrophe, he firmly upheld the surgeon's orders.

But after those first two days in which the only visitor allowed was Lady Skeyne, the flow of Sandra's friends began again, and she was not allowed much time to think, or become bored. Nevertheless it occurred to Jill more than once that her patient was far from being happy or contented, but that her unhappiness was nothing whatever to do with her health or inactivity. There were faint shadows under her eyes—as if she was not sleeping very well, though she denied the suggestion that she was having bad nights, and Nurse Farrow, who still looked in on her once or twice during the night, insisted that she always seemed to be asleep.

Jill noticed too, that there was a certain eagerness about the way Sandra went through her morning's mail, and how when there was an airmail envelope she snatched the letter up, tearing it open eagerly, only to throw it carelessly into the heap which would later be handed to her secretary, who now came down every other day for instructions.

Plainly, the letter she was expecting and hoping for did not come, and Jill wondered if it was Glyn Errol whom Sandra wanted to hear from, and if the evident fact that he had not written was the reason for that rather unhappy look in the dancer's eyes. Being Jill, it pierced her conscience to know that her speculation was more than half hope. Because if Sandra was really fretting because no letter had arrived from Lord Errol, that meant——

Well, what did it mean? That a girl who is interested enough in one man to be unhappy when he is away, is not likely to be falling in love with another?

So what? Jill asked herself sharply. Surely she did not want Sandra to be miserable?—to which the perfectly sincere answer was that that was the very last thing she wanted. But she had discovered that she was not the only person to notice there was something wrong with Sandra.

Lady Amanda was staying in the neighbourhood now, and a frequent visitor to her convalescent goddaughter. She usually came in when she could be sure that "the crew", as she termed Sandra's younger friends, had departed.

She was on the point of leaving one evening when she met Jill on the landing.

"Ah, Nurse! Good! You are the person I am wanting to see," she announced.

"Yes, Lady Amanda? Is anything the matter?" asked Jill, who had grown to like the forthright old lady very much.

"That's exactly what I want you to tell me!" Lady Amanda lowered her voice, glancing behind her to make sure that the door of number 25 was securely shut. Then her shrewd bird-like glance seeking Jill's: "What is wrong with Sandra?"

"There's nothing to worry about," Jill assured. "She is getting on very well indeed."

"Um! She looks a bit peaky to me," said Lady Amanda, frowning. "Perhaps it's because she is tired by the time I see her—too many visitors in the day, all talking like the parrot house at a zoo."

"She doesn't tire easily at present," Jill assured. "Of course when she is allowed to move about and is using up her energy she will only be allowed to see very few visitors at first. But the doctors have been so keen to keep her amused—and she likes people to come."

"Um!" Lady Amanda was silent for a moment; then: "I think she's got something on her mind," she announced. "Of course," she added briskly, "it may be my imagination—though I'm not given to over-exercising it." She chuckled. "Perhaps she's falling in love. What do you think?"

"I—wouldn't know." Jill was conscious of that odd too-familiar lurch of her heart. Yet, why should the old lady's suggestion worry her—hadn't she been suspecting the same thing? The difference was that she was certain Lady Amanda was not thinking of Glyn Errol, and the old lady's next remark made her more certain still.

"Wouldn't be the first young woman who had lost her heart to an attractive doctor, eh? You must see a lot of that kind of thing." Lady Amanda's eyes, bright and clear as a girl's, met Jill's smilingly. Jill was thankful to find that she could meet them steadily and smile back.

"Yes," she heard herself saying serenely. "But it doesn't usually last, you know. Anyhow, I don't think you have any need to worry, Lady Amanda."

"Bless you I am not *worrying*," her ladyship assured. And then, with a disconcertingly shrewd stare: "You are not looking too well yourself. I should think you need a rest after six weeks of that dear, but exacting, young woman."

"Oh, I'm fine, thanks," Jill protested.

Lady Amanda frowned thoughtfully. "Do they ever give you a holiday?"

"Yes. I shall be getting a fortnight next month."

Lady Amanda nodded approvingly. "And well earned, if ever a holiday was. Though, of course, not nearly long enough. Well, go on taking care of the child—I shall not see her again yet. I am going back to London to-morrow, and then to see my youngest nephew in Sussex. His wife's just presented him with twins—clever gel—too bad they are not grandchildren, but I must be satisfied with being a great-aunt I suppose."

She is an old pet! thought Jill when, having rung for the lift and seen Lady Mandy's upright figure disappear from sight, she turned to go back to her patient. An old pet! But she let her imagination work overtime, whatever she might say. Or—didn't she?

II

On the Friday morning Dr. Falconby informed Sandra that Mr. Carrington had spoken to him on the telephone, and as there were no longer any possible ill effects from her fall she was to stand up—with help, he added with a half severe, half humorous look—as a preliminary to what she very quickly learned would be the slow, hard process of being able to move about without having to depend on other people's support.

After her recent experience she had not even the confidence of the toddler who has no idea that his first steps will land him with a bump on the floor.

"The floor seems much too near," she told Jill, "and—much too hard."

But she soon got over her first nervousness, and by the Monday was able to dispense with Sister to support her on the other side, and to walk slowly across the floor with only Jill's arm as her prop.

This time Jill took her as far as the window, where she sat down on the wide seat and gazed rather wistfully out into the gardens. "I wonder when I shall get down there," she murmured.

"What an impatient person it is!" exclaimed Jill. "If ever anybody wanted to run before they could walk you do! Didn't learning to dance teach you that Rome wasn't built in a day?"

"I hated all the grind," Sandra admitted frankly. "I truly believe, my dear, that if Madame hadn't bullied me terribly—she was Russian and a real devil to work under. She herself had learnt in the Imperial Ballet School in what in her day was St. Petersburg, when she was much younger than any of the children she was teaching, and she really could be fiendish to us! She used to gibe at me—and tell me that anyone as lazy and clumsy as I was would never get to the back of the corps de ballet, much less ever become a ballerina. 'Ballerinas are born not made—and they work and work and WORK!' she used to scream at me—and one day I lost my temper and screamed back that I would be a ballerina—that I was born to be one, and she was an old liar! She slapped my face," Sandra laughed reminiscently, "but after that we were friends. And long afterwards I heard that she had told my mother I had the temperament of an artiste! "

"And now no one would ever dream of scolding you for your dancing," Jill said.

"Don't you believe it," Sandra retorted. "When I appeared in that first season under Errol's management he used to criticize me unmercifully. And never yet has he admitted that I couldn't do better. He enjoys being unpleasant to me."

"But everyone else says you will be the greatest ballerina of the century," said Jill. "Look at the book that Russian man has written about you."

"Errol says it's all—or a lot of it—sheer nonsense. That it's my personality and not my dancing that 'gets 'em'. He swears I am not fit to be a board under Fonteyn's feet! And sometimes I think he's right—at others I know he is only doing it to make me determined to get better and better; and then I tell myself that it's just because he gets a kick out of being hateful to me."

"He sounds thoroughly objectionable. I wonder you don't hate him," exclaimed Jill warmly.

"I do—sometimes." Jill kept her eyes on the flower-beds below, speaking with what Jill could not help feeling was deliberate indifference. "And I should love the chance of getting even with him—perhaps some day I shall have it."

Again Jill was sorely puzzled by the odd relationship between those two. But of course it was quite possible to feel that you hated someone you—loved.

"Shall we walk back? " asked Sandra, holding out her hand.

Jill helped her carefully to her feet again, and with an arm about her shoulders began to guide her. "This time we'll go to the door, and that will make it a little longer than yesterday. If you feel you can——? " she suggested.

"Of course I can," laughed Sandra.

They had almost reached the door when someone tapped on it, and in answer to Sandra's quick "Come in" it opened, and Vere walked in.

Before Jill could prevent her Sandra dropped her arm and darted forward with an exclamation of pleasure, and almost losing her balance landed laughingly in Vere's quickly outstretched arms.

"Hello there! Be careful," he warned.

She clung on to him triumphantly. "That's the very first time I have walked alone——"

"And suppose you had fallen?"

"You were there to catch me!"

There was a hardly perceptible pause. Jill, standing in the background feeling the quickened beating of her heart die down, was conscious in every fibre of her of that little tableau! Sandra's lovely laughing face raised to the dark handsome one above her, while he held her looking down with the half quizzical, half tender look he might have given to a naughty but forgivable child. It seemed to Jill to be quite a long time —a full minute at least—before he removed those slender, clinging hands, and putting one of them firmly through his arm, led Sandra to the chair that waited for her, and put her into it.

Then: "Good afternoon, Nurse." He appeared to become conscious of Jill's presence for the first time. "There appears to have been a considerable advance since I last saw Miss St. Just."

"She is getting on marvellously, but—not as fast as she thinks or would like to," said Jill evenly.

If he was going to have her on the carpet again for not holding on to the patient more firmly—to blame her, in fact for the second time for Sandra's stupid, split-second impulsiveness, he was evidently prepared to save it up until he saw her alone. She could have slapped the other girl. Who would have dreamt she would do a thing like that?

But apparently Vere had no intention of scolding to-day. He told Sandra that he had already seen both Dr. Falconby and the masseuse, and, without addressing Jill again, settled down to chat to his patient, telling her that he had seen Lady Amanda yesterday evening.

"I understand you are going to her as soon as you leave here," he said approvingly. "That seems an altogether excellent arrangement; and as there are no complications, I propose that you should remain down here for another week, and then —you can continue your treatment in London where I can keep an eye on you! and gradually resume your normal routine."

"That sounds as if you had finished with me," said Sandra.

"From a professional point of view—almost," he agreed.

"Then how soon can I start work?" she asked eagerly.

His laugh was genuinely amused. "Good heavens! You must walk—better than you appeared to be doing just now!—before you can run, and run before you can dance," he told her.

Sandra glanced after Jill, who was going quietly out of the room. "Nurse says I want to run before I can walk."

"Nurse is right, I think," she agreed.

Appearing not to hear, Jill shut the door behind her, and shutting it had the odd feeling that, with this case at its closing stages, another part of her life had finished—like the ending of an act when the curtain begins slowly to descend.

When it rose next she supposed there would be no question of Vere Carrington coming on to the stage again. Which was just as well considering the stupid round of applause her heart had given when he entered just now. . . .

Chapter XIV

I

BY the next day, by means of that sort of odd telephone system which sent important news, as well as often unimportant gossip, circulating through the clinic, it was known that the hospital's most glamorous celebrity would be leaving it in the middle of the following week.

Mr. Carrington had brought another difficult case to a most successful conclusion, and Broad Meadows was—as Judy said—"no end bucked with itself, for having helped."

It was Jill's free afternoon, but in spite of that small exhibition yesterday, she was not in the least afraid that Sandra would do anything more to retard herself; she was much too excited over what she called her order of release, and keen to do everything to help herself get back to work as soon as possible.

For once Jill was really glad to be free. Without analysing her mood she knew that she wanted to be alone—to get away from everyone. To try to find some peace for her overstrained nerves and aching heart.

With her bathing suit on under her frock, and thermos, and a few sandwiches in a basket on her arm, she left the nurses' quarters with the determination to take a punt and go across to a small island which had always been a favourite haunt of hers.

There were over fifty acres of park land included in what had once been the Broad Meadows Estate and now belonged to the clinic. It was useful to let quite a lot of this out for pasturage, and a portion had even been ploughed up for crops to help the funds of the hospital which—being outside State control—could always do with extra funds, goodness knew. Through all this land, narrowing almost to a stream when it reached the gardens, the river flowed at its most exquisitely lovely.

There were boats and punts, some of which were privately owned by the better-off members of the staff, but the others were there for anyone who wanted to use them.

No one was ever quite sure where the man who looked after them came from—he seemed to have made the unofficial appointment for himself. His name was Small and he was a character, living alone in a very small cottage, and perfectly content to manage on his old age pension and the tips he collected for "keeping an eye on them boats", so long as he could remain undisturbed near the beautiful river he adored.

"A lovely day, miss," he told Jill. "Fine for a swim or a row."

"I thought I might swim," she said. "But I think I'm far more likely to put out to the island and laze."

What a summer! There seemed no chance of the weather breaking—these blue skies and sunshine ought to make one glad to be alive, thought Jill as she punted herself slowly across the broad silver ribbon of water that sparkled in the sunshine. A little unconscious sigh escaped her—life ought to be perfect when you were doing the work you cared for most.

And yet she knew that her natural response to the beauty of her surroundings was lacking in some essential appreciation that would once have been there, and there was no real spark of interest when she wondered what her next case would be.

She would miss Sandra. But Sandra would take up her own full life, go back to her interrupted career, and once again have the world at her feet. When there were free seats available she might remember the people who helped her to use those magically endowed feet again, and the staff at Broad Meadows might benefit. Of course she would be just as likely to forget them all as part of a nightmare of illness and uncertainty that she wanted to put behind her altogether.

But there was one person she would never be likely to forget—besides she would be seeing him quite often.

Suddenly Jill found herself remembering—Sandra tottering forward into those arms which were so quick to catch her—Sandra laughing up into Vere's face—and Vere, with that half tender, wholly inscrutable expression as he half smiled down at her.

It was crazy to let the memory hurt her like it did—to be tortured by the knowledge of how often those two might see each other in the future. Yet she had stopped telling herself there was any cure. One had never been found yet. Throughout the ages the unloved had gone in search of charms which would create love—but there did not seem to have been anything done about charms to cure the most unbearable pain in the world—or to fill an empty heart.

She reached the island and landed, making the punt fast.

Almost as soon as she set foot ashore it was obvious that she had the tiny domain to herself, and, grateful that no one else had had the idea of coming this afternoon, she sought out her favourite spot, which was just out of sight of the opposite shore under the shade of a tangled mass of greenery.

From where she sat down she could see the forget-me-nots and the spiked leaves of yellow iris growing at the water's edge. A small clearing on her right was glowing with the tall rose-madder flowers of the willow herb; the air was full of soft murmurings from the river; the undergrowth full of the subdued movements and twitterings of unseen birds.

Jill had come in search of peace, and it was here all around her. Yet while she sat, hands clasped about her knees, watching the movement of the glittering water through the trees, she found it quite impossible to empty her mind as she longed to do, so that only a vague knowledge of the loveliness of her surroundings remained in it. Thoughts crowded in, refusing to be locked out, and between her and the perfection of this summer afternoon came the vision of a dark, square-jawed face lit by eyes that could harden to the glittering blue grey of the coldest steel, or soften and deepen to the hue of a dark sapphire.

More and more as those days had passed, deny it as she would, the knowledge that Judy was right had forced itself upon Jill. He was not inhuman and he was capable of being as vulnerable as any other man to the spell of a girl's charm and beauty. And when added to that was the knowledge of all that his skill had done, was it not only natural for him to feel that he had a personal stake in the future of the life he had helped to re-create?

The echo of his voice came back to her. "*You can continue your treatment in London where I shall be able to keep an eye on you——*"

Yes, he would be able to see Sandra in London as often as he wished to. It was not just a matter of them each being caught back into their own lives, or of her just going to him for a routine check-up over the next few months. She was going to live at her godmother's house, because, Jill had already gathered, during her absence dry-rot had been discovered in some of the floors of the flat in the converted Georgian house in Mayfair which was her home. And even if a busy man like Vere might, under ordinary circumstances be likely gradually to forget the existence of a patient, he was a personal friend of Lady Amanda's and—Lady Amanda was interested in bringing those two together.

Mr. Carrington would, Jill felt sure with a new hopeless bitterness, be given every help to make up his mind to turn his back on bachelordom.

She sprang to her feet with a subdued cry of protest. It was just crazy to sit here torturing herself. Haven't you learnt yet that you have got to snap out of it? she asked herself furiously. What Vere Carrington does with his life is nothing to do with you—you never had, and you are never likely to have a say in it.

Even if she could not lock her heart against him, surely she could have learned to control it by now? All this time she had kept her heart locked up—now she must shut it tight again and—forget. The trouble was that the lock was so awfully frail, and always bursting open to show her the image in the secret shrine inside.

Summoning all her common sense to her aid she decided to go for her swim now. She adored swimming and was like a fish in the water. Loosening her frock she slipped out of it, left it with her tea basket and was soon swimming away from it. Though the current could be tricky hereabouts, she was a strong swimmer and knew every trick of the river—or thought she did.

It was some time since she had been in last—as a matter of fact this was only her second swim this summer, for she had not taken enough time off since she had been nursing Sandra.

There was nothing like exercise for banishing the blues, she decided, and her spirits rose as she darted hither and thither, wishing Judy or Ken or both of them were here to race. Then realizing to her surprise that she was suddenly feeling rather tired she turned on her back and floated, gazing up at the sky.

And then at last the peace she had longed for seemed to encompass her. This was heaven, or surely very near it; everything—worrying, the need to plan for the future, or even think about it, rescinded—there was the sky, and the sun, and the river; and just herself to enjoy them.

She could think of Sandra with the deep affection the other girl had won from her. Sweet, lovely Sandra, who deserved to have the world to dance on! And Vere! She drew a deep breath. Would she forget him if she could? Was she going to be selfish enough, because she could mean nothing to him, not to want him to be happy? There were more questions crowding in on her. This time she tried to face them calmly. If she knew that Vere would be happily married to Sandra she ought to be glad that he had found her.

But were those two suited? It was so difficult to see Vere as the man who would be content to have a wife half of whose life was lived in another, very different world from his. They were so alike in some ways—but not in the ways that make for peace and companionship. Young as she was, a great many human problems had passed before Jill's eyes. She knew that it takes a very deep and generous capacity for giving to make a successful marriage. A man like Vere needed a wife to whom his career—his work—meant as much as it did to him; not one who would keep back half herself, perhaps more than half, for her own career.

But there was nothing she—Jill—could do about it. And anyway she had been long enough in the water. She took a plunge, and coming up shook the water from her eyes and began to swim back, telling herself that for the present a cup of tea, even out of a thermos, was a goal worth winning.

It was only there that she discovered how far out of her planned route she had come. Floating away she had left the island to her right, and was in full view of the path that led to the boathouse. It would, in fact, have been much shorter to swim straight for Broad Meadows, but, having left her clothers, to say nothing of her tea, on the island—back there she must go.

And then without any warning she felt a violent pain in one of her legs. There was just time to think: But I've never had cramp in my life! before she felt the water closing over her head.

She came up fighting blindly, and hardly knowing she had cried out for help, heard an answering call.

"Hold on! I'm coming——"

It won't be any good, thought Jill with curiously little fear. Not a bit of good . . .

II

"What the dickens did you think you were playing at? Of all the complete idiots! You deserve a good shaking!"

Jill came from what seemed an immeasurable distance to find herself staring up into a pair of furiously angry steel-grey eyes.

"What do you mean by running such risks? Do you *want* to be drowned?" Vere demanded.

"No—o! Oh!" There is nothing picturesque or attractive about being sick—but when you feel as if about half the river Thames is in your tummy——!

Oh dear! Why couldn't it be someone else watching me! she thought miserably.

Far from being someone else, though, it was Vere Carrington. "You'll be all right in a minute——" he told her unsympathetically. A very wet Mr. Carrington with a lock of his thick damp hair fallen forward over his forehead and his white silk shirt and grey trousers looking as though they had just come out of the river—which they had.

Of course they had! He had fished her out and brought her safely back to dry land! Realizing suddenly that she was on grass belonging to Broad Meadows, she struggled to her feet.

"You're soaking!" she exclaimed. "You must get a change."

Her own sense of humour had entirely evaporated, but if Vere's laugh was a little grim it was still a laugh. "I shall survive——"

At that moment old Small came almost running towards them.

"What's happened?" he demanded breathlessly as he drew near. "I was having me tea—I'm a bit hard of hearing, and the young man who just brought me groceries said someone was drowning. Not when I'm about I sez——"

"Well, someone *was* drowning," said Vere shortly. "Get me a blanket quickly. I want to get this young lady up to the hospital."

"Dearie me, Nurse, it's you!" The old man stared in horror.

"A blanket!" barked Vere.

"Yes, sir." You wouldn't have dreamed Small was nearly seventy the way he obeyed that order.

"But—I can walk," protested Jill, struggling uncertainly to her feet.

"Can you?" Vere had the blanket about her, and lifting her bodily strode away.

She lay very still, quite limp; that slow, painful, *frightening* throbbing of her heart which she had been conscious of when she came back to life, had quickened until it seemed as though it must burst its way through her breast; her head was swimming and she hoped desperately that she was not going to be sick again. But above and beyond it all was the wild sweet knowledge that it was Vere's arms that were holding her, Vere's shoulder against which her head was resting.

Just for this once, out of all her life, she was in the arms she loved, close to the heart which she would have given her life to know belonged to her.

And then like a smothering curtain sudden blackness descended upon her. . . .

Chapter XV

JUST for once in her life! And she had lost those magic moments by fainting.

Jill lay staring out of the window opposite her bed. She had never known what it meant to feel so bodily weak, and yet her mind was so terribly alive.

She felt that as long as she lived she would remember those moments when she had stared death in the face—felt herself going down, knowing that it was for the last time! felt herself grabbed by the hair and struggled wildly.

Had he slapped her face? She seemed to have a vague remembrance of it. Her next memory began when she had lain on the grass, and ended with her knowledge of strong and determined arms holding her as though she weighed no more than a baby.

They had all been perfectly sweet to her, and were treating her as though she was of the utmost importance.

Matron had come and looking at her with quizzical affection said: "What an honour! To be pulled out of the Thames by Mr. Carrington. But I would rather you did not try to drown one of my best nurses——"

But when Jill said, "I must have been crazy! I quite forgot the current. Can I get up, Matron?" Miss Travers had shaken her head.

"Certainly not. You are remaining there—Doctor's orders. And believe me, the doctor is an unreasonable man."

Jill had never known Dr. Falconby be unreasonable, but she felt too tired to ask what Matron meant, and it was only Judy whom she had the courage to ask:

"What about—Mr. Carrington? Is he—all right?"

"Of course he's all right," retorted Judy, "he doesn't go fainting away."

Jill sighed. "Shame-making, isn't it?"

"Not under the circumstances," said Judy stoutly. "Mr. Carrington's the hero of the hour, of course—and hating it! I wouldn't mind giving him a life-saving medal myself—only he would probably hit me over the head with same! Honestly, ducky, I wish you wouldn't, though—I'd just hate you to be drownded." Judy spoke lightly, but there were actual tears in her eyes.

Jill had never dreamed how many friends she had, or how popular she was. She wished though that she could be allowed to get up and go back to her case, but Doctor Falconby informed her that she was suffering from shock, and had apparently been suffering from overstrain "before your attempt to drink up the Thames", and so she must do as she was told.

It would have been almost unbearably frustrating, at any other time, to have to lie here knowing that at the end of the week her most interesting case (besides she was fond of Sandra) would be departing, and perhaps she would not even be able to say good-bye.

And meanwhile for two days her colleagues were always snatching time to come along and cheer her up. Ken came, of course, sat on the bed, and in the middle of teasing her mentioned casually that he and Judy were going to have dinner in Windsor.

So he was not dropping Judy, and she had a very happy look about her. Jill hoped that was going to develop——especially when Judy began to ask her if she knew of any books about South Africa!

But there was one person who did not come near her during those four days. She wondered if he still came down to Broad Meadows; but somehow she could not make herself ask. She knew now that she had allowed herself to dream of working with him again in the future oftener than she had realized she was doing. But that had been before Sandra's accident; and now:

"Of all the complete idiots! You need a good shaking——"

Having made up his mind to that he was hardly likely to want her on a case again. Jill gave a dreary little laugh, breaking off to turn her head sharply as the door opened.

"Good afternoon," said Mr. Carrington. "Someone said

you were asleep. But as I am rather pressed for time, I had to risk waking you up."

He has a habit of appearing abruptly! thought Jill. This time there was no Sandra to tumble into his arms—only a girl whose foolish heart went racing to meet him.

"I was not asleep, thanks," she told him, hoping that she sounded calmer than she felt. "I was lying here wishing someone with enough authority to tell me I could get up would come along."

Vere raised his brows as he sat down on the chair next to the bed. "Too bad that I am the only answer to your prayer," he said coolly. "For I am the last person to tell you any such thing. I am glad to find that my orders are being carried out to the letter, and that you are being kept out of mischief."

So it was his command which had kept her here; and he was the "unreasonable man" Matron had referred to.

She said, summoning her courage: "But I am perfectly well, sir. I—could have been about again the next day."

"Probably. But you happened to be suffering from overwork and overstrain, and heading—unless we don't know what we are talking about—straight for a breakdown."

"But I didn't—I mean I wasn't trying to drown myself." She gave him a look of mingled indignation and horror.

"I am not suggesting anything like that. Or that you have suicidal tendencies, Nurse," he assured. "But when a young woman, who is normally as good a swimmer as I am assured you are, gets into difficulties in full sight of land, there is something very wrong. When I reached you, you were as exhausted as though you had swum half the Channel! And you hung on to me like any fool who falls into the water by mistake. I don't suppose you recollect that I had to be—decidedly drastic with you."

So she had not imagined that slap! And when she was on terra firma he had threatened to do it again! Jill knew herself to be emphatically not the kind of young woman to get tough with with impunity, and it brought a shamed sense of outrage to know that deep in her secret heart the idea of even being slapped by Vere Carrington could thrill her.

Was it really possible, she wondered unhappily, that a normal, independent young woman of to-day could actually feel that being knocked about—well almost!—by one man was preferable to being kissed by any other. If he guessed, she felt that she would die of shame. Only fortunately he was obviously miles from guessing—she was sure of that.

"I'm—very sorry if I tried to drown you, too," she said in a surprisingly small and weak voice.

His lips twitched. "You are forgiven—under the circumstances. But I am not going to apologize for—chastising you. However," his eyes met hers, and though they were smiling, and his glance lacked none of its usual penetration, she had a sudden odd suspicion that he was slightly embarrassed. "I have an apology to make, which is rather overdue."

"An apology?" she repeated.

"Yes. I was coming to make it when you—caused a diversion. Rather luckily, as things turned out, I had been told that you had gone down the river, and had come in search of you."

Up to that moment she had sustained his level glance steadily, but now she dared do so no longer, and looked hastily away. "I—don't understand," she murmured.

"I have owed you an apology," he said quietly, "since the day of Miss St. Just's accident. I understand from Matron that you left your patient most unwillingly that day. You had told me so, and—I should have accepted your explanation. I was needlessly unpleasant. I hope you will forgive me." With one of those sudden brilliant smiles that—as Judy would have said—"knocked you clean out" he held out his hand. "Shall we be friends again?"

Hardly knowing what was happening Jill put her own into it. "But—of course," she heard herself stammering. "I——" she broke off, conscious of that firm, cool hand clasping hers.

It was the briefest of contacts. If she had not been feeling so chaotic herself she might perhaps have noticed that he released her fingers rather quickly. An instant later he was on his feet, but instead of making one of his abrupt exits he remained looking down at her, his face inscrutable. She would have received a decided shock if she could have read his mind and realized he was thinking suddenly how very young she looked—absurdly young, lying there with her gold-brown hair curling about her face, her eyes wide above the shadowed hollows above her beautifully moulded cheek-bones. Not at all the efficient young nurse whom he was used to seeing in uniform, and had once seen jolted from her usual serenity into just indignation.

Somehow the picture of her facing him in furious self-defence, showing him that she was no spiritless yes-woman, had remained in his mind; and being a strange, unpredictable man he had remembered it with something oddly like approval; especially after his interview with Matron.

But now, lying back on her pillows, a Shetland wool bed-jacket tied demurely under her chin, she seemed to have become a young and somehow vulnerable girl.

"You know," he said, the startling revelation coming abruptly upon him, "I can behave very badly. And did—that day."

"Oh no!" Jill exclaimed, before she could stop herself. "You—thought I was in the wrong——"

He gave her a quizzical look. "Are you making excuses for me?"

"No." Courage came flowing back into her, and she sounded serene once again. "I would not take the liberty of making excuses for you; though I admit that sometimes you need them."

The moment the words were out she wondered if she had taken leave of her senses, and afterwards she never knew how she managed to meet his eyes and keep her own smiling.

For an instant a little crease formed between his brows, and then he laughed. "You are a courageous young woman! Perhaps it is good for all of us sometimes to see ourselves as others see us! But, after all, you knew from the beginning that I was 'a difficult man', did you not?"

She hesitated. "Not so difficult, I hope, that you won't let me thank you for what you did? Because, you know, you saved my life."

This time his frown was unmistakable. "You have no idea," he told her, "how really difficult I shall become if you ever refer to that again. Kindly forget it—and do not exaggerate. I must go now. You are to remain where you are until Thursday. I have already spoken to Matron regarding what I think should be done about you."

Her heart missed a beat. What on earth did he mean?

"But Mr. Carrington——" she cried.

Vere had reached the door, and he turned rather impatiently. "Yes?"

"Can't I go back to my case—on Thursday?" she asked desperately.

To her relief he half smiled. "You are very persistent."

"But of course. Miss St. Just is going on Friday."

"So she is. Very well—I suppose, if Matron permits, you can resume your duties for one day." Without waiting for a reply he went out, shutting the door.

There was something frighteningly definite in the sound. Jill sat up, pressing her fingers to her temples.

What was Vere Carrington proposing to do with her life? *"I have spoken to Matron regarding what I think should be done about you."*

But her future was nothing whatever to do with him! . . .

And then she remembered. If she had known before that, however hard she tried to deny it, her life belonged to him, now he had the right to think that it did; and in any case he had always taken it as a matter of course that what he said went.

She thought, trying to work up a spurt of anger: If he thinks he can kick me around, he is wrong, even though I might not be here if it was not for him.

But she was nearer to panic than she had ever been—even in those unforgettable moments in the river. What had Vere in his mind, to make him even take an interest in her future—surely he did not think that she was really ill?

Chapter XVI

I

MATRON came in to see Jill again the next morning and put her mind a little at rest.

"By the way," she said, "Mr. Carrington has decided to be annoyed—or shall I say slightly acid, with me. He says you have been overworking (of course *he* has nothing to do with that!) and that you are too thin, overstrained, and if I can't send you away for an immediate holiday he advises me to keep you on very light duty until I can."

It was in her capacity as a friend and not as "Matron" that Miss Travers was speaking—ordinarily etiquette would have prevented the obvious criticism of a famous visiting surgeon to one of her staff. This conversation was off the record.

"The Great Man is undoubtedly right—whoever is to blame, and I suppose as he has dragged you back to life by the hair of your head, his words of wisdom deserve extra attention," she continued, her eyes a little worried. "You may not be the only overworked member of my staff, but it is true enough that you need a break, my child. I wish I could give it to you, but you know how things are—everyone's holidays are arranged——"

"But I don't want to go away yet," Jill protested. "Daddy's niece from Canada and her three children are there for the next six weeks. And my stepmother has her hands full."

"I see. If you did go, you would promptly be working even harder than you do here—or feeling criminal because you were not helping enough." Matron was slightly relieved. She knew the big rambling farmhouse in Westmorland where Jill's people lived, and decided that, with three extra children in it, it would be no place for a rest cure. "We must see you don't overdo things," she said decisively. And then with an abruptness that made Jill jump: "Are you worrying about anything?"

"I was only wondering if Mr. Carrington had—told you that I must give up nursing, or—something," Jill said truthfully. She was secretly thankful that this was true and she could ignore anything else that might be on her mind. Not, she told herself, that there was anything else; it was in her stupid heart that the trouble lay. Thank goodness Vere Carrington, for all his brilliance, could not diagnose that!

"Good gracious, no," said Matron laughing. "You certainly ought to be flattered at his interest in you. In spite of having you on the carpet—and then being put there himself by me!—he gives you full marks over our ballerina."

"Does he?" Jill asked.

"Yes." Matron was silent for a moment. Then she said casually: "By the way, have you noticed that romance is brewing?"

Jill's breath caught, but she managed not to change colour as she looked at her companion questioningly.

"Nurse O'Farrell and young Doctor Harding," said Matron, whose shrewd eyes missed nothing. "I wonder if it is serious?"

"Oh, I am so glad you have noticed!" exclaimed Jill. "I do hope it is."

"You know he is leaving soon to take up an appointment in Rhodesia?"

"Yes, he told me."

Matron hesitated. Then she said, watching Jill's face, "Mr. Carrington asked me if you were engaged to Kenneth Harding. I assured him he was wrong in thinking so, and that I had not noticed you giving the young man much encouragement."

Good heavens! Was there anything Matron did not notice? Jill wondered.

"You would not have thought about him?" the older woman asked.

"Not for a minute."

"Quite. I told Mr. Carrington I was sure he was wrong."

But Mr. Carrington had actually taken the trouble to find out what Matron knew about it! When she was alone again, Jill's mind reverted to that fact, and she thought a little sadly how ironic it was that Mr. Carrington should have rushed to the conclusion that she had another man on her mind, although of course a thousand times better than if he had guessed the right one.

Oh dear, oh dear! A sigh dragged itself from her. How difficult life could be, and—what a muddle. . . .

II

And so on the Friday Jill was there to see the patient to whom she had given so much of herself safely on her way.

Sandra greeted her delightedly, though she told her it was too bad of her to have deserted her for these last few days.

But she had made a big advance in Jill's absence, and could walk by herself quite well again now.

"And to think Vere saved you from a watery grave!" she said gaily. "He was furious when I asked him whether he would get a life-saving medal! You know that aloof expression he gets."

"Vere"—Sandra was evidently making strides in other things besides her convalescence. Jill wondered if he would come himself to fetch this star patient away. But when the time of departure arrived it was Lady Amanda who came to accompany her goddaughter back to London.

If it had been royalty that was taking its departure it could not have had a greater send-off. Every nurse in the hospital seemed to be there to bid Sandra Godspeed. There were flowers, and good wishes, and a graceful little parting speech from Matron.

Sandra was sweet to everyone, and her eyes were suspiciously bright as she threw her arms round Jill's neck and kissed her spontaneously. "Of course I shall see you soon again," she announced. "You will come and see me, Jill. And I shall come back to see you all. And when I can dance again we'll have a wonderful matinée for the hospital funds."

She meant every word of it, and would almost certainly do as she promised. Nevertheless, Jill was quite sure that as soon as she got away she wouldn't want to come back in a hurry, or think about the hospital more than she need do.

When she had gone, though, something certainly had gone with her. Everyone missed her to a greater or lesser degree; with her went all the glamour which had surrounded her, and the place seemed to drop back into its more utility self.

But though she tried desperately to ignore the fact, Jill knew that, where she herself was concerned, it was not Sandra's absence—though she truly missed her—which accounted for the strange emptiness of the days following the dancer's departure.

It was not Sandra of whom she thought every morning on waking; not Sandra whose absence made that blank in her life.

Matron had put her on a very easy case, and she would much have preferred one that would fill her mind and require all her energy. And yet she knew that the most interesting case would have called no exciting reaction from her.

And when she thought about it she realized with horror that the very work which had meant so much to her—that work around which she was still determined to build her life—had lost its savour.

Of course she was run down. After a holiday she would feel better; be able to take up the threads again and spin them into some kind of satisfying pattern. But her holiday was still three weeks off.

Vere Carrington had certainly been right in saying she needed it.

Vere Carrington——! She did not try to pretend that she missed him less than she did. She saw now only too clearly how every day that dawned had just been a waiting for that quick, light step of his. The opening of a door, the sight of him—even though usually his smile had been for Sandra, and her heart had only ached the more.

How inconsistent the human mind could be! She had left St. Monica's all that time ago, to avoid coming into contact with him; and now life was empty because she could not know he would be there for a few minutes out of each day. But even in those days when she had known he would not be coming, there had still been the knowledge that he would be back again, and the satisfaction of feeling that she was holding the fort for him. Sandra wrote a delightful letter of thanks—via Matron—to "everyone", and sent the kind of cheque for the non-paying side of the hospital which even in these slightly inflated days meant something substantial.

To Jill she sent a breath-takingly lovely dressing-case fitted with everything the heart could desire in toilet requisites all backed and topped in silver gilt.

It was a lovely present, and it was sweet of her to send it, but Jill's first involuntary reaction was a wish that she had not. Somehow she felt the day might come when she would not want something that constantly reminded her of Sandra. And then, feeling guilty and ungrateful, she shut the thought away.

It was not Sandra's fault if she was so attractive that even a man who had never bothered about her sex was caught in the net of that honey-gold hair. Jill wondered unhappily how close the meshes of that net had drawn? And if those two were still seeing each other—often?

It was no use trying to shut out those questions—they hammered at her mind too persistently. . . .

There was still speculation among the nurses as to what would come of what was still known as "the romance". After all, a surgeon did not need to pay as much post-operative attention to a patient as Vere Carrington had done. And it did not comfort Jill to remember that Mr. Carrington had always kept a strict eye on his patients, even, or perhaps especially, those who were non-paying hospital cases. And so naturally, as a friend of Lady Amanda's——!

But less than ten days after Miss St. Just went away the hospital had a nearer home romance to take its mind off the one they had so sedulously woven for her. The news of Nurse O'Farrell's engagement to Dr. Harding was announced.

Jill's pleasure in Judy's engagement was unmarred by any stab of envy. It was characteristic of her not to grudge her friend one iota of her new-found happiness. She was certain it was all exactly right for Judy, that Ken would settle down into the best of husbands and that Judy was one of those girls who are just made for marriage.

And although they were still capable of being very gay and very mad, being in love had had a decidedly steadying effect on both of them. There was one thing Jill was sure of—that whatever troubles might lie ahead those two would bring an unfailing sense of humour to the smaller ones, and care for each other well enough to face the bigger ones bravely. She was sure, too, that Ken would go ahead to the top of his profession.

Lucky people, to have been able to love on their own level, and not reach up to something beyond their grasp.

One afternoon during the first week of the engagement Jill was sitting in her bedroom, a blotter and the pad on which she had been writing home on her knees.

Having finished her letter she sat gazing out of the window to where among the trees the distant river wound between its banks. Her experience had left no fear of the water in her mind; strange though it might seem, the memory of that day only made her love her "sweet Thames" more than she had done before Vere had dragged her rather ignominiously out of it. For even if he had not meant it—if it had been just a touch of bedside manner when he had said it—that episode had led to that unforgettable moment when he had asked: "Are we friends again?" Had he really felt that they were friends? It did not seem much use if he had, she decided with a sigh. He had gone now; and it did not seem as though he were inclined to send any more of his patients to Broad Meadows.

How stupid I am, she thought impatiently. Even if he wanted to, he would have to wait for the right kind of case.

She picked up her pen again, but she was still watching the sparkling river through the leaves when ten minutes later she came out of her reverie with a start to find Judy standing beside her.

"Day-dreaming?" asked Judy. "I thought you were asleep or had gone out. Didn't you hear me hammering at the door?"

Jill looked unbelieving. "You must have muffled the hammer."

"Rubbish! You were miles away, ducky."

Jill coloured slightly. "I was probably searching for news to send home. Nothing seems to happen here any more. At least nothing worth writing about."

"I like that!" exclaimed Judy with mock indignation.

"Oh! I told Daddy your news last week," laughed Jill.

Judy sat on the edge of the bed. "I suppose you mean since the St. Just went away? It does make things rather quiet, I admit—we could do with a couple of celebrities to be going on with. Unfortunately no V.I.P.s are choosing the right complaints."

"Too bad they won't oblige." Jill rose and, crossing to the chest of drawers, put her unfinished letter away and came back with a carton of chocolates and a packet of cigarettes. "Which hand will you have?"

"What a friend in need you are! *And* a mind reader." Judy took a cigarette.

"Matches on the dressing table." Jill put the packets away again without helping herself from either of them. "I must go back to my patient in a few minutes," she explained.

Judy, watching her closely, taking fresh note of the shadows under her eyes and the new listlessness with which she moved, smoked for a minute in silence before she broke the silence.

"Jill——"

"Yes?" Jill turned, looking across at her.

"N—nothing," said Judy.

Jill frowned, surprised at the other girl's obvious embarrassment. "What do you mean—'nothing'," she demanded. "Of course it's something. Speak out like a big girl, and tell me what's on your mind."

Judy looked down at her cigarette, then, gathering her

courage in both hands: "As a matter of fact," she blurted out, "I was wondering—what was on yours."

Jill met the embarrassed eyes smilingly.

"Not a thing in the world." She laughed lightly. "My mind is almost a blank—I've given up thinking. My present case hardly requires it."

Judy was not deceived. Although she had been so very much occupied by her own affairs lately, she had still noticed the change in Jill, and she was certain that her friend was unhappy. "Well, you are getting much too thin," she said. "Are you sure you're not worrying?"

Jill shook her head. "You're dreaming. I may have lost a little weight, but wouldn't anyone melt away in this weather?"

"It's abominably hot," agreed Judy. "But——" she broke off, her eyes widening, as a sudden, startling thought occurred to her. Judy's strong suit had seldom been tact. With her, as with Shakespeare's Rosalind, it was too often a matter of "when I think I must speak", and she had often enough got herself into hot water by blurting out what was uppermost in her mind. Too frequently thought reached her tongue before her mind had time to digest it.

She said now, rather breathlessly: "Jill, darling—Ken asked you to marry him before he—fell for me, didn't he?"

"Who told you that?" Jill asked sharply. But the answer was obvious. Only one person could have done; and they said women were the talkative sex!

"He did," admitted Judy, already regretting her impulse. "I—challenged him one day with having been keen on you."

Jill was really annoyed. "And he had the exquisite tact to inform you I had turned him down. But honestly, sweetheart," she added, more gently, "you needn't mind. Ken 'got over' me very quickly. I just came along when he was looking for someone to fall in love with. So——"

"Oh! I'm not jealous!" cried Judy. "I was only—afraid that perhaps you—I mean——" hopelessly involved, she stammered her way to silence.

"You mean you were afraid I might be regretting having said 'no', and pining away for love of your young man? Darling!" Jill's laugh was slightly forced; she really was sick of having people think she was—interested in Ken Harding! "I promise you that I never would have married your young man under any circumstances. He's all kinds of a dear—but not my kind. Satisfied?"

Judy sprang up, throwing her arms about her. "I can't tell you how relieved I am. I couldn't have *borne* it if you were unhappy because of Ken."

"You prize idiot!" Jill laughingly disengaged herself. "Oi! Pick up that cigarette, you'll set the place on fire."

"Oh, golly!" Judy retrieved the cigarette which she had let fall in her excitement, and hastily rubbed her foot over the singed rug. Then sitting down again while Jill straightened her cap at the dressing table, she continued, more seriously:

"I do adore Ken. And I do mean to do everything in the world to help him when we are married. I hope he won't ever think *he* might have married someone more suitable."

"Don't be a goose," advised Jill. "You were made for each other. I'm sure you'll both make a go of it."

"Won't be for lack of trying on my part," announced Judy. "And Ken is the very best-tempered man I ever met." She pressed the end of her cigarette out on an ash-tray. "You see—although I may have seemed rather frivolous, I've always thought that marriage was frightfully important, though I've liked being a nurse—and never wanted to be anything else. I've loved my work, and I don't mind how hard it's been—but I'd never be first-class like you are, Jill. Sister is so right when she says really good nurses are born, not made."

"It's just a matter between a profession and a vocation, I suppose," said Jill.

"Yes. And with you it's a vocation. I couldn't have borne to think of spending all the rest of my life in hospitals," Judy said. "But you will go right ahead, and one day you will be a very nice, terribly efficient Matron of some enormously important place like Guys or The Westminster."

"Not if I stay here listening to your fairy tales when I am wanted elsewhere," Jill told her.

They parted a minute later out in the corridor and hurrying away Jill gave a soft, dreary little laugh.

"A very nice, terribly efficient Matron!"

Oh well! She lifted her chin. Thank heaven for work, anyway. Surely when it meant such tremendous service for others it could be made to fill one's life without leaving any room for regrets, or vain dreams.

It must do so. Because she knew so well that never, never would she be able to take second best. . . .

Chapter XVII

I

Two afternoons later Jill received a summons to Matron's room. When she got there Miss Travers told her that she wanted her to take her holiday at once. The nurse who had been due to go off to-morrow was anxious, for urgent family reasons, to postpone her holiday until the first week in August; and as she and Jill could not possibly be spared together, Matron wished Jill to do a swop and go now, instead of later.

The older woman did not explain that it had occurred to her this was an excellent opportunity for getting Jill away earlier.

"Smithson is only on routine work at present and can take your case," she said. "Will it upset your plans very much? If so, I am afraid she has had it, for I cannot make any other arrangements."

Matron was a dear, but Jill knew the difference between a request and an order! Besides, she was always particularly careful not to seem to take the smallest advantage of Miss Travers's friendliness. So she assured her that she would be quite willing to go, and was rather glad Matron seemed to have forgotten all about it being inconvenient to go home just now.

For her own part Jill knew at once what she intended to do.

Home was out of the question, and though she hated the idea of not seeing her people for several months more she was almost relieved. After all, she might be able to snatch a week-end later and go up North. But at present she did not want to be in the country; she wanted to go somewhere where there were more distractions, and less time to think. When she left Matron's room her mind was already made up to go to London. A friend of hers—Rosalind Greyson—with whom she had worked at St. Monica's, who had left to get married and subsequently lost her husband in a tragic train accident, had now gone back to nursing, taking private maternity cases. She had a small flat in a mews off Marylebone High Street, and she had only written a little while ago to say how glad she would be to put Jill up at any time, or, if she happened to be away when the younger girl was in town, the latter was welcome to use the flat at any time. Jill put a call through to her that evening. Rosalind was delighted at the idea of having her, and though she herself would be going off to a case in a few days, told her she was welcome to stay as long as she wanted to.

And so Jill packed up hurriedly, and, two mornings later, woke in the tiny spare bedroom of Mrs. Greyson's flat.

For the first three days the girls reminisced over old times, did a matinée, and a couple of other shows, and in spite of the noise of cars being brought home and "put to bed" at late hours, and being got out and hosed at early ones, Jill slept more soundly than she had done for a long time. Then Rosalind had to go off to her case.

"You won't get bored, will you?" she asked. "You have friends to ring up, of course? And you'll go and see them at St. Monica's, I suppose."

Jill made a non-committal answer, but privately she had no intention of going near St. Monica's—anyhow, not yet. For once she felt that she had had all she wanted of hospitals, nurses' gossip, and—doctors.

"Well, you ought not to feel strange," Rosalind laughed. "You are a stone's throw from the doctor's quarter—you can always take a walk down Harley Street if you want to see the great."

"Heaven forbid!" exclaimed Jill.

Nevertheless, to reach the centre of things— and even if she only wanted to look at the shops in Oxford Street, she realized that small maze of streets where the *élite*, and too often the not so *élite* of the medical profession put little brass plates with their names on outside the doors, would have to be traversed in one direction or another.

She had been so determined to lose herself in the vastness of London, and seek all the distractions it offered, as far as she could afford to; and it had never occurred to her for a moment that, trying so hard to forget Vere Carrington, she was practically landing herself on his doorstep. Of course she had always known he lived in Wimpole Street, but St. Monica's, being down by the river, had always seemed far enough away from that thoroughfare, and she had never thought about where it was situated.

It was no use worrying now. She told herself determinedly she hoped she would not meet him. Also, she knew at the back of her mind that Vere would not be at all pleased to find her taking her holiday in London.

The weather had broken for one day, and although immediately afterwards it resumed its golden glow, the rain seemed to have cooled the air a little. Jill had almost forgotten what the heat of streets can be; making her plans after Rosalind's departure, she knew that it still would be wise to get all the fresh air she could, and not return to Berkshire looking pale. But, after all, there were the parks, and it was always possible to take a bus to Hampstead or an underground to Kew.

Of course, she decided, there was tons to do. It had been wise to come to town where there were so many distractions and so much to think about.

And yet she still continued to think—much too often it seemed—about one person. She hoped she would not come face to face with him, and yet—if she were just to catch a glimpse of him without being seen herself——!

Then she asked herself angrily if she *had* to behave like a romantic teen-ager. Did every girl in love lose her sense of proportion? Yet she was still certain that, however it might hurt, she would not lose this love for the world; for in doing so she would lose half herself. She must keep her heart locked if she could. But she dared not desecrate the shrine which was lit by that ever-burning flame blown into her heart by the winds of destiny. She had given up all hope of being able to quench that fire, and, when a flame is very beautiful it is surely ungrateful to mind because sometimes

"Smoke gets in your eyes".

Yet she must try to forget sometimes, or she could not bear it.

And so she made plans to go about to see places and things which she had never really had time to get near when she had been at the hospital.

On the day after Rosalind's departure she went to see an exhibition of pictures in a gallery in St. James's—flower paintings by a famous French artist, which filled her with delight. There were not many other people in the gallery, and she sat down opposite a study of roses that glowed out of the canvas in such perfect loveliness, that it almost seemed possible to smell the flowers' perfume.

Lost in her delight she did not notice when someone sat down beside her, until a startled voice spoke, dragging her back to her surroundings.

"Nurse——!"

Jill turned her head quickly and met the bright, dark eyes of Lady Amanda Skeyne.

She rose quickly. "Lady Amanda!"

"Sit down, child," the old lady commanded, "and don't look as if you had seen a ghost. What are you doing in London? Up for the day——"

"No. I——" there was no help for it, Jill had to explain. "I'm—on holiday," she said.

"Alone?"

"I came up to stay with a friend."

"Hum! You look better. How long have you been here?"

"Four days."

"Why didn't you ring me up? Or ring Sandra——"

"I didn't know—that is I didn't think——" Jill stammered.

"I told you to come and see me. Of course you must," said the old lady firmly. "I tell you what—I am just going back to tea. Come with me." And as Jill hesitated: "Got another date?"

"No——"

"Then of course you must come."

And so, a quarter of an hour later, when they had walked round the exhibition again and Lady Mandy had seen a "sold" label attached to two of those lovely little canvases, Jill found herself leaning back on the deeply cushioned seat of a pre-war but still beautiful Rolls-Royce, being driven back to Lady Amanda's Belgravia home.

Travelling along Jermyn Street and up Duke of York Street the car was at once caught in the heavy stream of traffic in Piccadilly. London was still very full, and as usual the press of cars coming out of the side streets held up the main stream of vehicles; so that there was plenty of time for conversation.

While they waited at the approach to St. James's Jill's companion asked casually:

"How do you think Vere Carrington is looking?"

Jill, who had been watching the traffic, glanced round with a start. "I haven't seen him," she replied.

"Not since Sandra left the clinic?"

"No. There isn't any reason for him to come down. There are no patients of his there, and, of course, he is not one of the official consultants."

"I see. Anyone can use the private wing?"

"Oh yes. It's like any other nursing home."

"Hum! I think he's looking tired. He needs a holiday. I have told him so, but you might as well talk to the moon. Apparently he had arranged to go away for ten days this month, but he has altered the arrangement, and now says that he will go 'sometime'."

"He must need a holiday." Jill was grateful to hear how steady her voice was.

"He does. But perhaps there is a method in his somewhat indefinite postponement."

As the car moved slowly forward again Lady Mandy continued, still sitting perfectly upright as only her generation learnt to to: "He has certainly made a wonderful job of Sandra. She is to begin dancing again this winter, and is actually practising already."

"So soon?" asked Jill.

"Yes. She has twisted her surgeon round her little finger, and coaxed him to let her try—getting her own way as usual. I had no idea Vere could be so indulgent," the old lady laughed, and then becoming serious. "But I wish she would give up the whole idea and get married like a sensible girl."

"But—you couldn't expect her to give up dancing!" exclaimed Jill. "I mean, it isn't just like any ordinary career. Everyone agrees what a great artist she is."

"I know. She is beautiful on the stage—even though I am not a ballet fiend," agreed Lady Mandy rather testily. "I suppose Vere feels that having mended her up he ought to let her go on for a time. But I am sure that he would rather she did not."

Jill hesitated on the brink of panic; then something stronger than her fear of Lady Mandy's answer forced her to ask: "Do you mean—they are engaged?"

"No—not yet, unfortunately. But I have known Vere for

many years. His mother was a friend of mine, and I have never seen him show what appeared to be personal interest in a girl before. I am sure it is only this dancing business that has made him hesitate to ask her before this——"

"And—Sandra?" asked Jill quietly.

"My dear, how can she avoid thinking the world of him? Have you ever met a more attractive man?"

Jill forced a laugh, avoiding the question. "He is a—very brilliant one."

"Oh! I forgot!" Her companion gave her a humorous look. "You've seen a side of him that may not be so attractive. Sandra says he can be a martinet. But I am sure she is very attracted—it's only this dancing business again that keeps *her* from admitting it. They have been meeting a lot; Vere drops in two or three times a week, and I am sure *I* am not the attraction. The only thing is to keep my fingers crossed and go on manœuvring," she added frankly. "Arranging a marriage is rather like a game of chess, you must have infinite patience. But these two will not be the first to be gently coaxed into realizing they are made for each other. And you must confess they would make an ideal pair."

"Ideal."

"My dear child, how pale you are! London in this weather is not the best place for you to take your holiday!" exclaimed Lady Amanda.

"But—I've loved it," protested Jill. "It's—only that I have a slight headache. Perhaps looking at the pictures gave it to me."

"You must have a couple of aspirins when we get in," said Lady Amanda, whose kind heart would have contracted with horror if she could have realized how her bright gossip had tortured the girl whom she had taken such a fancy to.

II

Lady Amanda lived in Eaton Square, on the first floor of a great Georgian mansion which had been converted into flats to suit these modern and less spacious days. But though the tenants might sigh about the servant problem and high taxation, the whole environment emphasized the fact that happily the art of gracious living has not quite perished.

Jill, who loved beauty, looked round with a thrill of delight as she followed her hostess across the broad panelled hallway to the lift, which was lined with rose-coloured brocade and had been cleverly arranged to somehow give the impression of a large sedan chair.

"Young man who 'did' this house rather let himself go," observed Lady Mandy quizzically. "But had to keep his hands off my flat. I never trust interior decorators—except to let 'em carry out my plans."

It certainly did not look as though she needed advice, thought Jill when they had passed through the door which shut away the old lady's domain. The cream-painted hallway along which exquisite prints of the Old London pleasure gardens were hung at intervals, was carpeted in glowing plum colour; traversing it they entered a long sunny room decorated in robin's egg blue and silver, with outer curtains of thick cream corded silk patterned with wreaths of blue love-in-a-mist and pink rose buds, at the three enormous windows.

The briefest glance told Jill that every piece of furniture, from the golden walnut bureau to the carved and gilded mirror above the tall mantelpiece was in perfect "period", and yet there was nothing of a set piece about the place—if it was a drawing-room it still managed to look used, and as if it belonged to someone's home.

A big black and white cat was curled up on the deeply cushioned window seat. Lady Mandy glanced at him. "Puss occupying the most comfortable spot as usual!" she observed. "He's a frightful snob and prefers being in here. We'll go into the library. I always have tea there unless there are visitors, and I am not going to treat you as a visitor, my dear. Go through, will you. I will join you in a few minutes."

Jill went through the communicating door and found herself in a much smaller room, where another door evidently led out into the passage.

Here there were hundreds of books in breast-high shelves against the cream walls; deep sapphire carpets underfoot and again exquisite old prints and beautiful eighteenth-century furniture—though the deep settee and armchairs, covered in rose-coloured leather, were modern. The long windows were framed in rose-coloured brocade curtains, and Jill could not help thinking what yards of material those curtains must take. These old houses were hardly economical!

She went across and looked out. Beneath, the square glimmered greenly, almost deserted in the afternoon sunshine. How peaceful it all seemed! So far from the constant stir and rush that always contrasted with the seeming quiet of Broad Meadows, or the almost constant racket which surrounded Rosalind's mews flat. And yet, as far as she herself was concerned, how deceptive the peace was! For here she was again swept into the lives of Sandra St. Just, and with Sandra—Vere Carrington.

Suddenly that wound in her heart which Lady Amanda had inadventently set throbbing again seemed almost unbearable. But what was the use of being unhappy? What was happening was only what she had expected. How right Judy had been from the beginning.

She turned quickly as an elderly woman who looked like—and was—a lady's maid, came in carrying a glass of water and a phial of aspirin tablets on a small, very highly polished tray.

"Her ladyship says will you please take some of these, miss," the newcomer requested.

"Oh, thank you! But my head is not really bad enough to need them," said Jill; nevertheless she did as she was requested, dropping two of the tablets into water.

"Thank you." Holding the glass in her hand she smiled at the older woman. "I will take these in a minute."

"Shall I draw the curtains, miss—Nurse?" asked Bridges, who was Lady Amanda's personal maid. But Jill told her that she preferred the sunshine, and Bridges went away, thinking that if that was Miss Sandra's hospital nurse she was a very pleasant young lady—and very good looking.

Left alone Jill waited for the tablets to melt before she drank the contents of the glass down; her headache might not be very bad, but she was curiously glad to have something to soothe her nerves. She had just put the glass down and was going back to the window, when her eyes fell on a framed photograph standing on the top of the bookcases nearest to her.

For a moment she stood staring at it, her eyes wide, the colour coming and going in her cheeks.

The man in the photograph looked back at her, grave and rather detached, though his pictured eyes, seeming to gaze straight into hers, smiled faintly as she had so often seen the eyes of the original do. Her breath caught, and almost before she knew what she was doing she had moved forward as though drawn by a magnet and snatched the picture up.

There was no inscription on it. But it was here in Lady Amanda's library, and must belong to her—if Sandra had one it would be in her own bedroom. Staring down at it the echo of a deep, very charming voice came back with startling clearness.

"Good morning, Nurse" . . . Her breath caught, and the longing to hear that voice again dragged at her like an actual physical pain.

Lost to everything else she stood staring with the photograph in her hand, never dreaming there was anyone to see her; knowing nothing of the mirror hanging on the drawing-room wall which through the open communicating door reflected that portion of the library where she was. Even if the carpets had not been so thick the loud, heavy beating of her heart would have deafened her to any footsteps.

In the other room Lady Mandy had paused, involuntarily watching her guest with no intention of spying on her, but shocked at the revelation of suffering on the lovely young face on which she had never before seen anything except calm.

Good heavens! she thought. What a clumsy old fool I am! The child's in love with Vere, herself . . .

A minute or two later her hostess's cough sounded from the other end of the long drawing-room, warning Jill hastily to replace the photograph and hide her trembling hands in the folds of her skirt as she swung around to face her hostess.

"Sorry I have been so long," said Lady Mandy cheerfully, "but Sandra rang up to say she would not be back to tea. I forgot to tell you that the workmen are out of her flat and it is being put in order for her to go back to-morrow."

"Will she be—all right there?" Jill realized she sounded breathless, but Lady Mandy did not seem to notice.

"Splendidly, my dear. She has a couple of excellent maids. Besides Farrer, who is her personal maid and also looks after the housekeeping—the kind of treasure one seldom finds in these days! who fusses over her like a hen with a chick. Then there is Miss Johnson, her secretary."

"Yes, I have seen her," said Jill, who had herself quite in

hand again now. "And her maid came to fetch her from Broad Meadows."

"I believe she did. Do sit down—I hear tea on the way." Lady Mandy seated herself in a high-backed, winged leather chair and pointed to a more loungy one opposite.

Then a staid elderly manservant wheeled a tea wagon in by the other door, gravely placed a table containing plates of cakes, wafer thin sandwiches, and bread and butter within reach, and withdrew.

Pouring out tea Lady Mandy asked how Jill's head was, and being told it was better gave her guest a rather penetrating look when she rose to fetch her cup.

When the preliminaries were over she took up the conversation which the arrival of tea had interrupted.

"Yes, Sandra will be quite safe. After all, there will always be someone to read the Riot Act if she overdoes things. It has been delightful having her, but I shall not miss some of the people who have come to see her—nice people, no doubt, but a little fatiguing at my age. I must confess that unless I have to go out—or do an occasional theatre for my own pleasure, I like to spend my evenings with a book or a game of patience." She laughed ruefully. "I have reached the selfish age."

"I am certain you could never be selfish," Jill assured her warmly. She liked this charming, if somewhat autocratic old lady, better every time she met her.

Lady Mandy said: "I told Sandra you were here, by the way, and she said that if you go before she comes in she will never forgive you. She will be back about six—now, don't look like that! It is after five now, and surely you can endure me for an hour."

"I was thinking you might not want to endure me," said Jill.

"I like having you."

Since Lady Amanda was so obviously not the sort of person to say that unless she meant it, Jill supposed that settled it; and yet she would rather have avoided seeing Sandra to-day. But there was no doubt about her hostess being a very entertaining companion. The time slipped quickly by while the old lady talked about the fun she had had in her own youth, and how different and somehow much more important the London season had seemed to be then.

"There were more conventions surrounding a girl, of course

—and there were chaperones!" she said. "Thank goodness those have gone out of fashion. I really could not bear to tag round with some unfortunate girl, watching to see that she danced with the right men, and not too often with any one of them. I, of course, was an Edwardian—and dear me! how hard we fought for our freedom. Perhaps the young woman of to-day overdoes the freedom business a bit—nevertheless, I do hope she will not suddenly—or even gradually—throw it all away."

"Whatever makes you think such a thing?" asked Jill.

"Well—there's a queen on the throne again, and women are wearing bonnets; and—some of them at any rate—sighing for security. Crinolines are charming in the ballroom but not in the mind." Lady Mandy had attended suffrage meetings in her youth and remembered the time when a woman, no matter how intelligent, had no right to have a say in who ruled the country in which she had to live. "Everything in moderation," she added, "but you know, sometimes the pendulum can swing back so far and so suddenly that everything changes almost overnight."

"But—you think girls ought to marry and settle down——"

"If the right man comes along. After all, marriage is important. I'm old-fashioned enough to believe that a girl's love story is more vital than her career if it comes to choosing between them. But heaven forbid she should have to make marriage her career and be on the shelf if she didn't find a husband!" Lady Amanda laughed frankly. "You'll think I am inconsistent, but sort it out and you will find I am not. Now I must stop holding forth, because I think I hear Sandra."

The next moment the door opened and Sandra came hurrying in.

"Jill!" She caught Jill by the shoulders, reaching up to kiss her affectionately. "How lovely to see you! Look who's here——"

But Jill already knew who was there, and she wondered how much oftener would she have to thank the training which taught such rigid self-control, as she thanked it now when she turned, a smile on her lips and an agony of longing in her breast, to look across at Vere Carrington.

It was not because he was so terribly attractive with the grey blue of his eyes contrasting with the golden tan of his skin and the thick darkness of his hair—though all those things set her heart galloping.

It was because he was the only man in the world whose presence could fill her with a gladness that almost smothered the pain in it—just to know that she was in the same room with him once again.

Because, after all, he was the only man in the world who ever had, or ever would matter to her.

"How do you do." He shook hands in the brief, firm way she remembered so well. "How is Broad Meadows?"

"Just the same as ever," she told him, though she knew it was not, and never would be the same again.

"Isn't it nice to see her!" exclaimed Sandra, linking an arm in Jill's. "Lady Mandy, what do you think? This man was practically next door, and I had to almost use physical violence to make him come in to see you."

"How very unfaithful of you, Vere," said Lady Amanda. Then more seriously: "Were you in a hurry, poor man? And did this wretched child drag you away from something important?"

He smiled slightly. "I am always in a hurry, alas! I was thinking of coming back to see you this evening, but this young woman tells me you will neither of you be here."

"For once I am going out," Lady Mandy told him. "An old friend who is over from the States is staying at the Dorchester and I promised to look in after dinner. And as usual, Sandra will be gallivanting off somewhere. Ring for Jackson, Sandra—Vere will have some sherry."

"Thanks, not for me," said Vere quickly. "It is before my time for an aperitif."

Sandra glanced at the tiny diamond studded watch on her wrist. "It's half past six," she announced. "Surely you will have something?"

"Nothing at all."

"Awkward, aren't you?" She pulled a laughing face at him.

He said calmly: "Surely you discovered that long ago?"

It seemed to Jill, watching from the background, that they understood each other very well indeed, these two; and although Vere had said he was in a hurry he remained chatting to his hostess.

Sandra went across and sat down beside Jill, telling her again how nice it was to see her and asking how long she expected to be in London. "How wonderful it must be to escape for a little while," she said. "Isn't it marvellous to be able to do what you like?" But though she went on to speak of her own delight at the idea of returning to her dancing, and about going back to her flat, Jill felt that in some way which she could not have explained, Sandra was curiously detached—almost as though her thoughts were elsewhere. With Vere, perhaps—though she did not glance in his direction.

Jill wondered if it was just her own imagination working overtime which made her feel that, in spite of the attention he appeared to be paying to his hostess, his thoughts were wandering too. In spite of all her efforts she found her eyes straying towards him, and on one of those occasions, to her embarrassment, discovered him watching her.

Then rising abruptly, he announced: "I really must go now."

"Come again soon." Lady Amanda gave him her hand. "Remember I shall be a 'lone, lorn creetur' after to-morrow."

"So you will—but I am sure you will find life very peaceful," he said coolly.

"Yes, won't it be lovely for her?" asked Sandra. "She'll be able to put her house in order without a lot of untidy people cluttering it up. She has been a perfect Christian martyr enduring me all this time. By the way, you have not forgotten that you are coming to my party to-morrow—have you, Vere?"

"Unless something prevents me," he told her.

"You mustn't let it! It's my house-warming and to celebrate my real return to life. You of all people must be there."

"I will certainly come if it is humanly possible," he promised. "But remember that I am not always my own master. That I am the servant of emergencies which are none of my making."

"I feel it would almost have been better if she remained here," sighed Lady Amanda. "Do exert your influence to prevent her overdoing things when I am not there to ring the curfew."

"If she chooses to be a fool she has been told what will come of it." Vere spoke with his old abrupt asperity.

"Don't worry, darling." Sandra crossed over and leaning on

the back of the settee where Lady Amanda was sitting, put on arm round her. "I shall be the most obedient of Cinderellas and always retire before midnight."

For an instant Vere watched the tableau—it was a very pretty one, with the girl's lovely face bent down to the handsome old lady. But even while he watched it he was more aware of the other girl, sitting in a deep chair, her hands resting on the arms of it.

He had not addressed Jill since his greeting, but now he turned to her suddenly.

"What are you doing in London?" he asked. "Just up for the day?"

"No. I am—staying for a little while," she replied.

"I see." His tone was non-committal, but it seemed to her that he did not approve. Then he bade his hostess farewell, and as Sandra walked towards the door with the evident intention of seeing him off, nodded briefly to Jill and followed her.

Sandra was only gone for a minute. She came back singing a gay snatch of song.

"Jill, darling, come to my room and talk to me while I dress," she begged. "I really must rush or I shall be late for my dinner appointment."

Jill shook her head; somehow just then she felt she could not bear it if Sandra should talk about Vere. If—there should be something she was likely to confide to her.

"I must get away myself," she said. "I'm sorry, but I—can't stay any longer."

"Well, *you* must come to my party to-morrow," Sandra urged, and as Jill hesitated: "Don't say you've another date, please!"

"No——" Jill almost wished that the urge to truth was not quite so strong in her, and yet——

"Then you'll come! Seven o'clock—wait, and I will scribble the address." Sandra darted across to the desk and seizing a piece of paper began to write rapidly. Watching her Jill could not help noticing how graceful every movement she made was. A lovely, lovely thing! "There." She turned, thrusting the folded paper into Jill's hand. "It will be fun."

Fun!

Jill wondered, as a few minutes later she left the house and turned her steps westward. It would be a change, anyway, but perhaps one of those emergencies of which he had spoken would prevent Vere Carrington from going.

She was too honest to pretend she wanted that to happen; she knew only too well that her only real reason for consenting to go to Sandra's house-warming was because it would give her the chance of seeing Vere again.

Chapter XVIII

SANDRA'S "flat" was really a maisonette near the Piccadilly end of Park Lane. The building, with its lovely sweeping bow windows leading out on to a balcony long and wide enough to be almost a terrace, looked straight over the sweep of the park. There was no longer a garden between it and the road, but the enormous room with its polished floor strewn with beautiful Chinese rugs was a veritable bower of blossom and greenery when Jill followed her name across the threshold the next evening.

Feeling unusually and rather frighteningly shy she had purposely come late to Sandra's party, hoping that by doing so she would be able to slip in unnoticed. And luck seemed to be on her side, for several other people had arrived at almost the same moment, and it was with four other girls that she left her wrap in the room off the hallway which had been set aside as a powder-room.

The moment she entered the reception room she realized how wise she had been not to take her hostess's insistence that this was just "an informal Bohemian little affair" literally. The clothes, of the women at any rate, were anything but informal, and Jill remembered the reflection of herself, which she had seen in a long mirror a few moments before, with relief. Thank goodness! she had decided only that morning to be extravagant and buy a new short evening frock that would do later on for the hospital ball. She was wearing it now—a dress of dark amber-coloured moiré poult, which a loose Chinese coolie jacket of the same material lined with black satin turned a low-cut sleeveless dance frock into something for dinner, or a cocktail party. The outfit had seemed a particularly alarming extravagance, and only a recklessness which she had not attempted to account for had induced her to choose it; but she was glad now. With it she wore high-heeled amber and black grosgrain sandals, a pair of her few hoarded gossamer fine nylons, and an amber necklace and earrings which had belonged to an aunt—the kind of old-fashioned jewellery that was in fashion again.

Sandra, in the middle of the room, surrounded by a little crowd, freed herself to make one of those darting rushes across the floor which made her somehow look as though she was just floating through the air.

She looked quite breath-taking this evening in a midnight blue chiffon ballerina frock that emphasized the natural whiteness of her skin and the honey-gold of her hair.

"Darlings, how lovely of you all to come," she greeted. "Jill, my precious, come at once and be introduced——" and before Jill could prevent it, or even guess what was going to happen, the other girl had turned her towards the room, a hand on her arm, saying in her clear, pretty voice:

"People, I want you all to meet a very important person. My nurse, Jill Foster. She didn't only help to *nurse* me with the most wonderful and untiring patience, but she made life feel as if it could be worth living when I wanted to die of sheer boredom."

"Hooray for Nurse Foster. Here's to her and all pretty nurses," exclaimed a dark young man whom Jill had already met when he had come down to Broad Meadows, and knew as the author of a book called *A Ballerina Speaks*—a short appreciation, half biographical, of Sandra.

Just then, to Jill's relief, some more people arrived, and she was able to lose herself in the crowd and finally land up in a corner of the room where she could observe without being observed herself. Used, like every nurse, to hiding her light under a bushel, her hostess's extravagant eulogy had made her want to fall through the floor with embarrassment. She searched the crowd anxiously, and seeing no sign of the one person she wanted to see, drew an illogical breath of relief. She felt that she just could not be too grateful he had not been there to hear Sandra; sure that he would have thoroughly disapproved of her being dragged, even for the briefest moment, into such a blaze of limelight.

But search as she would from her point of vantage, she caught no glimpse of Mr. Carrington's tall, perfectly groomed figure for the next quarter of an hour. If he was there she was sure she could not miss him, and calming down she thought: I hope Sandra does not propose spotlighting him—because there will certainly be an explosion afterwards, if she does.

Although she could not help being interested, she felt rather like a fish out of water in this environment where everybody seemed to know everybody else, and—from the scraps of conversation which floated to her from all round—seemed to be discussing their friends and acquaintances with uncompromising frankness, when they were not talking with passionate interest about themselves. It was her first glimpse at close quarters of the theatre, the ballet, the cinema, and musical worlds, with a sprinkling of writing people—and although she found it intriguing it was also slightly disillusioning. But presently her sense of humour took charge, and she began to enjoy herself; though she was still a lonely and quite dry island in a seething sea of very strange fish.

To give Sandra her due she was an excellent hostess and had determined above all things to introduce Jill to people who might really interest her, but she had speedily become caught up in welcoming the constant stream of new arrivals and trying to talk to a dozen people at once, and she had almost forgotten Jill's existence. Added to that, she was constantly watching the entrance, an unusual anxiety behind the smiling surface of her eyes.

After a time, in spite of the wide open windows, with her both natural and trained propensity for fresh air, Jill began to feel the overheated atmosphere, heavy with the mingled scent of flowers and the perfumes the women used, almost overpowering. Escape by the door appeared almost impossible by now—Sandra's "informal house-warming" having turned into a milling crowd, all talking at the top of their voices, packing the room and spilling out into the hallway beyond. Jill looked anxiously towards the window recess, and gradually edging herself that way, finally found herself on the threshold of the balcony.

People were mad! she concluded. Not a soul seemed to have

hought of going out there. Talk about the herd instinct! And it was terribly bad for Sandra to be on her feet all this time in this atmosphere! However, there was nothing she could do about it, though she wondered if she might not have to pick up the pieces later, and if it would not be just as well to stick around.

She stepped out on to the balcony and walking across rested her hands on the stone parapet, drawing in a deep breath of air—even if it was mixed with petrol there was at least still a percentage of purity in it, and it was getting cooler now, thank goodness!

"I am glad to find one other sensible person in London——"

Jill jumped round as if she had been shot, a hand to her heart.

"Mr. Carrington! Where on earth——?"

Vere had drawn his long length from the deep cane chair in which he had been lounging.

"I did not recognize you for a moment," he said coolly. "I am afraid I made straight for this oasis as soon as I arrived—about a quarter of an hour ago. Will you tell me why people go to parties? Or does this kind of thing interest you?"

He had pushed the chair towards her, and she sat down in it, conscious of how grateful she was for support for her knees, which felt suddenly unsteady.

Couldn't one be one's age! And sensible, instead of trembling like any Victorian miss, because one particular man was about? How she envied people who could be calm and sensible about being in love!

A thought which showed that Nurse Foster, in spite of a couple of medals and a lot of experience, was still oddly young and innocent not to realize that love has to go through several stages before it becomes "calm and sensible"—if it ever does. That if it starts off that way it may be affection and respect; it certainly is not the most disturbing emotion in the world.

But she had plenty of outward self-control and her face was deceptively calm as she glanced up at the tall man who stood looking so intently down at her.

"Ye-es, they interest me," she admitted. "Especially when I look on from a safe distance."

There was genuine amusement in his short laugh. "'Distance lends enchantment to the view'?"

"Well—I can breathe now. And I can recognize several people whose photographs I've seen in the papers—even some I have seen on the stage."

"Does that thrill you?"

"They *are* interesting, you know. They do things I couldn't do in a thousand years—act, and dance, and write——"

And not one of them does a day's work worth one hour of yours, my dear! he thought. But he admitted: "All very good for the *morale* of the country—when they do it well. Personally I should like to infuse a little more health into the activities of some of them—Hello!" He turned as a servant with a tray of glasses paused just inside the window. "I could do with one of those. What about you?"

Jill said gratefully: "If there is any orange juice."

There was. Vere got her a glass and, nursing his own drink, drew another chair up and sat down. She felt suddenly as though she had been transported into some dream; was it really possible that she was sitting on a balcony overlooking Hyde Park with Vere Carrington—or would she wake up in a minute and find herself somewhere quite different? She studied the strong, handsome profile beside her, as he stared out across the park, a half smile on his lips, those brilliant eyes narrowed a little. She had never seen him quite relaxed before, and she wished that the silence could remain unbroken—quite sure that he had forgotten her and feeling at liberty to give herself to the joy of being near him.

But he had not forgotten her. Though he was not looking at her he still carried that picture of her in his mind, and found it an unusually pleasing, if a slightly disturbing one.

It was the first time—except for those few minutes yesterday, when he had hardly noticed what she was wearing—that he had seen her out of uniform.

One somehow did not think of a nurse apart from her uniform! Yet he had recognized her at once, this girl who would have made a study in black and amber, with her soft hair curling above her clear brow, and her eyes in which the tints of her golden dress seemed to be reflected. Very lovely eyes between their thick fringe of lashes——

Yet in spite of the unacknowledged fact, that she had clung to his mind so consistently, he would have been amazed if he could have seen his impression put into words like that.

Then, glancing round at her with one of his swift illuminating smiles, he asked:

"Why do we make rash promises?"

"Goodness knows," said Jill. "But do you?"

"Rather. I promised to stick this party out—and the one that is going to follow it."

"But—Sandra isn't giving another, is she?" Jill's eyes opened in dismay. "She will be a wreck."

"She is pretty strong," he said casually. "I confess I am amazed myself at the extraordinary come-back she has made; but of course I don't need to be a 'psychiatrist' (overworked and too often unnecessary 'science'!) to know that half her delicacy was sheer worry about the future. She really has a marvellous constitution."

"I know she has," admitted Jill. "But—isn't this kind of thing rather soon? She has never been off her feet."

He shrugged his shoulders. "She will have to learn by experience. When she finds that if she is stupid enough to burn the candle at both ends her precious work will suffer, she will organize herself all right. She may not care about obeying doctor's orders, but she does care about her career."

Was there just a shade of bitterness in his voice? Had he learnt to resent that career? Jill was not sure whether she wanted to answer those questions or not. But she knew with a sudden fierce intensity that she did not want him to be hurt—and that Sandra had no right to hurt him. No! not for all the careers in the world.

Reaching that conclusion she reached, all unknowingly, the very height of love, which is selflessness. But then she never had been a selfish person, and had long ago given her life to service.

"Now," he demanded abruptly, "tell me what you are doing in London? I gathered yesterday that you were staying up here—is this an extra holiday?"

Jill shook her head. "No—it's just my ordinary vacation." She explained how it had come about, and saw a sharp little crease draw itself between her companion's strongly marked brows.

"I should hardly have thought London in this weather the place for an overworked young woman to have a 'break' in," he observed. "Rest and fresh air——" he paused. This was not the hospital, and it was rather unfair to lecture her.

"But I get plenty of fresh air all the year round," she told him. After all, for the first, and maybe the last time, they were meeting on neutral ground.

He frowned, and then laughed. "I did not know you could produce such a feminine argument. O.K. I won't scold you now. But I thoroughly disapprove."

"I—wanted to—have a real change," said Jill defensively.

Before he could reply a shadow fell across the threshold of the room and Sandra stood looking at them in surprise.

"So this is where you got to, Vere!" she exclaimed. "And —Jill too. Jill, darling, I was so afraid you had just vanished quietly away, and I did want you to stay. Vere—you're not to going to be mean and desert? They are beginning to thin out now and there will only be about eight of us for dinner. Jill—you *must* stay. I forgot to tell you I expected you to."

Vere looked at Jill. "Of course she will stay," he said.

She could not have received a bigger shock if someone had fired a gun, but before she could make any comment he was speaking to Sandra again.

"Sit down for a minute." He indicated the chair he had vacated.

"I can't. Take Jill along to the garden room. I will gradually send the other dinner guests along there," she said. "I don't want to make it too obvious that there is a private party." As she went back into the room Jill noticed that her smile faded and her face seemed to set as though she were tired, or—annoyed. Could it be because Sandra had found her out here with Vere? She glanced quickly at her companion, but he, at any rate, appeared calm and unruffled.

Yet somehow Jill felt that the *tête-à-tête*, which had been so wonderful to her, was spoiled.

Chapter XIX

THE crowd in the reception room had thinned considerably and people were steadily taking their leave when a few minutes later Vere piloted Jill across it into the hall.

"This way——" he turned off, traversing a short passage and going up two or three shallow steps. Obviously he knew his way about, and he seemed quite at home.

Of course, Jill told herself, Sandra had been superintending the putting in order of her home for a week or two, and no doubt he had come here either with, or to see her—which proved yet again what strides their friendship had made. For who could have imagined a busy man like Mr. Carrington finding time to pay social visits—unless he had a very good reason for doing so. And that he had "a very good reason" for putting himself out was something she must learn to take as a matter of course.

The room he led the way to was not large. A charming place with soft green walls and Parma violet coloured curtains and upholstery. There were two settees and several deep comfortable chairs. It was evident the room received its name from the fact that over one wall and round the windows climbing indoor plants were trained, some of them bursting into bloom, against painted wrought-iron trellises.

Sitting down in a corner of one of the settees, Jill glanced about her with a sigh of pleasure. What a lovely home Sandra had—how long did she propose keeping it?

Suddenly she wished someone else would come; her pleasure at being with Vere—a happiness which she realized could only have ever been vicarious, was gone, and she felt an acutely unhappy embarrassment. She wished someone else would come quickly, and almost immediately had her wish.

Two people entered—a man and a girl. The girl Jill recognized as Gay Trefusis, a well-known actress; the man introduced himself by a name belonging to an even better known producer.

Two people from the world Sandra had made her own; that world that was so far removed from Jill's, and from—Vere's.

Oh! if only he realized how far! But did men who were in love ever see things clearly?

Very soon Sandra joined them, bringing three other people.

In a brief lull in the conversation Gay Trefusis said inconsequently: "We're a man short, Sandra."

"I know. Does it matter?" Sandra spoke rather shortly, and Gay gave her a surprised look. Catching it, she forced a laugh. "Superfluous women are common in this country—one more or less doesn't count."

Jill wondered uncomfortably if she made the odd girl out, but it was too late to do anything about it.

Vere gave their hostess a searching look.

"You have been overdoing it," he said.

She shrugged her shoulders. "I feel fine, thanks."

But she sat, her cigarette gone out between her fingers, very plainly cross about something, while the others—almost as though they were used to her moods—laughed and chatted round her.

And then the door opened and a man's voice said:

"Thanks, I'll announce myself."

In an instant Sandra was on her feet, and though she dropped back into her chair immediately, Jill had seen the sudden transformation of her face as she looked across at the newcomer.

Jill had only seen him once before—at Broad Meadows—but it did not need a second glance for her to recognize Glyn Errol, the man in whom Sandra had shown such a very strong interest, and whom she, Jill, had wondered if the ballerina could possibly have been in love with.

"Hello, Sandra." He moved forward with that air of complete self-possession that Jill had found irritating on their first meeting and still did. "Sorry I could not get here before—I've been in Paris all day."

"In Paris?" Sandra had given him her hand and he retained it while she looked up at him. "I thought——"

"That I only got back from America yesterday? Right again—but I found an important communication waiting, and I flew over—faithful as ever to your interests."

"My interests!" she repeated. But two excited little spots of colour showed in her cheeks.

"Yours, oh precious jewel!" He bent and kissed her cheek lightly. "Tell the child about it later. Who don't I know here?" He waved a gay hand to the ones he did know, and it seemed only Jill and Vere were not included in his acquaintances.

Sandra said: "You know Jill Foster. You met her at the nursing home. You remember Lord Errol, Jill?"

Jill admitted, without any show of enthusiasm, that she did. But Glyn gave her a smile of recognition.

"By Jove! The young and efficient nurse. Sandra, what company are you bringing her into?"

Sandra ignored the remark. "And here is someone very, very important," she said. "Mr. Carrington—Vere, this is Glyn Errol, perhaps you have heard of him. He has certainly heard of you."

"Yes I have. How do you do? You must be proud of yourself giving us back our ballerina."

It might have been a gracious speech, but somehow it was nothing of the kind. Jill had never dreamt that anyone would dare to be patronizing or insolent to Vere, and her hands clenched against a primitive desire to slap Lord Errol's handsome face.

Vere, never moving a muscle, merely bowed, but just for an instant the two men looked at each other, as men only can look when instant and violent antagonism has sprung to life between them.

"I am naturally pleased if any efforts of mine have helped to put Miss St. Just in circulation again," said Vere quietly.

"But good heavens, Sandra! Why didn't you tell us that this was the great surgeon?" cried Gay Trefusis, who was entirely uninhibited and said whatever came into her mind without considering whether it made her hearers comfortable or otherwise. She stared at Vere, her china-blue eyes wide with admiration. "I didn't catch your name, Mr. Carrington—I'm just crazy about the medical profession, do come over here and tell me all about it."

"Darling, he doesn't go in for mental cases," said Sandra. "You're not a bit in his line."

There was a general laugh, and Jill drew a deep breath, grateful to the blonde actress for making a diversion. Of course nothing would have happened if she had not done—probably, apart from Vere himself, no one except Jill had noticed that touch of insolence in Glyn's manner. And Vere was a rigidly controlled and highly civilized person. Anyway, this was not the jungle, where two male things who take a dislike to each other fight it out on sight.

But during the evening she noticed that these particular men, seated one on either side of their hostess, hardly exchanged a word.

When dinner was over, as Sandra and her guests left the dining-room, Jill found herself beside Vere.

Glancing up she met his eyes and to her dismay felt the colour deepening in her cheeks.

For a moment he stared down at her, and then:

"Don't go overdoing your 'holiday'," he said, and turning abruptly away, rejoined Sandra, who broke off her conversation with Errol with a dismayed:

"You are not going, Vere?"

"I am afraid I must," he replied. "Nice of you to have let me come to-night." He held out his hand to her. "Now—please remember!"

"To obey doctor's orders. Yes, I will—truly," Sandra promised eagerly. "Don't thank *me*—it was sweet of you to come—I shall see you soon again, won't I?"

"I expect so." Again one of those smiles which Jill always felt were specially reserved for Sandra, softened his face. Then bowing to the others he went quickly back into the hall.

Jill would have dearly loved to excuse herself then, but Sandra had already followed her other guests back into the garden room. As she, Jill, heard Errol make a low-voiced remark to Sandra, and though she could not catch what he said, Sandra's reply, spoken with unusual sharpness, reached her:

"You are the last person who should dare to criticize him!" And then she went over and sat by the dramatic critic, ignoring Errol.

The zip seemed to have gone out of things; Jill noticed that Sandra looked pale, and although she was laughing and talking with her companion, experienced eyes could see plainly she was dropping with tiredness. Jill only wished she still had the authority to order her to bed.

Then, as Errol took Miss Trefusis's empty cup and rose to put it down, Sandra suddenly broke off what she was saying and got swiftly to her feet.

"Darlings," she said. "I love you all, but I am going to send you away now. It is time good girls were in bed, and though I've had a lovely time I shall be like a rag to-morrow if I don't go bye-byes soon."

"Obeying doctor's orders?" Errol's sarcastic mouth curved into a not very pleasant smile.

"How right she is!" said Gay Trefusis. "I bet he would only have to murmur the smallest order to me, and I'd *crawl* to obey. You've lost all my sympathy, Sandra," she added, kissing her hostess good-night. "When I think how sorry I was for you! And all those weeks Mr. Vere Carrington was calling upon you every day—I think it's just too bad that I was on tour. Can't someone think up a simple operation with a long convalescence for me? Nurse—can't you?"

Jill shook her head. "You wouldn't enjoy it at all really," she assured smilingly. "Don't come with us, Sandra," she added. "I'm sure we can find our wraps ourselves."

When they emerged into the hall Sandra was there talking to Glyn, who looked anything but pleased.

Jill said her farewells and thanks, and left the others. As she crossed the street at the side of the house she saw several cars parked there, and concluded they belonged to Sandra's now departing guests. Foolish of Sandra to have let people stay so late! It would have been much better if the party had ended before dinner.

It was a lovely night and she decided to walk at least half-way home, turning westward along Park Lane. She had hardly gone a hundred yards when a low-slung shining black and silver car drew almost noiselessly to a halt at the kerb, almost on a level with her.

"Has no one ever told you that nice young women are not safe walking about alone at this hour?" asked an amused voice. And as she made to quicken her steps without looking round: "O.K. Nurse—it's only me——"

She stopped then and turned to find Lord Errol standing beside the car.

"Oh, it's you!" she exclaimed, half laughing, but not at all anxious for his society.

"Hop in," he urged, "and I will take you wherever you want to go. Please! I want to talk to you—about Sandra."

And so, still rather reluctantly, she let him help her into the car and gave him her address.

He drove on for a few minutes in silence before he asked:

"How much has Doctor Carrington been seeing of Sandra since she came back to town?"

Jill felt herself bristle and sat up a little straighter. "I am afraid I really don't know," she replied coldly. "I don't keep Mr. Carrington's appointment book."

"*Mr.* Carrington," he repeated with a short laugh. "Sorry. I really never can understand why, just because a doctor takes to surgery, he should object to being called doctor."

"Does he object? I never heard he did. It is just a matter of etiquette," said Jill, rather coldly, sure now that she never could like this arrogant man. What had *he* ever done that gave him the right to speak in that tone about a man like Vere.

"Hello! Are you on the side of the handsome doctor, too?" her companion demanded; and as she made no reply; "I've nothing against him as long as he sticks to his job, and does not upset my plans. Look here—he is not going to continue snooping round and interfering, I hope, preventing Sandra from working?"

"Hasn't she told you that she has permission to get back to work again?" Jill asked.

"Yes, but——" He frowned, stopping the car as the lights flashed red ahead of them. "Exactly what does that mean? What sort of job has this fellow really done? Has he just patched her up, and is there any chance of her going phut again as soon as she does any real dancing?"

"Surely you can *see* the kind of job he has done?" demanded Jill. "A magnificent one! As far as I know there is not the smallest chance of her 'going phut', but common sense should know she ought not to overdo things at first."

"What about October?" He gave her a quick side glance as they moved off again, and then his tone altered, becoming warmer and more friendly. "I'm asking all these leading questions with a motive. I want to fix something important up, but it is no use if she is going to let me down again. I will tell you in confidence. They want Sandra at the Paris Opera;

it will only be three nights a week for one month, but after that I plan a come-back season for her in London. You may, or may not, know that she leaves her business in my hands, and it's important we should not be let down flat again as we were when she had that fool accident."

"I think you ought to feel lucky that she was not killed," said Jill. He really was hateful! Remembering what Sandra had told her about his dislike of any illness she hoped fervently the other girl had entirely got over caring anything about him—whatever her change of heart had led to.

Almost as though he read her thoughts, he said: "You think I am callous, and I don't suppose I can make you understand how desperately important I think—or rather know—Sandra's career is. An artist such as she is does not belong to herself. She belongs to the world. One day she is going to be a very, very great dancer—a real ballerina. I've watched her since she was a kid, and I know."

"But she might want other things besides dancing," said Jill.

"What kind of things?"

"Marriage, for instance."

His face darkened. "Not to—look here, tell me the truth. Is she in love with this surgeon fellow?"

"I don't know," Jill answered shortly, "and I am afraid, Lord Errol, I should not tell you if I did. Thank you very much for the lift—if you will put me down here, it's only a step."

But he insisted on taking her right into the mews. "No ill-feeling," he said as he shook hands. "And—I am sure I can trust you not to repeat what I have said to you. Forget it, will you?"

"Yes—if you want me to," Jill promised. After all, she could do no good by telling Sandra of this interview.

But when she was safely in Rosalind's flat and the headlights of Lord Errol's car no longer lit up the cobble stones below, she sat down and, lighting a cigarette, pondered over it thoughtfully before she undressed.

It did not matter in the least if Vere upset Lord Errol's plans—but it did matter if Errol should upset Vere's life.

Was there any chance of his doing so?

And once again, realizing how utterly unlike the two men were, it seemed to her that if it were only a matter of Sandra's heart there couldn't be any doubt which of them would win.

She had told Glyn: "She may want something besides a career. . . . Marriage——"

Marriage to Vere—something worth giving up any career in the world for—something better than even the most fulfilling work. To be his wife. His companion——

Jill, her usual splendid self-control deserting her, covered her face and wept bitter searing tears.

Chapter XX

SHE woke the next morning with a headache and took herself severely to task.

There was no sense in crying for the moon (it was Nurse Foster who was in charge now; not the girl whose breaking heart had overflowed last night). The moon was out of reach, stretching up for it was hopeless.

She had made no plans for to-day, and since the idea of wandering round picture galleries, looking at shops, or going to a matinée seemed equally futile, she decided to go to Hampstead and try to get rid of the cobwebs by a brisk walk across the heath.

But she felt curiously listless, and it was nearly ten o'clock when she finally emerged from the yellow-painted front door at the foot of the steep flight of steps leading down from Rosalind's domain, and shut it securely behind her.

Far down the mews a chauffeur was hosing a car, otherwise the place seemed almost deserted that morning; then, as she walked towards the exit, a black saloon began to back slowly out of one of the garages and she had to pause.

The driver brought his car adroitly round and opening the door beside him got out. Then:

"Hello!" he said. "What are you doing here?"

The Rolls engine was purring softly—she wished it was a motor cycle because she felt as though only something really raucous could possibly drown the noise her heart was making.

Vere Carrington thought how pale she was, and frowned disapprovingly.

"I—live here," said Jill. "I mean I'm staying here." She pointed towards the yellow door.
"Good heavens! What an atmosphere! I should forbid people to live in mews by Act of Parliament if I had my way," Vere exclaimed.
She could not help smiling at his irritation. "It isn't really as bad as you would think."
"Well, there is precious little air here," retorted Vere. "I yanked my chauffeur and his wife out of it and found them a flat in civilized surroundings. He is on holiday at present, and I am doing my own chauffeuring."
"Not all of it, surely?" she asked, glancing involuntarily towards the ablutions which were still going on further down.
"Oh, that fellow along there looks after the cleaning. Which reminds me, I must speak to him. Stay where you are for a minute."
He strode away and Jill looked after him, smiling again. Odd that in spite of everything his very presence near her could transform whatever the surroundings were into something celestial. And she actually liked to have him order her about. She accepted his coolly curt direction to remain where she was as she would have done a royal command.
He only kept her waiting a few moments before he was back beside her. "You look as if yesterday's dissipation had not done you much good," he told her uncompromisingly. "You know you should really have gone to the seaside, however loudly the joys of London called. What are you proposing to do with yourself to-day?" And when she told him he stood looking down at her half thoughtfully, filling her with the fear that that penetrating glance might read more than she wanted it to.
But her spirits were rising in the strangest way, and suddenly she wanted to laugh aloud. He seemed to take it so much for granted that he should catechize her; and when his next question came her lips twitched.
"Got friends in Hampstead?"
"No. I was just going for a walk—Sir."
"For heaven's sake don't call me Sir—we're not in hospital," he softened the asperity of his tone with a smile. "I tell you what. I am going down into Suffolk for a consultation. It is not exactly a beautiful drive until we leave what William

Cobbett called 'the great wen' behind us, but after that it's exquisite. Come with me. You can wander about while I am 'consulting', and then we will have lunch somewhere and drive back in time for me to keep an appointment with Lady Amanda——"

"I am having dinner with Lady Amanda," Jill told him. "Until then I'm free. She said not to dress——"

"Good. Get in—I'm due for a drink with Lady Mandy, so I can deposit you safely with her."

Doctor's orders again! And so—Jill supposed—one did not waste time arguing. Besides, what madness to make any kind of demur with all those lovely heaven-sent hours stretching ahead.

With a quiet "thank you" she got into the seat beside the driver's. However hard and cruel and—unequal life can be, it has its compensations. "Once to every man"—and to every girl! To this girl, anyway, for here surely was a day she would remember for ever.

Vere pulled on his gloves, easing those long legs of his under the wheel, and a moment later they were turning into the bustle of Marylebone High Street.

She thought: All these days, and I never even dreamt that he kept his car a few doors away from me.

She was secretly amazed at the calm way he took it; for a man who was anything but patient, and so apt to fly off the handle, he took the irritation of repeated hold-ups and the general bad manners of so many of the other drivers with amazing calm. He talked very little, intent on his driving, and leaning back beside him she was conscious of those strong, firm hands resting lightly on the wheel—hands she would have trusted to guide her through chaos itself.

She could watch, too, the reflection of his face in the wind-screen—that beloved face which was always in her mind. Once or twice his shoulder touched hers, sending a little bitter-sweet thrill through her. She knew that in spite of the ugly, often sordid streets she would have gladly had this drive go on for ever.

He spoke of the East End as they went through it—of those days and nights of war of which the scars still showed. He had worked in that part of London for a time and spoke with admiration of the endurance and team spirit of the people.

"Grand people these Londoners—whatever their faults!"

And yet a van driver cursed the "posh" car as it passed, and a handful of urchins threw dust—with no thought that the man at the wheel had done more splendid work for "the people" in one week, than all the demagogues, politicians, or street corner orators in a year.

But finally London was left behind, and those sprawling outer suburbs faded behind while the country stretched ahead

They had been driving for over two hours, had passed through exquisite winding lanes into the rolling Suffolk countryside, and through an old market town dreaming in the noonday heat, where time seemed almost to have stood still, leaving England beautiful and serene—a land of dreaming spires and gracious old houses, with a ruin here and there to take one still further back into the past, before they reached the village where, in the great house behind its high walls, Vere was due to give his verdict.

He left Jill at the village inn with the promise to come back to her as soon as possible.

"Don't you think the local doctor will expect you to lunch with him?" she asked.

"I have already made it clear I could not," he answered. "An honest excuse—I really thought I should have to get back earlier, but I found unexpectedly that I had most of the rest of this day to myself. If you are starving, have a sandwich or something. I'll come back as soon as I can and we will drive on to a place I know, where they'll give us something decent even if we are rather late."

And so—more than an hour later—Jill found herself facing Vere Carrington across a luncheon table in the raftered dining-room of an inn where one almost expected to see ladies and gentlemen in the costumes of the age of that great and imperious lady who surely never expected to become "Elizabeth the First" walking in the gardens that were ablaze with all those flowers which must have blossomed there in those more spacious days.

A very different Mr. Carrington from the one Jill seemed ever to have known before. Not even on that day when he had come to see her at Broad Meadows to "apologize" to her, had he been so friendly.

For the first time she discovered that they had tastes in

common—that they liked the same books, the same plays and even shared the same prejudices.

And watching the light and shade on the charming young face opposite him, Vere realized again—without the shock which the discovery had once given him—that his companion was an extremely pretty girl. Though, he decided, perhaps "pretty" was an inadequate word. She was strikingly lovely, with those high cheek bones and her golden brown eyes—eyes which he had noticed last night were only a shade deeper than the dress she had been wearing.

Last night when he had gone back to his house, and this morning while he was dressing, he had remembered that girl in her amber dress with curious distinctness, still feeling the slight but definite shock her appearance had given him.

It seemed that Nurse Foster had a somewhat varied personality. It was a little difficult to reconcile the calm, reserved, so very efficient young woman in her starched uniform; the dripping wet, frightened girl who had clung to him so desperately in the water; that sweet, oddly childish figure lying back among her pillows in the neat white-walled bedroom at Broad Meadows, and that vivid lovely in her amber dress at Sandra's party. And yet they were all Jill Foster, and each of them had clung to his mind with strange insistence. Though the only one he had knowingly remembered quite often was the one he had dragged out of the river. Which—since he had saved her life—was surely only natural, even for a man to whom a nurse was just a machine—or was she?

Although there was a strong strain of impulsiveness in Vere Carrington's nature, he almost always kept a rigid control on it—and if anyone had told him when he went to fetch his car that morning that he would be lunching with Jill a few hours later he would have considered them quite crazy. And yet here he was looking across the table at her, and finding it oddly satisfactory to have her there.

She was amusing, she was intelligent, and she was certainly charming to look at. A man must be very difficult indeed to please if he asked more than that of the companion of a summer's day. He did not regret bringing her—and she looked better already.

It never occured to him that some of the delicate colour in her cheeks might be brought there by his unconsciously intent scrutiny. But the pleasantest interlude must come to an end some time, and when they had finished their second cup of coffee it was time to return to London.

Vere paid the bill, and went to see that the car was filled up, while Jill went to powder her nose and re-tie the silken square with which she would keep her hair tidy on the drive back.

But when she went down again he was not by the car, and turning into the garden at the side of the inn, she found him standing contemplating the herbaceous border thoughtfully.

He came out of his reverie with a start.

"What a lot one misses in London," he said. "I sometimes think people who have a country house and a garden get the best of things."

"It would be heavenly," Jill agreed, and thought: With the right person to share it. Was he thinking that? His next words made her wonder with the first sharp little pang of pain she had felt since she came out with him.

"I think I shall have to buy a cottage," he said, "and grow roses in my spare time." He seemed unwilling to drag himself away, and turning, paced the path beside her.

And then suddenly: "By the way, Sandra stood up to that party last night pretty well, don't you think? Or did she collapse after I left?"

"No. I think she was tired, though," said Jill quietly.

He frowned. "Who is that fellow Errol? He seemed very possessive." And as Jill told him what she knew about Errol: "Of course—I ought to have remembered." He glanced at his watch. "We must be on our way, if you are not to be late at Lady Mandy's."

Jill went to open the car door, but he was before her, and for a moment their hands met on the handle.

The wild, frightening thrill of the unexpected contact set her pulses racing. He did not touch her again as she got in, but leaving her to settle herself in the seat beside the driver's, went quickly round to the opposite door.

They drove off, and noticing his silence during the first mile or so, she wondered in panic if he could possibly have noticed—or guessed how disturbed she was—could have felt that sudden leap of her pulse beneath his touch.

Then he began to talk again, and when he relapsed into

silence for the second time she told herself that it was only because his thoughts were elsewhere. With Sandra?

Although she knew she was being foolish, somehow it seemed as though, from the moment he had mentioned the other girl, a blight had fallen on the day—her golden day which she was so certain would never come again.

The village where they had lunched was right off the beaten track, approached by the kind of roads which are marked secondary on the map, though unless you want to speed along, and simply out to get from one place to another, they can be so very much more attractive than the wider, smoother surfaced main thoroughfares.

There was one stretch of lonely, but particularly lovely country which Jill had noticed on the way, and where there seemed literally nothing to spoil the lanes and the stretches of fields, except an occasional tiny hamlet or a country house set amid its woods or behind high walls.

They were back in this lonely stretch when the car slowed down and Vere brought it to a halt. "This engine feels a bit odd," he said. "I think I had better have a look."

He got out, and opening the bonnet began his examination. After a little hesitation Jill opened the door beside her, and followed him.

"Is there anything wrong?" she asked.

"Yes. It is just as well Hanson—my chauffeur—will be back at the end of the week," said Vere, frowning. "What an extraordinary thing it is that you cannot trust people to do the job they are paid to do in these days. That fellow in the Mews is responsible for giving this thing the once-over when he fills her up. He told me she was O.K. before I brought her out, but—though my knowledge of car insides is rather elementary, it is perfectly obvious she couldn't have been. Hang it! I hate taking machinery to pieces, but I shall have to put this right. I hope you have plenty of patience. But maybe," he glanced at his wrist watch, "we shall not get to Lady Mandy's too late."

"Can I help?" Jill asked. "I have lots of patience, by the way."

"Know anything about cars?"

"I am afraid I don't," she admitted. "But—I can hold screwdrivers or spanners, or—whatever the tools are."

"Well, you can't. Not at this operation. Just wander round and look at the pretty flowers, and leave me to use bad language on my own," he told her firmly. Then as he looked at her, his frown gave place to a half smile. "This is one of those times when I can do without a nurse on the case."

Human nature is an odd thing. It was going to be rather awkward if she arrived in Eaton Square late for dinner, but suddenly Jill's spirits were soaring again.

"Mustn't I even watch you?" she asked. "I love all those intricate-looking bits of machinery."

"Well, I hate them," he retorted. "Go for a walk or you will hear things that are not good for you."

Jill laughed. "I often have. One has to learn not to take any notice."

But realizing that he really wanted to be left alone she turned and strolled away.

It was an exquisite evening. The sun was not due to set for a couple of hours yet. White clouds chased each other leisurely across a sky of that particularly delicate shade of blue which East Anglian skies seem to have taken out a patent in. Those perhaps necessary but, nevertheless, deplorable despoilers of the countryside who hack away destructively with billhook and spade, seemed to have left the ditches and hedgerows just hereabouts as untidy and beautiful as nature meant them to be.

Jill wandered slowly on, conscious all the time of the man on the road behind her.

She had never thought of him as being an impulsive person and she wondered what had made him ask her to accompany him to-day. It—couldn't be because he had wanted to find out about Sandra and Glyn Erroll. He could have done that easily without bothering to ask her. But why waste time probing for the why and wherefore? She had had her day; for a little while she and Vere Carrington had met on equal ground. Not since that long ago brief period at St. Monica's had they seemed so near being really friends—and then it had not been as it had to-day. For to-day they had talked of subjects apart from their work—had got to know things about each other that they might never have found out otherwise.

Yet—did it make it any easier to find out how many tastes they had in common, and to remember how few he and Sandra had?

In spite of everything, Jill admired Sandra and genuinely liked her, but she had had every chance to sum the other girl up; she knew Sandra was far more of a specialist than Vere was. Vere's work meant a great deal to him, but he had outside interests—though Jill would never have said that the ballet was one of them. He was—she had gathered to-day—a great reader, he knew a lot about pictures (not the kind that move and talk, though!) and he took a secondary interest in the living theatre. But Sandra's dancing was her whole life; far removed as the other girl's world was from hers, Jill understood that Sandra St. Just was not just another charming and clever dancer. She was a born ballerina, and to the born ballerina her art counts above everything. No home or children will thrust it into the background, and if it came to choosing it will always be her career—her art—that wins.

What would she have left to give to a man who loved her—a man whose interests were far removed from hers?

If Vere loved her—Jill broke the thought half angrily. What was the use of letting her mind go round and round the subject? She could not alter things; she could not help him, if——

Deliberately she switched her mind back to her surroundings. As she walked along, the air was filled with the sweet subtle perfume of honeysuckle, and she saw that the hedge beyond the ditch by which she was strolling was one mass of the honey-coloured and white blossoms.

It was a widish ditch, but the temptation of the flowers called to her, and scrambling across it she caught hold of an overhanging branch. Pulling herself up by it she was intent on gathering her posy, when a voice behind her said: "So that is where you have got to."

She looked over her shoulder, still with enough presence of mind not to let go of the branch.

"Oh! You've finished."

"Yes. When I looked up and found an empty road I thought you had been spirited away. Come on, there's a good girl. If we get a move on we shall still be in time."

That was all very well. But having got up the bank she had to get down. She did not feel it would be an exactly graceful performance and she wished he was not there to see it—or that she could tell him to go for a walk as he had told her to!

However, there was no help for it, and tucking her posy into her belt she began to lower herself, gingerly feeling for a footing.

"You are going to land in that ditch," Vere warned, a hint of amusement in his tone.

Jill felt herself going pink with annoyance. Why on earth had she done this? Anyway it was too bad of him to stand there deliberately watching, and laughing at her.

"And," he added, "there are nettles, and probably frogs."

"Oh!" She turned, lost her grip and slipped.

"Careful!" She felt firm hands on her waist, and then for the second time Mr. Carrington had lifted her bodily and set her on her feet on the road.

"What a girl you are for getting yourself into difficulties," he was laughing frankly now as he looked down at her, his hands still on her waist. If only she had not been so terribly conscious of those firm, strong hands. She looked up blindly, and then——

She was in his arms and his lips were on hers, close and warm and demanding.

Who can measure the length of a first kiss? For Jill, at least, time stood still, the earth disintegrated beneath her feet and she was up there among the blue and white and gold of the sunlit firmament. Such wild happiness could not be found on earth; here with Vere's arms about her was all she needed of heaven.

And then above the wild, sweet beating of her heart his voice came to her again, and she knew, as every lover has known from the beginning, that the earth was good enough for them both.

He was saying: "I believe I have wanted to do that ever since I dragged you out of the river."

"You—haven't?" Still within the circle of his arms she drew back, her eyes widened.

"Jill—you're incredibly sweet." He bent, kissing her again quickly. "How dare you look so innocent when you ought to be slapped for upsetting my life like this." But in spite of that not very chivalrous speech there was something in his eyes that gave her courage.

"What about—upsetting my life?" she asked.

"Darling! Have I?" He studied the flushed face upraised to his intently. "Don't you rather dislike this 'difficult man'?"

Her eyes answered before her lips. "I—should have been much happier all these years if I could have managed to dislike him."

"Years!" he repeated. "You can't mean that—you have been caring for me?" There was such sincere amazement in his tone that she had to laugh a little shakily.

"How blind—and rather dense—clever men can be!" she sighed. And then her hands closing tightly on his shoulders: "Oh! my dearest, I can't believe that——"

"What can't you believe?" he urged.

But this time her courage failed; or perhaps it was only her voice. The warm yielding of her mouth beneath his told him all he wanted to know. How right she was! he thought as clearly as it was possible for him to think in the rather chaotic jumble of emotion her nearness brought. What a blind idiot he had been! When he had only needed to stretch out his hands and take the gifts that made his life complete. Every impulse urged him to tell her how much she meant to him—that if he lost her now nothing could ever fill the gap that would be left in his heart. For the first time he realized that work was not enough—if one had to go on alone. If he had been in any state to analyse his feelings he would have supposed that he had always intended to marry one day; goodness knew, far more than just one or two women had shown him plainly—perhaps too plainly—how ready they were to say "yes", but Vere was only just on the brink of learning why he had held back, that deep down in him had been the knowledge that somewhere in the world there was the one woman for him, and the hope of finding her.

Perhaps that was why, though he had come very near to realizing that, if he allowed her to, Sandra could weave a spell about him, he had drawn back before it even had a chance to begin to act.

And here, close to him all the time, had been the one girl who could share his mind, fill his heart, and set his senses reeling. Yet when he had begun to suspect how possible it was to care for her—when he had looked back on that moment of near panic when he swam out to her, and remembered her unconscious in his arms, he had deliberately turned away from the idea. Blind, wasteful fool!

Even now he could not begin to tell her all she meant to him. "My sweet," he said. "I simply hate taking you back to London; I wish we could stay here for ever, however damp it may become. But, apart from Lady Mandy, there may be an important telephone call waiting for me. We must go——"

"I know we must," said Jill.

But knowing it they lingered for a few more magic moments. Then putting her firmly away from him, he said with a touch of his old manner:

"Come along, young woman! March!"

When they were in the car he sat for a moment, his hands gripping the wheel, his eyes on her face, as loth as she was to let this enchanted hour go completely.

"Do you know how adorable you are?" he asked, and as she shook her head. "Look at me, Jill——" his hand went out, tilting her chin upward, "Are you happy——?"

Her breath caught. "So happy that—I'm frightened."

"Then don't be," he told her. "There's nothing in the world to be frightened of—except that if I kiss you again now we will probably arrive back about midnight, and we both have our reputations to think of, Nurse Foster. Do you think we had better be sensible?"

"I'm afraid so——"

"I wonder how often what you say will go, my beloved," said Mr. Carrington, starting the car abruptly. After all, there was plenty of time to tell her all that she meant to him; all their lives.

If only he had said that to her. But neither of them realized how the fact that he had refrained from just that little reference to their future—making a dream into a concrete thing, might complicate their lives.

He had asked no promise; he had made none; but neither of them thought of that—then.

For Jill, as they drove back, there was neither past nor future—only the wonder of the present; the memory of Vere's kisses—of that new look in his eyes, and that new note in his voice.

Chapter XXI

ALTHOUGH the roads approaching London were much clearer than on the journey out, Vere talked hardly at all, but scarcely noticing his silence Jill sat back, utterly content. The streets which she had found a little sordid earlier might have been paved with gold; for as long as Vere was beside her, as long as she could be sure of his love the widest and most arid desert would have seemed like El Dorado.

For that journey to go on, for them to travel to the end of the world together, was all that she wanted. To-day she had discovered that dreams—even the ones you dared not put into words, could come true.

But Vere drove fast, and the time seemed woefully short before they were in Eaton Square.

Stopping the car, he turned to his companion. "Did you go to sleep?" he asked. "Or were you merely paralysed with horror at sight of the speedometer needle?"

She laughed, meeting his eyes. "Neither. I was—just in a trance."

"Then come out of it and congratulate me for having brought you here safely—and almost punctually," he told her.

She glanced at her watch. "Goodness! We must have travelled."

He was already helping her out of the car, and as they ascended the steps his hand was still beneath her elbow. Crossing the hall she found herself controlling the impulse to draw closer to him. They had to wait for a few moments for the lift to come down, and he told her quickly:

"Listen, Jill. Unless I have to leave first I shall drive you home, but just in case I can't, give me your telephone number —write it on a piece of paper and give it to me."

"But—what will Lady Mandy think if she sees me?" asked Jill.

"Nothing. You will just say, 'Here is the number you asked me for—in case I forget.' Intrigue is the spice of life." His eyes teased her. "Anyway, it isn't Lady Mandy's business."

Just then the lift arrived, but so, alas, did a third party—a complete stranger bound for the floor above Lady Skeyne's flat—and those precious moments that they might have had alone were filched from them.

Neither were they any luckier as they went along to Lady Amanda's door, for Bridges, her maid, had just emerged on her way out for the evening.

She turned back quickly to open the door for them with her latchkey, and there was the butler in the hallway.

"Good evening, Price," said Vere without a trace of disturbance in his manner. "Has anyone telephoned for me?"

"Good evening, sir," replied the butler. "No, sir."

"Good. If anyone does, just take a message, will you?"

"Very good, sir. Her ladyship isn't out of her room yet, but Miss St. Just and Lord Errol are in the drawing-room. Her ladyship said to let her know as soon as you or Nurse Foster arrived."

Vere frowned slightly as they followed Price, who had already turned to lead the way.

It was only afterwards that Jill felt there had been a slight tension in the air as she walked towards the drawing-room door beside him, but subconsciously she was remembering for the first time since he had kissed her that she had been practically certain he cared for Sandra.

"All right, Price," he said. "Don't bother to announce us."

"Very good, sir." The old man moved aside, and Vere opened the door himself.

Jill was slightly ahead of him when they entered. The long, sunny stretch of the room lay before them. Two people were standing near the windows—so close to each other that it would almost have been possible to mistake them for one. Then in a flash Sandra had pulled herself free of Glyn Errol's encircling arms.

There was a hardly perceptible pause, then calmly putting a strayed curl back into place Sandra said:

"Oh! there you are—did you meet on the doorstep?"

"No. We arrived together." Vere appeared entirely unembarrassed, but Jill was quite certain he had noticed that Sandra was being kissed. How heavenly to know that, apart from the fact that he disapproved of Glyn Errol, such a discovery meant nothing to him!

It was Jill's face that was flushed, and she had the impression that though Sandra was carrying it off with such perfect *sang froid* she was upset.

"You met Glyn last night," she said, waving a hand towards him.

"Yes." Vere nodded briefly to the other man, who returned the nod, keeping his smile for Jill.

"Got over your party, Nurse?"

"Yes, thanks."

Vere said easily: "I think she was feeling a little 'morning after' when I met her."

"Well, she doesn't look it," laughed Sandra. "She looks absolutely sunburnt."

"She certainly looks better than she did," said Vere calmly. But he did not explain where she had acquired her sunburn.

At that moment Lady Amanda entered. "How nice of you to come, Vere," she gave him her hand, after greeting Jill affectionately. Then: "So you are back from America, Glyn. Did you come by air?" she asked with decidedly less enthusiasm.

"No. On the *Queen Mary*." He kissed her hand lightly. "Hope you will forgive me butting in, Lady Mandy, but when I telephoned Sandra and heard she was here, as I had something very important to discuss with her, I could not resist following her, and—taking the opportunity of paying my respects to you at the same time."

"Nice afterthought," Lady Amanda told him drily. "I won't throw you out this time."

There never had been any love lost between them, and Glyn accepted the old lady's cool greeting philosophically.

Lady Amanda told Jill: "Go along and take off your hat, dear. Price will show you my room." And as Jill went out again, his hostess told Vere: "That child is looking very well, don't you think?"

"Very well," he agreed, meeting her direct, rather inquisitive stare calmly.

"But I don't think a fortnight is nearly a long enough break for her," continued the old lady. "She was looking tired out when Sandra left Broad Meadows weeks ago."

"Why can't she have longer, Vere?" asked Sandra in her impulsive way. "You ought to tell Matron she needs it."

Matron was going to be told something which would give her much more of a shock! But Vere gave no sign of knowing anything like that, as he said: "It is hardly my business to tell Miss Travers what she must do about her staff."

"But you ought to feel rather responsible about Jill," said Sandra.

"Why, on earth——?" For once he showed that he was startled.

"Well, you hauled her out of the river, didn't you? And once you save someone's life you must surely feel some interest in them," she said.

"What's that?" demanded Lady Amanda.

"Nothing," said Vere. "Your goddaughter talks too much."

Just then Price came in with a tray of drinks, and informed Vere: "St. Monica's on the telephone for you, sir. They would like to speak to you personally."

"Do you mind, Lady Mandy?" asked Vere, and receiving permission, hurried away.

Jill, in the bathroom next to her hostess's bedroom, was washing her hands and redoing her face, smiling happily at the girl in the mirror—that quite new Jill who had been reborn such a little while ago. The Jill who had a song instead of a pain in her heart; who no longer felt afraid of anything in the world; except, perhaps, that she might wake up and find it all a dream.

Putting her comb back into her handbag she remembered Vere's request, and, taking out her diary, wrote Rosalind's telephone number on one of the back pages and tore it out.

She was smiling when she emerged into the hall, where Price was hovering near the front door.

"Hasn't it been a lovely day, Price?" she asked (though of course he could not possibly know how lovely!)

"Beautiful, miss. I have a note for you,—mi—Nurse," the butler told her, holding out an envelope. "Mr. Carrington asked me to give it to you."

"Oh!" Her heart missing a beat, she took the grey envelope, and, as the butler faded discreetly away, tore it open quickly.

Vere had written:

"I am just scribbling this in the library. Emergency I was fearing has occurred, and I can't stay to see you again. If I am not kept too late shall ring your bell and you must come down and talk to me. Shall be operating all to-morrow, but if I can't see you to-night ring me before 8.30. In haste, darling."

Her first letter from him; and if it was not all that a love letter should be, she was one of the few girls who could understand that his doctor's mind had been three-quarters on the emergency which awaited him. Nevertheless, he had written.

She read the last line again, and kissing it hurriedly thrust the letter into her bag. But though her face was serene her step was less light when she re-entered the drawing-room.

Sandra, her feet tucked under her, was in a deep chair with its back to the window recess, while Lady Amanda sat opposite, and Errol in another chair near.

He rose as Jill entered, and Sandra said:

"Jill, aren't you sorry for doctors' wives?"

"Why?" asked Jill.

"Well, they can't ever make sure where their husbands will be from one minute to another. Vere's just had to go racing off to his old hospital."

"But 'Vere' is a bachelor, is he not?" asked Glyn, a slightly unpleasant edge to his voice. "Though whether a gay one or not, I wouldn't presume to say; though I should guess the odds are against the gaiety."

"Well, I am sure it is not our sex's fault that he is a bachelor of any kind." Sandra gave him a half annoyed, challenging look. "He's a terribly attractive person."

Now what is she up to? wondered Jill. Surely Sandra was not trying to play the two men up against each other? Very excusably, the thought annoyed Jill. Supposing things had been as she, Jill, had all this time been afraid they were (she could acknowledge at last that "afraid" was the operative word) how would Vere be feeling after coming in and finding Sandra being kissed by Glyn Errol? Hugging her own secret, she could be angry with Sandra simply for what she might have done to Vere, if he had been in love with her.

Instead—— Suddenly realizing that Lady Amanda was watching her, Jill felt herself go scarlet, as though the old lady were a mind reader.

Lady Amanda said: "Give Jill a drink, Glyn." And as he fetched her one, and they were all seated again: "Too bad that Vere had to rush off. I should have thought his work ought to be finished by this hour, but apparently he was expecting something of the kind. I rather wonder that he did not hold out—stick completely to his private practice."

"Private practices can be rather precarious since the Health Service, I should imagine," observed Glyn. "Anyway I suppose the great surgeon wants to earn an income—even if he already has one."

"I am sure Mr. Carrington would hate not having his hospital work—even if it earned him practically nothing, as it used to do." This time it was Jill who had an edge to her voice. What a hateful man this was! If he was jealous of Vere he might have the decency to hide it! And they said women were cats! Then to her added annoyance she found him looking at her with raised brows, an amused smile on his lips.

"Three to one, I think," he said, "though Lady Mandy hasn't *said* anything in favour of the gentleman's bedside manner." And, changing the subject abruptly: "By the way, Lady Mandy, I met a friend of yours in New York——"

After that, conversation seemed to flow more smoothly, though there was a sense of strain in the air. Sandra almost ignored Glyn, who rose presently to take his leave.

"You're not coming along, I suppose, Sandra?" he asked.

"No. Though I have not been asked, I am having dinner with Lady Mandy," she told him.

"What time can I come to see you in the morning, or would you prefer to come to the theatre? We really ought to get this Paris contract fixed."

"Oh, Glyn, I don't feel like talking business." She made a little negative gesture. Then she added teasingly: "How do you know I have not entirely forgotten how to dance? Hadn't you better wait to find out?"

"You are in a tiresome mood, my sweet," he told her. "I shall ring you in the morning."

She shrugged her shoulders. "O.K. But don't blame me if I am sound asleep."

"If you are I shall wake you up."

"And I shall be furious."

"I'll bear it." Although there seemed to be sparks between them he took his leave gracefully, apparently in perfect good humour.

"I could kill Glyn sometimes," exclaimed Sandra. "It's really impertinent of him to dislike Vere—isn't it, Jill?"

"I expect Mr. Carrington will survive," said Jill quietly.

Lady Mandy made no comment, though she looked sharply from one girl's face to the other. She still wanted Sandra to marry Vere, but she would never remind Jill of the fact again. Poor child! she thought, I don't believe she is getting over him.

She had heard from Price that Nurse Foster and Mr. Carrington had arrived together, and concluded they must have met downstairs. And the girl had stars in her eyes—even now there was an aura of happiness about her. Just because he had been there! Poor child! But Lady Mandy was sure she need not feel really guilty; after all, nurses were just capable machines to Vere, he was hardly likely to fall in love with one. Nevertheless if he *had* saved her life—Sandra had told what she knew of the story after he went out of the room, and Lady Amanda thought she understood the situation better now. Only natural the girl should feel he was wonderful.

"It really is too bad Vere should have had to go off like that," complained Sandra again. "I believe he lets himself be put upon."

"Vere is one of the kindest men—though sometimes you would not think it," observed Lady Amanda. "Hand me my work-bag, Jill, dear, and come and sit down and tell me what you have been doing."

But Jill was not ready to say more than that she had been in the country, remembering Vere had not mentioned their being together.

"How dare you arrive on the doorstep with my handsome surgeon," laughed Sandra. "Did he say anything about me and the party, by the way?"

"I—don't think so." Jill really *had* forgotten.

"Why should he, you little egotist?" asked Lady Mandy.

Sandra laughed. "Aren't I one of his most successful

cases?" She sank into a chair, tucking her feet up under her and lighting a cigarette.

Jill was surprised at the strength and suddenness of her desire to slap her, and realized with a shock that she was learning what it meant to feel possessive.

While Lady Amanda observed: "Sometimes I think you deserve a good slippering, Sandra." And then changing the subject: "Well, are you going to do this season in Paris in the autumn?"

There was a moment's silence while Sandra thoughtfully watched the smoke curling upwards from between her fingers. Then: "I am—not quite sure," she said. "That will depend."

Her godmother glanced at her quickly. "On whether you feel strong enough?"

"Oh, I shall be strong enough!" Sandra assured. "It's the dickens getting back into things, but I feel fine. No, whether I go to Paris or not will depend upon—circumstances."

A startled question battered at Jill's mind.

What circumstances? Were they anything to do with Vere? Surely Sandra was not developing a personal interest in him? Poor Sandra! That would be too ironical.

Chapter XXII

I

IN spite of Sandra's gaiety at the beginning of the evening she was unusually quiet during dinner, and most of the conversation was between Jill and her hostess.

If Lady Amanda noticed how withdrawn her goddaughter seemed, she made no comment, seeming quite content to leave Sandra to her own thoughts while she talked to Jill. Afterwards they went to the library to have their coffee and smoke the Turkish cigarettes which were Lady Mandy's "specials"—she always smoked one after her lunch, and after her dinner.

When she had finished hers Sandra rose, saying: "Darling,

having eaten your lovely dinner I simply must run home to bed. I don't know why, but I am dropping with tiredness."

Lady Amanda told her: "I don't believe you have recovered from that party yet."

She laughed. "Between you and Vere, I don't believe I shall ever hear the end of that party. He rang me up afterwards and instead of saying 'Thank you' nicely, scolded me for thoroughly overdoing things. No wonder you said he was a difficult man, Jill."

"Did you, Jill?" asked Lady Amanda.

"I—think I did," said Jill, her colour deepening.

"I am sure he is," said Lady Amanda calmly.

"Can I give you a lift, Jill?" asked Sandra. "You do go in my direction, don't you?"

"Not really, thanks all the same," Jill answered. "I shall get a bus. And I think I ought to be going, Lady Amanda," she added. "You look tired, and I am sure you want to be quiet."

And although her hostess protested, she went to put on her hat.

She and Sandra left together, and as they emerged into the square Sandra said: "You might as well come along—you can drop me and take the car on." As was so very usual, she got her way. The drive to her own flat was so short that there would have been hardly time to say much. It occurred to Jill that the other girl was depressed, and when she was driven on after leaving her in Park Lane, she wondered if Sandra's unusual lack of spirits was anything to do with Lord Errol. If being kissed by him made her as unhappy as that, there did not seem much sense in it!

Then leaning back in a corner of the car, her eyes closed, she forgot all about Sandra and her possible—or impossible—love affairs. She was back again on that deserted country road, with Vere's arms around her, Vere asking: "Do you know how adorable you are, Jill?"

Although she had never denied her love for him, never until now had she dared to give herself completely up to it. It was almost frightening to find how intensely single-minded it was possible for her to be; to know that nothing else in the world counted beside just one man; that she would follow him barefoot to the end of the world if he wanted her. Everything she had ever been or was capable of being, she had given him in that first kiss, and she knew that she would never really belong to herself again. No wonder that knowledge was rather alarming, to anyone as independent as Jill.

She was jolted back from her dreams by the chauffeur pushing back the screen and asking: "Which end of the mews, miss?"

She glanced out quickly. "This one. But don't go any further. I'll get out here." She was already on the pavement; Jill tipped the chauffeur and, followed by the man's cheerful thanks and "good-night", she walked quickly away.

Walking down the cobbled incline towards the yellow front door of number thirty, she glanced quickly in passing, towards Vere's garage. The doors were drawn back, as he always left them when the car was out. She thought: Surely he will bring it back later. He didn't need the telephone number—he could just ring and I would come down. But obviously he had expected to be very late.

There were three steps leading up to Rosalind's domain. Reaching them she stopped with a startled exclamation as a figure, who had been sitting on the top of them, rose.

"Jill—at last! Thank goodness! I was beginning to wonder if you'd come back with the milk."

"Judy! Good heavens! What on earth are you doing here?" cried Jill in amazement.

Judy laughed. "It's all right. Shure, I haven't been dismissed from the hospital with ignominy. I got leave until to-morrow, and as 'me young man' was coming up to Town, I thought it would be a good opportunity to see you. You can put me up, can't you?"

"Of course I can," Jill told her. "But where's Ken——"

"He had an important dinner," Judy explained. "Something to do with that Rhodesian job, and he was going to come here afterwards. That's why I've been obliged to hang round."

"You poor lamb!" exclaimed Jill. "Come on in. Are you starving?"

"No, I had a snack before I came," said Judy.

Jill unlocked the door, and as they went upstairs explained where she had been—keeping her explanation, however, to the evening's activities. Much as she loved Judy she had no intention of telling her about Vere—yet; and though she was genuinely glad to see the other girl, she could not help wondering if her presence here might not be a little complicating, if Vere should do what he had first suggested he might and ring her door bell later on.

But she was in the mood not to cross bridges until she came to them, and soon the two girls were chatting happily while she made coffee in the kitchenette and they went into the sitting-room to drink it.

Judy told Jill that the doctor who owned the nursing home in Salisbury where Ken would later take up his new post had unexpectedly come to England on his way back to South Africa from a conference he had been attending in Sweden.

"Sounds a bit roundabout," she said. "But apparently he decided to spare a couple of days to see his people, and thought it was a good chance to contact Ken. So they are having dinner together. Ken wasn't sure what time he would be through—hence my decoration of your steps."

Jill laughed. "Well, what's the news from the home front?"

"More wedding bells. Who do you think?"

"You tell me," said Jill.

"Sister Hudson! Isn't that nice? There's hope for everyone."

"Don't be a cat, Ju," reproved Jill. Sister Hudson—excellent in her way—was no favourite with the nursing staff, but a very important person in the hospital. She was fortyish, and a decided dragon.

"Well, no one will weep—unless Matron sheds a tear. She doesn't really like changing staff," said Judy. "But she won't have married nurses—even part-time. So what?"

"Well, you know," Jill refilled their cups, "I think she is right. Could one run the two careers? Seems to me that each one of them is a full-time job. And however much I—or anyone else—hated giving up nursing——" she broke off, wishing suddenly she had not embarked on the subject.

But Judy did not notice her confusion.

"I am perfectly certain I couldn't do the two things. Besides, it can't go on after the babies start coming along," she said frankly. "Fancy having an important case and half your mind on little Willie's first tooth."

"Judy. You crazy girl," Jill laughed.

But Judy regarded her unsmilingly. "I'm serious. Me! Marriage is a full-time job, and grievous as it is to lose good nurses—well, what would you do about it?"

"I am sure you are right," Jill told her, not really answering the question.

Reaching for a cigarette Judy asked: "You are near the *élite*, aren't you, ducky? My taxi brought me through Wimpole Street. Seen his nibs anywhere about? Hang! my lighter's gone dry."

Thankful for the excuse to get up and look for matches, Jill turned away, feeling her cheeks burning. She had herself in hand in a moment, and as she gave Judy a light, answered calmly:

"He was at Lady Amanda's to-day. Only for a few minutes, though. He had gone by the time I took off my hat—emergency hospital call."

"He's rather marvellous," said Judy admiringly. "Most men in his position wouldn't be available at that hour."

Rather marvellous? Of course he was! The most wonderful person in the world! said Jill's quickly beating heart.

"And the lovely Sandra?" enquired Judy.

"She was there, too."

"Which probably accounted for his presence. Wonder how that's going on?"

"I rather think," said Jill, with commendable coolness, "that you're going to be disappointed. Unless I am very much mistaken, Sandra is interested in someone else."

(And so was Vere! Judy had a shock coming to her.)

"Oh! don't say my lovely romantic arrangements for them are going West," she pleaded.

"I wouldn't be surprised," said Jill. "Listen! That's your young man."

Judy ran down to open the door and came back in a few minutes, pink and bright-eyed, her arm in her beloved's.

Ken was his usual cheerful, exuberant self. He greeted Jill with: "Hello, beautiful. Aren't you sorry you let your girl friend get away with me?"

"Not in the least," she told him. "I frequently congratulate myself on the escape I had."

"No! How hurtful of you. Judy, darling—comfort me."

Sitting next to her on the settee, he laid his head on hi[s] fiancée's shoulder.

"I am going to make some more coffee," announced Jill returning to the kitchenette. It was wonderful to see thos[e] two so happy. More wonderful than ever now, because ther[e] was no little pull at her heart strings caused by the knowledg[e] of her own loneliness.

The other two seemed to be talking quite sensibly when sh[e] went back into the room.

"Oh, Jill," said Judy. "Ken thinks we'll have to be leavin[g] England sooner than we expected."

"Before the end of the year?" asked Jill with a little pang knowing that, whatever might be happening to herself, sh[e] would miss Judy badly.

Ken nodded. "About the end of next month. You wouldn't feel like coming too?"

"Good heavens!" Jill exclaimed. "Where are you goin[g] to? Utah?"

"Nurse," said Ken gravely, "you flatter your sex if you think I was contemplating taking a *brace* of wives with me. It i[s] merely that my future partner thinks we might be needing [a] capable young woman to join our nursing staff."

Jill shook her head. "It wouldn't be me, Ken. I—wouldn't think of leaving England."

"Pity. Sounds like a good job," said Ken. And then, chang ing the subject: "By the way, as Judy has parked herself o[n] you for the night, I propose we hit the town to-morrow. I'l[l] get some matinée seats, and we'll go out to lunch beforehand O.K.?"

Jill hesitated. "I'm—not quite sure what my arrangement[s] are for to-morrow evening," she said. "I shan't know unti[l] the morning."

"Well, that's time enough," he said cheerfully.

"But wouldn't you two be better on your own?"

"No, we would not," said Judy firmly. "Three's never [a] crowd when you're around."

"It's sweet of you," said Jill. "If I'm free, of course I'd lik[e] to come."

It was well after midnight when Ken finally rose to take hi[s] leave, and Judy went downstairs to see him off.

As soon as she was alone Jill opened the window softly an[d] ooked out. Although the mews was so dimly lit she could just see that the doors of Vere's garage were still open. He was very late! She drew back into the room, shutting the window again. He would not be likely to disturb her now; she would have to be content with to-day's memories and wait until the morning to hear his voice. It seemed a very long time, and she wondered if it was not going to be rather difficult to make that telephone call without letting Judy hear who she asked for.

Meanwhile the engaged lovers were lingering over their good-night. As they seemed to have the deserted mews all to themselves, Ken had drawn Judy close into his arms, while, lost to the world, they were murmuring sweet, absurd things to each other, and not even noticing the long, silent car which turned in at the top of the hill, until the driver suddenly turned on his headlights, and Judy started back into the doorway as if she had been shot.

"Good-night, Ken," she called softly.

But Ken's voice was clear as he answered: "Night, darling. I'll be along as early as I can."

The flat door shut, and he went striding up the mews, inwardly cursing the darned chauffeur who had arrived so very tactlessly.

The car had already turned into one of the lock-up garages, and as Ken drew even with it the man who had been driving it came out and paused to slide the doors into place before locking them.

Ken, stopping to light a cigarette, glanced at him casually, and then, as someone else drew a curtain back from a window above, saw the other man clearly, and noticed, first that he was not a chauffeur, and then, with a start, recognized him.

"Good evening," said Vere coolly. "Dr. Harding, is it not?"

"Yes, Mr. Carrington. Gosh, sir, you're the last person I—er—expected to see."

Wondering how much the big man had seen, Ken was for once in his life slightly embarrassed.

"It's a small world," said Vere drily. From his tone no one, least of all the person concerned, could have guessed at the seething rage within him.

"Yes, rather. I—as a matter of fact my best girl's staying

over there." Ken jerked his head in the direction of Rosalind's front door. "I—was just saying good-night to her."

"Really." Vere locked the garage doors with careful deliberation. "Well, I'll say good-night to you."

"Good-night, sir." Ken strode on, since he was obviously not required to linger.

It was a little over ten minutes later when Vere let himself into his house and went up through the silence of it to his private quarters. Turning on the lights in the book-lined sitting-room, he flung hat and gloves into a chair, and, going across to the fireplace, stood, his hands gripping the mantelpiece, staring unseeingly at the picture above it. He was curiously pale, his mouth set grimly.

"I was saying good-night to my best girl——"

When his headlights had so suddenly picked up that little tableau, he had seen only a girl, enveloped in a man's embrace being unresistingly kissed. Then he had caught the flash of the light dress she was wearing as she ran through the doorway behind her.

It was quite inevitable that as he stood there remembering another picture should rise in his mind. The broad landing outside the door of Sandra's room at Broad Meadows—a man and a girl standing very close together (or seeming to do so and the girl snatching her hand hurriedly from her companion's clasp.

He had thought then that there was something between those two.

But—only a few hours ago it was he who had held Jill in his arms, felt the swift, warm response of her lips beneath his. It was incredible that within those few hours she should be giving the same response to another man.

He told himself bitterly to be his age. Would she be the first girl who enjoyed having two strings to her bow? Heavens! had he not learnt about women in his life; watched other men being fooled, and told himself how wise he was to have made up his mind to remain wedded to his work?

This afternoon he had called himself a blind fool; to-night he knew exactly how blind, and how big a fool he was.

But Jill! Jill! Surely it could not be true!

Never in his life had he understood that it was possible to feel this kind of pain, and, lashed to a sudden fury against his own suffering, he asked himself why he had not rung that bell—made her come down to him, demanded an explanation. He had meant when he drove into the mews to see if there was still a light in her window, and if there was, to call her down. He had felt he could not go to bed without making quite sure of her—telling her: *"I suppose you do understand what it all means, my darling? No more nursing—and just how soon are you ready to give it up and marry me?"*

He did not even speculate now on what her answer would have been. Anyhow, he told himself savagely, it was over. If she had felt any triumph at bringing him to her feet, it would be short-lived.

He supposed that Harding would tell her of their encounter, in which case she could hardly be stupid enough not to put two and two together. But meanwhile——

II

Contrary to her expectations, when she went to bed that night Jill slept soundlessly and dreamlessly.

She woke with the sun streaming into the room, and knew at once that there was something special about this day. Something had happened that made everything, including herself, quite different.

Then she remembered. Someone had said yesterday: "*Jill, do you know how adorable you are*——" and the world had been made anew.

She sat up quickly, reaching for her watch. It was seven o'clock. Vere had said "before eight-thirty." That meant, if she rang just after eight——

But how far away that seemed! Nevertheless she curbed her instinct to get up at once and do something to kill the time, remembering Judy in the tiny spare room across the landing. It always took an alarm to wake Judy, but perhaps it would be better not to risk disturbing her. Anyway, Ken had said he would not be round until mid-day, so if Judy wanted to stay in bed late there was no need to call her yet.

For the next half-hour Jill lay back on her pillows. She read Vere's letter again, and, holding it against her heart, wondered why she had never realized that, once given the cue, she could be as sweetly foolish and sentimental as any girl who is starry-eyed with love.

But up to yesterday she had only known love as something which hurt and tore and ate one's heart away with longing that could never be realized. Now everything was different, because Vere's lips, and his eyes, and that new unsteady note in his voice told her he loved her.

At seven-thirty she got up and went softly along to the bathroom. When she had had her bath there was still no sound from Judy's room. She put on the kettle, and, still in her dressing-gown, her heart hammering, she went to the telephone and dialled the number Vere had written across a corner of his note.

Wimpole 89771.

A man's voice—not the one she was hoping and longing to hear—answered after what seemed almost an eternity, and was in reality only one minute.

"Wimpole 89771."

"Could I speak to Mr. Carrington?" she asked.

"Mr. Carrington has gone out, madam," was the reply. "He doesn't expect to be back before this evening. Can I take a message?"

"No, thank you. I'll—ring again." She replaced the receiver slowly. What had happened? Work, of course; and he could not very well leave a special message. Her heart felt suddenly as though a leaden weight had been laid on it. Something was wrong! Then she told herself not to be stupid. Of course he would get in touch with her—then she remembered he had not got the number. Well, but he would come—as soon as he could. She would just have to wait.

She went to put on the kettle, forcing back that strange frightening premonition of disaster; the superstitious dread that she had been too happy.

On her way to finish dressing she heard a click below, and, looking down the stairs, saw that the post had come. She could not think, with Judy in London, of anyone who would be likely to write to her here. The letter was probably for Rosalind, but as she wanted the milk and would only have to reach a hand round the door to get it, she went down, and naturally the first thing she did was to pick up the letter.

It was a square envelope of thick white paper—unstamped,

She turned it over, and her heart gave a little leap as she saw her own name in Vere's firm handwriting. He must have sent it by hand.

Sitting on the stairs she tore it open eagerly. Outside, all the usual noises were going on. Men's voices, the sounds of opening and shutting doors, of the starting up of car engines—the swish of a hose.

But to Jill, reading those lines which seemed to have been written in such very black ink, an impenetrable silence seemed to have descended over everything.

"DEAR NURSE,

I feel that I owe you an apology, and hasten to make it. I am afraid I entirely lost my head yesterday. I am quite sure it was not the first time such a thing had happened to you—you are an attractive young woman. That, however, does not excuse me to myself.

Please forgive me, and forget about it.

VERE CARRINGTON."

Jill sat, staring down at the paper in her hand. It wasn't true! It couldn't be!

"I lost my head——"

But he had said——

What had he said? That she was "adorable"? What had he done? Kissed her, as a man kisses a girl who obviously likes it and—wants it to happen again. A girl to whom such a thing has happened before! He had made not a single promise. Asked nothing from her in words. But he had left her that note yesterday; the note in which she had read between the lines things that had never been meant to be there.

And whatever may have been in his mind, she was certain it had not been what she had hoped and believed; he had gone away and thought about it; and—decided it was not worth while.

Oh! It couldn't be true!

You idiot! she told herself, furious with pain, as Vere had been last night, can't you see how true it is? That the only true thing is—he doesn't want you? . . .

Chapter XXIII

LOOKING back, she never knew how she got through that day without betraying herself to Judy. Fortunately, though Judy told her she looked pale, that young lady was fully concerned with her own happiness, and though both she and Ken had protested when Jill said she could not go out to lunch with them because of her other appointment, they had gone off happily together.

While she was shut up alone that afternoon, Jill made up her mind to return to Broad Meadows the next day, though her leave was not up until Monday.

The merest chance of encountering, or even glimpsing Vere again was more than she could bear.

She tried for her pride's sake to answer his letter—to tell him that she quite understood and, of course, she would forget. She would sign it: "Sincerely yours, Gillian Foster."

But somehow, when she sat down to it she could not form the words. It would just have to remain unanswered.

She did manage to write short notes to Lady Amanda and Sandra, telling them she had been obliged to return to Berkshire in a hurry.

But though she fought not to think about what had happened, to stop asking herself whether there was any other reason behind that sudden change in Vere, she could not shut the thing out of her mind, any more than she could shut him out of the heart he had so cruelly thrown back at her. The added torture of lacerated pride added to her suffering when she remembered how she had confessed her love for him.

And then it would begin: But he had said he had wanted to kiss her since he had pulled her out of the river. And he had not kissed her as a man who just loses his head kisses a girl.

Jill was pretty and attractive enough for several men to have lost their heads at different times—she had often been told that she was cold, ungenerous, inhuman! All the old stock phrases dear to the philandering male. She had been implored more seriously to give her heart; but the only person she had given it to had not wanted it—not for one little minute. If only she could have believed he had meant it all, even just for that brief time, it would have been a little easier. She told herself that it was sheer folly to believe there could be anything else behind that letter of his; that the only possible thing to do was to accept it at its face value. And yet deep down in her something went on asking Why? reminding her he was not the kind of man to behave that way. What was behind it?

Unfortunately, Ken had not thought of mentioning his meeting with Vere, or Jill would have had enough imagination to realize he might have thought she was the girl who had been with him; and by the time she got back to Broad Meadows the incident had gone out of young Doctor Harding's mind.

She was welcomed at the hospital with open arms. Matron did not even scold her for coming too soon. And Jill was not at all sorry to find that she had been switched from Private back to the short-staffed main building, where she was promoted to Sister Hudson's ward.

Matron told her frankly: "You are being pushed on sooner than you would have been otherwise, and it is up to you to make good. I know you are not afraid of responsibility; but it is very hard work. Your health may not stand up to it; we will see."

There was certainly plenty to do, and however wearisome the routine, she was on her mettle to make good. There was blessedly little time to think, and as she could not afford not to sleep at night she had to do something about that.

She had been on the new job over a week and was busy in her office one afternoon when Ken Harding tapped on the glass-panelled door and came in.

"May I beg a few moments of your valuable time, Sister?" he asked, his eyes contradicting the gravity of his tone.

"Certainly. What can I do for you, Doctor?" she asked, and shaking her head at him: "What are you up to now?"

"I'm serious for once," he assured her. "Getting a heck of a sense of responsibility, I assure you."

"Then sit in the chair," she advised. "It's more dignified."

But he remained on the desk where he had perched himself, swinging his long legs. "Listen, Jill, you remember what I said in London? Do you happen to know of any 'clever and very reliable, fully qualified and experienced nurse, who would like to be the second in command with a chance of later becoming full Sister-in-Charge of a private hospital in Salisbury, Rhodesia?' The job is open—or will be at the time I am due to arrive—and Sheldon has written to remind me to, if possible, bring someone along. They want an English girl."

Jill looked at him in silence for a moment, conscious of an odd feeling of uncertainty. Would this be a way out—a chance of escape? She would not have dreamed of thinking of it once. But now——

"Matron—might know of someone," she said.

"You *wouldn't* think of it yourself?" he asked. "Judy went crazy with excitement when I told her, and sent me right to you. Why don't you think about it, Jill?"

Jill looked out of the window beside her. "I—don't know, Ken, my dear. Wouldn't it be rather like deserting—Matron——"

"You know perfectly well Matron would not stand in your way."

And she knew very well that it was not only the thought of Matron that held her back. Could she really be mad enough to dread the idea of putting thousands of miles between herself and Vere Carrington?

She picked up a pencil, and for a moment was silent, drawing straight lines on the pad in front of her.

Ken watched her, disappointed. "Are you thinking about leaving your people?" he asked.

She shook her head. "No. There are the others, and I go home so seldom; they wouldn't really miss me." She put the pencil down and looked at him. "But it is a matter of—pulling up roots. Perhaps I am less adventurous than I ought to be. Do you want me to make up my mind at once?"

"No. There's plenty of time—at least you needn't let me know until the end of the month. I'll write and tell them I'm looking round for someone."

"I won't keep you as long as that," she promised. "I—I just want to think it over."

"It would be grand if you came," he said. "I'm all for it. The idea of Judy having you near appeals to me as much as it does to her."

She smiled at him. "Thanks, Ken. I know it's a wonderful chance. I'll—think about it."

She did think about it; sitting by the window in her bedroom long after lights out, watching the moonlit river between the trees.

Which was the worse—never to see Vere again; or to come face to face with him and perhaps betray her real feelings?

It was no use telling herself that one day she would succeed in rooting him out of her heart, living her life without a thought of him. If that had ever been possible all hope of it had gone. However little those moments in his arms had meant to him, they had bound her to him irrevocably. She knew that if she married anyone else she would be betraying—not Vere, who cared nothing for her, but all that was most sacred in herself.

She still had work—duty!

But what cold little words those had become, against that burning ache in her heart.

Chapter XXIV

I

JILL continued to think a great deal about Ken's offer to go to Rhodesia, but she got no nearer to making a decision, though she rather despised herself for hesitating. Here was the chance to cut clean away from the past—to begin life in a new land; and yet she had not the courage to take it.

What good could she do by staying here? All that would come of it was that some day she was practically certain to come face to face with Vere, and experience all the humiliation such a meeting must bring. And yet I am so weak, she told herself bitterly, that I would rather risk that than know I should never see him again.

And so, in spite of their fullness, the days dragged on until it was nearly a whole month since her holiday, and at the end of the week she would be due for a week-end of freedom.

She had no idea of what she would do with it when it came, but there was no thought in her mind of going anywhere near London. Since she came back to Broad Meadows, she had heard nothing from anyone she knew there; not that she had really expected to. Sandra was, in her own words, the world's worst correspondent, and Jill did not expect Lady Amanda to write.

And then Friday morning's post brought Jill a letter with the London postmark, addressed in the old-fashioned flowing handwriting which she remembered seeing more than once when Sandra was in the clinic.

With very mixed feelings and rather unsteady hands, she opened the pale-grey envelope. Lady Amanda had written:

"DEAR JILL,

I have been wondering how you are getting on, and if your fortnight in town really did you any good. When will you be free next? If you are not making other arrangements I should be delighted if you would come to me for a week-end. I am afraid I cannot offer you much excitement; Sandra comes in and out but she is very much back into her own life, and splendidly well. *My* life is quieter, but less entertaining, and I should be glad of some young society. Come, my dear, if you can and *when* you can—if you think you can bear an old woman's company for a day or two. A few hours notice of your arrival is all I shall need.

Sincerely yours,

AMANDA SKEYNE.

P.S. As usual Vere Carrington is working like a black! It's high time he had somebody to look after him. He looks to me as if he was thoroughly overdoing things, and not at all happy, though he would probably slay me for daring to suggest anything of the kind!"

And so he seemed "not at all happy". Yet he was the last person to show his feelings; could it be Lady Amanda's intuition, or just her imagination, which made her think everything was not well with him?

Jill, who was in her office, folded the letter hastily and

called "Come in" in answer to the tap which had sounded on the door.

Judy said breathlessly: "I've no right here, darling—but I had a few minutes and I couldn't resist flying across to show you this." She held out a newspaper, pointing to a paragraph beneath the headline "To-day's Gossip". The Paragraph was headed "More Wedding Bells?" and, following the announcement of a society engagement, read:

> "In the platinum-walled precincts of the discreet Colonnade restaurant, where almost everyone who is anyone seems to be lunching in these these days, I saw our loveliest ballerina—glamorous honey-haired Sandra St. Just—lunching with Mr. Vere Carrington, the famous orthopædic surgeon. Mr. Carrington quite recently operated upon Miss St. Just for a stiffened knee joint, which other doctors had declared would lame her for life. Said to be the most brilliant man in his particular line in the world, he is young to have attained to such eminence, and one of the best looking specialists in the medical profession. We buttonholed the enchanting Sandra when her escort was obliged to hurry off to keep another appointment, and audaciously enquired if we might expect a romance. To which she replied that we were entitled to expect anything which we fancied, but for her part she was much too busy to think about such things. She added, however, that it might be possible that she would have some 'exciting news' for us, before long."

Jill sat stiffly in her chair, thankful that the paper was hiding her face from Judy's eyes, and when she lowered it a moment later she was able to force herself to smile and say quite naturally:

"I do think journalists are the most impertinent people under the sun."

Judy nodded. "But I told you he was human! And she practically admits it, doesn't she? I do hope it will be a success—I can't see him liking being married to a girl whose career is frightfully important, can you? Of course he will be proud of her, who wouldn't be? But—I bet there's a tug-o'-war sooner or later. I wonder who will win." She laughed. "It's thrilling, though, isn't it, to think the romance started here."

"If that is what Sandra meant I hope they will be happy," said Jill quietly. "And now run away for goodness sake! I'm terribly busy."

"O.K. See you later." Judy went blithely out of the room. As the door shut behind her Jill picked up the paper and read the paragraph through again. "*Some very important news.*" So—this time it was not just a matter of his "losing his head"! Suddenly, pain quickening her imagination, Jill asked herself if it was not possible that his feeling for Sandra was at the back of the whole thing. She remembered how his face had set and his whole manner altered after they had entered Lady Amanda's drawing-room that afternoon when Sandra had broken away so quickly from Lord Errol's embrace. Had the sight of her there suddenly shown Vere clearly what she meant to him; that it was Sandra he really cared for?

Jill reminded herself that she had suspected often enough that he was falling in love with his beautiful patient. And when a man as busy as Vere found time to be seen often in the company of one girl, he must be very interested in her indeed.

And so—it looked as though Sandra had won.

And loving him as she did, Jill reached in that moment the very height of love. "Dear God; let her make him happy," she prayed silently. "Only let her make him happy."

And then suddenly her mind was made up. She knew that she meant to do two things. She would go and spend this week-end with Lady Amanda. However much it hurt she wanted to know all about what was happening. And before she went she would tell Ken definitely that she would go to Rhodesia. . . .

II

When Jill arrived at the Eaton Square flat on Saturday afternoon, Lady Amanda welcomed her warmly.

"Delightful of you to come and relieve the monotony for me, my dear," she said. "I have missed seeing you."

Jill was touched—even if she did not quite believe in the "monotony"; for Lady Amanda had always seemed to her to be a person with plenty of interests to keep her from getting bored. And yet it did not occur to her to wonder why this charming old autocrat should have suddenly decided to ask her to come and spend the week-end with her; she had too much on her mind just then to think of sifting for motives.

"But I must say," Lady Amanda continued, "I should like to see you looking more robust. Why, you are thinner than you were when I last saw you."

"I have had two wards to look after, and that means a lot of exercise," Jill told her smilingly. "You knew I had become a Ward Sister?"

"Yes, you told me in your letter. Congratulations—but I still think you need thoroughly well feeding up."

"Oh! I eat plenty," said Jill, feeling a little guilty, because she knew that was one of the biggest lies she had ever told. She hated food in these days, and, though it was breaking all Matron's rules, snatched a sandwich whenever she could avoid a meal.

When her guest had gone to her room, Lady Amanda sat frowningly regarding a vase of flowers on the table opposite where she was sitting in the library. She was really concerned. The girl looked as though a puff of wind would blow her away; not only had she lost flesh, she looked—different. Lady Mandy did not like those hollows above the beautiful moulding of Jill's cheek-bones, and although her charming face still wore that expression of calm serenity, her eyes were tragically unhappy. Could it possibly be as bad as all that? Was the child breaking her heart for——

The thought was interrupted by Jill returning, and almost immediately Price brought in the tea wagon.

"Are you really enjoying your new job?" Lady Amanda asked as Jill, who had come across for her cup, carried it back to her chair.

"Yes, it is wonderfully interesting," said Jill.

"Better than the Private Wing?"

"There is more variety. With twenty-four patients in each ward. I shall," Jill hoped she was succeeding in sounding cool and natural, "miss it." And as her hostess gave her an enquiring glance: "I haven't told you that I am leaving Broad Meadows next month? I am going to South—or rather Central Africa, to take up a post in a private clinic and nursing home just outside Salisbury."

"You are leaving England? But, my dear child, why on earth——?"

Jill explained about Ken and Judy, and the chance this new post offered of a much more important one in the near future. "Besides, I think change is good—don't you?" She added: "I've always been rather attracted by that part of the world. It will be thrilling to put down roots in a great new Dominion."

"I suppose it is only natural to feel like that when you are young, and ambitious," said Lady Amanda a little flatly, though she could not think why this news should bowl her over so completely. In spite of the comparative shortness of their acquaintance she had grown very fond of Jill and now she had an odd feeling somehow of being partly responsible for the girl. Of course it was absurd, she thought, because Jill was old enough to know her own mind, and it was not as though she was going among complete strangers. She would have her friends with her—be still doing the work she loved.

If it was another, unrequited, love that was sending her overseas——

Involuntarily as, having finished her tea, she rose to get her embroidery, the old lady's glance moved to that photograph of Vere that still stood where it always had done—which just now happened to be behind the chair where Jill was sitting.

It was not the first time she remembered looking through that communicating door and seeing Jill with the cool, serene mask her profession had taught her to wear fallen from her face, and Vere Carrington's photograph clasped between her hands. . . .

As the old lady turned back to her chair, the silence, which had grown rather lengthy, was broken by the opening of the door leading from the hall to the library, and Sandra came quickly into the room.

"Lady Mandy, darling, I'm so glad you're in. I didn't have time to telephone." She bent to kiss her godmother affectionately before she turned to greet Jill with that impulsive out-throwing of her hands which was characteristic of her when she was glad to see anyone.

"Price told me you were here, Jill. What fun——"

"She is staying the week-end," said Lady Amanda. "I was going to telephone *you*, and ask if you could come to lunch to-morrow. As you are here you had better stay to dinner."

"Exactly what I intended to do, darling, unless you throw me out."

Jill felt a pang of shame, because Sandra was so clearly pleased to see her, and she could not entirely reciprocate. When you are eating your heart out for someone it does not make you very happy to meet the person who is going to have all those things you would almost give your very soul for. Jill knew she could control her jealousy—hating it, as she did, she must control it. She had known, of course, that she would meet Sandra during this visit, but—somehow she wished that she had been more prepared for the meeting. She could not doubt the reason for that new air of confidence—a something difficult to define, which she had never noticed about Sandra before. Then, catching the other girl looking at her, she forced a smile.

But this time there was no response in kind from Sandra, who continued to regard her frowningly. Then:

"What on earth have you been doing to yourself, Jill?" she asked bluntly. "You could slip through a crack in the floor-boards."

"Yes, is it not appalling?" Lady Amanda looked up from her *petit point*. "She ought to take cod liver oil or something."

Jill's laugh was genuinely amused. "I don't know why you all think I am fading away," she said. "I do assure you I'm absolutely sound."

"Well, I hope you will get fatter in Africa," said Lady Amanda.

"Africa?" Sandra repeated. "Why should she go to Africa to get fatter?"

"Apparently she is going there to live," said Lady Amanda. "Tell her, Jill."

So Jill repeated her story again while Sandra, after an exclamation of amazed protest, listened wide-eyed.

"I think you must be crazy," she said at last. "Does Vere know about this?"

Jill felt herself change colour. "Why should he?" she asked, rather quickly.

Sandra had not noticed that painful flush, but Lady Amanda had, and thought unhappily: "So that *is* it!

"But he'll be furious," cried Sandra. "He thinks you are such a good nurse. He was agreeing with me only yesterday, that I should never have got well so quickly, or so thoroughly, if it had not been for you."

So he did acknowledge that! She was a good nurse—an excellent machine! A wave of bitterness welled up in her.

"That was—kind of him," the words were out before she could keep them back.

Sandra looked at her in surprise. "Are you being sarcastic, Jill? Aren't you and Vere friends any more? Has he been treading on your toes?"

"Don't be silly," said Jill. "I was not—being sarcastic. It is very kind of Mr. Carrington to give me credit for——" She broke off, knowing to her horror that she dared not trust her voice further.

At that moment Lady Amanda dropped her scissors, and she was grateful for the chance of stooping to recover them; by the time she straightened again her lips were steady.

Sandra laughed softly. "Oh! Vere's really a darling," she said. "He's being very co-operative with me, and everyone is going to have such a disappointment. You've heard the rumours that are flying round, darling?" She looked at her godmother.

"What rumours—I seem to hear so many. From the marriage of Royalty, to——"

"Oh, I forget you only read the very respectable press," said Sandra. "The papers that don't go in for gossip columns. But—it's really too funny, in spite of the cheek of it all! I'm supposed to be going to announce my engagement to Vere at any moment——"

"Well," demanded Lady Amanda bluntly, aware of Jill's suddenly whitened face and thinking it was best to get the thing over and done with, "are you going to?"

"Good heavens, no!" Sandra's great eyes widened. "Now Lady Mandy, my precious, can you imagine a more unsuitable match? In any case I don't think Vere is a marrying man—I rather gather from some remarks he has let drop recently that he—doesn't care for women (incidentally I'm not just a female, I'm a devastatingly successful case, and he's ready to forgive me a lot!). And so when I showed him a silly paragraph in *The Daily Hour Glass* the other day he entered into the joke.

"What is the child talking about?" demanded Lady Amanda.

"I'll explain." Sandra slipped from her chair, sitting on the carpet cross-legged, which was a favourite habit. "Some impertinent journalist—or columnist, or whatever he calls himself—has seen me out with Vere several times lately, and the other day at the Colonnade he had the audacity to ask me if there was 'a romance'—you know," she glanced briefly towards Jill, "the way they go up to a film star who happens to have been seen twice with the same man, and ask those kind of questions? I'm not out for that kind of publicity and I object, so I strung him along. I said demurely that I was not aware there was—or something of that sort, and added that I should, however, have some very interesting news to announce soon. So, of course, the dear thing believed I was only denying it on principle, and would be flashing a diamond ring about shortly. Whereas my news is quite different."

Lady Amanda had been too conscious of Jill sitting there, tensed and white as paper, but suddenly she forgot all about her as she said sharply:

"You are not going to tell me you are engaged to Errol; if so——"

"No. I'm not engaged to anyone except—oh! I've the most wonderful news." Sandra sprang to her feet in one bound. Light as thistledown, graceful as a lily, she stood poised, her cheeks pink, her eyes shining. "It isn't to be published for a few days, but I've signed a contract with Serge Boronoff——"

"Good heavens!" said Lady Amanda. "I thought he was dead."

"Darling, of course he is not. He's still the greatest ballet impresario in the world. He lives in New York. And I'm going to America to dance for two years under his direction. It will mean all the great classics—Sleeping Beauty, Nutcracker, Swan Lake, and those things (I care for them so much more than the modern stuff) being put on magnificently. He'll probably kill me with work and abuse me like a pickpocket, but I'm tough enough to stand it. And he swears I shall be a really great ballerina at the end of it all. I'm crazy with joy that he should think enough of my work to sign me up."

"But, my dear child," said Lady Amanda, to whom all this was so much double-Dutch. "I thought you were going to Paris in October. What about Errol?"

Sandra's face set, though for an instant just the shadow of a guilty expression flitted across it.

"It is his own fault," she said. "My contract with him lapsed while I was laid up; and he was so angry about my accident that he did not bother to have another one drawn up. And then—after having been quite beastly—he took it for granted that things would just go on in the same way. At first I thought I might let them, then Boronoff came out of the blue—he was on a private visit to London from New York, which is now his headquarters. He made this offer, and of course I accepted. I am sorry about Glyn, but I feel the change will be good, both for me and my work. So—that's that." She drew a deep breath as she moved across to the hearthrug.

Watching her, Jill was still aware, even through the chaos of her mind, of the dancer's exquisite grace. She seemed to float rather than walk over the carpet. Yet there was something more than just grace and beauty about her to-day. She was not cruel—she would not deliberately dance on another's girl's heart. Although what she had just heard left Jill stunned, some instinct told her that Sandra had changed. As lovely, even lovelier than ever, there was a new decision about her, even a touch of hardness.

Jill had always felt "the St. Just" liked her own way and would get it—but this impression was different. Sandra had been like a spoiled child; now she had grown up, and from now on she was going to be capable not only of knowing what she wanted, but of managing her own life.

But—how would Vere feel?

Lady Amanda's embroidery had fallen into her lap, but still, while she studied her goddaughter intently, she was fully conscious of Jill's white, strained face

Hum! she thought. Well, what next?

Chapter XXV

I

So it had all been a myth—an absurd half-hoax invented by Sandra; and Vere had been "co-operative".

Changing from her suit into something more suitable for dinner Jill, recovered from the first shock of Sandra's announcement, could hardly have told yet how she felt about it. Except that the reason which had finally forced her decision—the knowledge that she could not bear the torture of remaining when Vere and Sandra were married—had been quite unnecessary.

He was as free as he had even been, and she was going thousands of miles away. But how senseless to feel, even for an instant, that could possibly make any difference. If the whole world was between them they could not be farther apart than they were now—than they had always been.

Always? Except for those few minutes—that golden part of an hour, when he had held her in his arms and kissed her lips. It was no use his denying it—in those moments she *had* meant something to him.

If a man is sufficiently attracted to lose his head once, isn't there the chance that, some day, given the opportunity, he may do it again?

Meeting her eyes in the mirror, Jill went scarlet with shame. What has come to me? she thought, and shut down her heart against the answer. Whatever happened, she decided, she must not let her hostess or Sandra guess that she was unhappy.

Sandra had suddenly remembered that she had made an appointment at home to have some shoes fitted, and had gone flying off, promising to be back in time for dinner. When Jill went into the drawing-room Lady Amanda was not yet down, but the other girl had returned, having changed her frock meanwhile.

She was sitting in a high-backed chair which was upholstered in cream brocade, and in her full ballerina-length sapphire-blue organza dress, she made a picture to rejoice the eyes of any artist. She was lovely and sweet. How could one blame any man for falling in love with her, or understand how he could resist doing so? But when, of course, the man happened to dislike women——

Anyway, thought Jill, with that new-found bitterness, I can be thankful to him for not loving Sandra and—spoiling my affection for her. How ungenerous and cheap it had been to —actually feel jealousy. Jill, who had never dreamt herself capable of such a thing, felt a surge of quite unmerited self-contempt. For, after all, however high a standard she might have set for herself, human nature has its limits.

"Hello, Jill," Sandra greeted. "I do feel a heel—never writing to you. But you know me—writer's cramp is my occupational disease if I scribble five lines!"

Jill laughed. "Buy a typewriter."

"Worse and worse! Do you know I thought of you last week-end, and wished you were with me," said Sandra. "I flew to Paris—and incidentally spoiled Errol's week-end. I didn't know he was there, and we met, and quarrelled all the time. Of course," she added calmly, "he is never going to forgive me when he knows what I have done." She rose, and slipping a hand through Jill's arm drew her over to the window. "I'm so glad to have a few minutes alone with you, Jill. You're so sensible."

Sensible! thought Jill.

Sandra continued quickly: "I haven't really a conscience about him, but I suppose I ought to have told him about Boronoff. You see—he's still expecting me to dance in Paris though of course there is nothing in writing. Anyway (you are the only person I can talk to about this) sooner or later I had to get Errol—out of my hair."

Jill gave her a quick look. In the turmoil of her own mind, and her recent belief that Sandra was going to marry Vere after all, she had forgotten to think seriously about the other girl's feeling for Lord Errol.

"Tell me, Sandra," she asked. "Are you in love with him?"

Sandra was silent for a moment, looking down at her hands as she clenched and unclenched them. Then: "I—suppose so," she admitted. "He had the power to hurt me as no one else could, and—he used it. Perhaps I could have forgiven that—we are such fools over men!—if he had not chucked me over as he did when I was ill, and then taken it for granted that I was still there to be his nice clever, dancing puppet."

So Sandra could feel bitter too! Jill was startled at the intensity of the other's voice.

"But—I think he cares for you," she ventured. "Oh! I wouldn't have you marry him if I could prevent it, but I think as far as he is capable——"

"You've said it!" Sandra flung up her chin. "And I'll tell you how far he is capable—I shall never be human to him while he can pull the strings and make me part of the art he is crazy about. When he thought I was not going to dance any more, he didn't feel a bit sorry for *me*. But when I got better he thought everything would go on just the same. This will teach him a lesson. He has felt me slipping away from him and began to think he would make sure of me in another way. I *am* mad about this Boronoff contract, but I've also got to protect myself."

"I don't understand," said Jill.

"Well, do you remember the afternoon you and Vere walked into this room and—found us together?"

"Yes," said Jill briefly.

"Thank heaven you did. Errol was using storm tactics. He had just asked me to marry him, and I was terribly near to saying yes. But I escaped that time—and now I shall be away from his influence on my dancing life for two years. He will have to sit back and see someone else taking direction."

"And afterwards?" asked Jill.

Sandra shrugged her shoulders. "I don't know. If he ever wants to come back into my life it will be on very different terms—my terms. Meanwhile I am going to try to forget him."

But would she succeed? Jill wondered. Did any girl—really succeed?

II

Lady Amanda had tickets for a matinée the next afternoon. She had arranged to take Jill herself, but in the morning she announced that she thought she had a cold coming on, and had telephoned Sandra to ask her to go instead.

"I told her to take you to tea at the Savoy," she announced. "I don't think she should come back here in case I am—catching."

Jill was rather surprised. It was the first time she had ever heard Lady Mandy mention feeling off-colour, and it amazed her to find such a very strong-minded old lady quite jittery about a cold. But her hostess firmly refused to have her temperature taken and said she would probably be quite all right by the evening.

So, without any real inward enthusiasm, Jill went off to meet Sandra.

Her guest had no sooner gone than Lady Amanda got up and dressed with surprising alacrity.

But she was so quiet while her maid was doing her hair that the woman asked anxiously if she was sure she ought not to have stayed in bed.

"Certainly not, Bridges," she snapped. "Don't talk to me—I want to think."

She had a lot to think about, and most of it made her unusually uncomfortable. That girl's face! She had caught a full glimpse of it while Sandra was explaining all that nonsense about her rumoured romance with Vere.

And how right I was! she decided. She's eating her heart out for him. But what about him and Sandra? He certainly has not made any move to make those rumours come true. Of course the little baggage seems to have made it clear that she is not interested in him in that way—oh! bother! What a mess! But then, of course, her thoughts ran on, Vere was not the kind of man to wear his heart on his sleeve.

The day had turned very dull, with a drop in the temperature which advertised the advent of autumn. Lady Amanda ordered Price to put a match to the fire in the drawing-room and was sitting beside it at work on the lovely chair-back which was growing beneath her hands when the visitor she was expecting was announced.

She watched him crossing the room and wondered if she was getting over-imaginative or if he really had changed a lot. Those lines at the corners of his eyes suggested sleepless nights, and he, too, seemed thinner. Overwork, of course. All doctors were overworked in these ridiculous days.

"Nice of you to come, Vere," she said. "Am I being a nuisance?"

"You could not be a nuisance," he told her with a slight smile. "Or if you were—I should not notice it."

"A backhanded compliment." She pointed to the chair opposite. "Too near the fire?"

"No. It really is chilly. You have the right idea," he told her.

"Glad you think so. I wondered if I only felt chilly because my blood was thin."

He raised his brows. "What's the matter, Lady Mandy? You surely haven't taken to counting years?"

She laughed. "Time I did, perhaps. Cigarettes beside you—no, I won't, thanks."

He lit one for himself, asking: "Well—what did you want to see me about so particularly? Nothing wrong, I hope? You are not feeling——"

"My dear young man," said Lady Amanda, "I have nothing wrong with my bones, and if I felt ill otherwise, I should send for my usual G.P. This interview is not going to be nearly as easy for me as if I was asking for any kind of diagnosis." And as he looked at her in surprise: "Vere—I've known you almost since you were in rompers. But I suppose there are some impertinences the oldest friend should not commit. Probably you will snub me——"

"I can't quite see myself——"

"Wait a minute. I am going to ask you a very straight question. Are you in love with Sandra?"

"Good Lord, no!" he exclaimed. And then: "I am sorry to be so emphatic—I know it sounds unflattering. Sandra is a darling. She is also a credit to me. But—I've no time for that sort of thing."

"But you must contemplate marrying some time," said Lady Amanda.

"My work is——"

"Nonsense," she interrupted. "Every normal being wants something besides work, and I should say you are fairly normal."

It was, perhaps, just as well he was used to her. "Surely

you didn't send for me to discuss my—emotional reactions?" he asked.

"I sent for you to solve a problem," she said. "You are not in love with Sandra. Once I hoped you would be."

"My dear old friend, I am sorry——"

"It doesn't matter in the least, but I *must* know if you are in love with anyone else," said Lady Amanda firmly.

He flushed darkly. "What the——"

"Devil is it to do with me? Nothing, I suppose—except that I am an interfering old woman, and I hate waste. However, consider that last question unasked. Ring for some tea, will you. It is early, but I feel a cup would be pleasant."

He pressed the bell, glancing at his wrist watch.

"I have an appointment in twenty minutes," he said. As a busy man perhaps it was justifiable for him to feel annoyed at having his time wasted. Besides, the subject Lady Amanda had chosen was the last one he wished to discuss. He did not like to think that she might be getting just a little eccentric, but——

Lady Amanda guessed exactly what he was thinking, and was suitably amused, though she was worried because she had not yet solved the problem she had set out to solve.

"By the way," she said, calmly going on with her embroidery, "Jill Foster is staying with me."

"Really. They seem to have a lot of free time at Broad Meadows."

But she had seen him pause in the act of lighting another cigarette.

"She is a Ward Sister now." Lady Mandy re-threaded her needle. "She's leaving Broad Meadows, by the way."

"Leaving——?" He looked at her quickly.

"Yes," Lady Amanda stopped sewing. "She's going to Rhodesia. It appears one of the doctors at Broad Meadows is taking up an appointment there."

There was a very slight pause. Vere rose and stood by the mantelpiece, flicking his cigarette ash into the fire. "Is she going to be married, then?" he asked.

"Not to that particular doctor," said Lady Mandy. "Or to any other—as far as I know at present. This Doctor Harding is marrying one of the other nurses—a great friend of Jill's, and Jill has been offered rather a good post. I suppose it means she will settle out there. She means to devote herself to her work, but all men are not fools. One of them will snap a girl like that up, I am certain."

Vere threw his half-smoked cigarette into the flames as the tea was brought in.

Watching Lady Amanda pour it out, he asked casually: "Did you say Harding? He was the young R.M.O. at Broad Meadows, if I remember rightly. I—rather fancied there might be a case between him and Nurse—Sister Foster."

"Well, you were wrong," said Lady Amanda curtly. "But I'm pretty certain, in spite of all she says, there is someone else. Jill is very unhappy, and my guess is she is going to Rhodesia to try to forget."

He took the cup she handed to him, and put it carefully down on the mantelpiece, but not so steadily that some did not splash into the saucer.

"Perhaps," he suggested, "she—did care for Harding, and would rather——"

"Don't be dumb."

"What?" He glanced round, hardly believing his ears.

"Don't be dumb!" repeated Lady Amanda. And then, as their eyes met: "Listen, Vere, I told you I was an interfering old woman. And arranging other people's lives is always a stupid business. Jill Foster is breaking her heart for someone whom I am afraid I persuaded her was—destined for someone else. She has never confided in me, but all this talk about work, and this wonderful new appointment, does not deceive me in the least. In my opinion it is not a nice successful career she wants at all—it is just a very stupid man."

III

It was somewhere round six o'clock when Jill got back to the flat in Eaton Square.

Price opened the door for her, remarked on the chilliness of the evening, and requested: "Would you be good enough to go straight into the drawing-room, her ladyship says."

"Oh!" said Jill. "Is her ladyship up?"

"Yes, miss. She's up."

Jill went quickly along the hall. It was still broad daylight outside, but in spite of its long windows the drawing-room was not very light when the sun was off it. Glancing towards Lady Amanda's chair Jill saw it was unoccupied, and for a moment thought the room was empty. Then:

"Good evening——"

Her eyes on the tall figure coming towards her a hand went involuntarily to her throat.

"G-good evening," she stammered. "I—didn't know—I thought——" She swallowed hard. This would never do. "Does Lady Amanda know you are here?" she asked.

"Yes. I was waiting for you." He glanced at his wrist watch. "You are late. I had to put off my last appointment."

"I—am sorry." But why should she be sorry? The first shock of this meeting passed, she caught desperately at her pride. "You were—the last person I expected to find here," she said.

"Why? I come quite often."

There was a moment's silence. He wondered how much of a fool he was to be here. But since Lady Amanda had told him certain things there was something else he must know.

"Will you please sit down." He pointed to a chair.

He had never seemed more curt, but it was because her knees felt suddenly unsteady that she obeyed. Then she wished she had not, because he stood before her, suddenly seeming enormous.

"What is all this about Rhodesia?"

"Oh!" She heard herself laugh nervously. "I just—wanted a change."

He frowned. "It sounds mysterious."

"Not at all," she began with a touch of spirit.

"No? But you are not going to marry Dr. Harding?"

"Marry Ken?" she stared at him. "He has been engaged to Judy O'Farrell for—oh! ages." After all, this was no time to beat about the bush.

"Then will you kindly explain why he was kissing you outside your flat on the night after you—had been down into the country with me?"

She stared up at him in such undisguised amazement, a blind man could hardly have mistaken it. "Ken—kissing *me*! But Judy was there. I found her when I went back. I—oh!" she sprang to her feet. "Judy went down to see him off." Sudden light burst in on her, dazzling and confusing. "You don't mean you——"

"Jill," he took her roughly by the shoulders. "Was it Judy—whatever her name is—I saw in Harding's arms? Good God! And I thought——"

"You thought it was—me? But how could you—how could you? When——"

"I was crazy," he said. "I've been crazy ever since. I owe you an apology." Absurd that a conventional thing like that should be the only thing he found it possible to say, when there were a thousand others on the tip of his tongue.

Jill turned away, the sudden joy and relief that had welled up in her dammed back.

"It doesn't matter," she said. "Now——"

There was a very slight pause: then:

"And you are going to Rhodesia?" he asked.

"Yes."

"And you are very keen on your profession, are you not?"

He really had no right to cross-examine her, she told herself. And to seem—actually annoyed.

"It is a—very important job?"

"It—will be."

"So important that you would not be persuaded to give it up, Jill?"

She looked up then, and their eyes met.

"My darling," he said. "Of course you can't go—I need you far too much."

"You—need me?" What was the use of trying to repress her singing heart—to tell herself that she must have some pride. She stammered: "But you said that—I was to forget——"

"That," said Mr. Carrington, with startling humbleness, "is because I am a very stupid man——"

"You are not! You—Oh! Vere——"

She was in his arms again, and her lips were telling him without any words how right Lady Amanda had been.